Thomas Ingoldsby

The Ingoldsby legends

Mirth and marvels

Thomas Ingoldsby

The Ingoldsby legends
Mirth and marvels

ISBN/EAN: 9783337153526

Printed in Europe, USA, Canada, Australia, Japan

Cover: Foto ©Andreas Hilbeck / pixelio.de

More available books at **www.hansebooks.com**

THE

INGOLDSBY LEGENDS;

OR,

MIRTH AND MARVELS.

BY

RICHARD HARRIS BARHAM.

[THOMAS INGOLDSBY, Esquire.]

IN TWO VOLUMES.

VOL. I.

PHILADELPHIA:

PORTER AND COATES.

1885.

CONTENTS OF VOLUME I.

First Series.

MEMOIR OF THE AUTHOR.

RICHARD HARRIS BARHAM, a celebrated humorist, better known by his *nom de plume* of "Thomas Ingoldsby," was born at Canterbury, December 6, 1788. At seven years of age he lost his father, who left him a small estate, part of which was the manor of Tappington, so frequently mentioned in the *Legends*. At nine he was sent to St. Paul's school, but his studies were interrupted by an accident which shattered his arm and partially crippled it for life. Thus deprived of the power of bodily activity, he became a great reader and diligent student. In 1807 he entered Brasenose College, Oxford, intending at first to study for the profession of the law. Circumstances, however, induced him to change his mind and to enter the church. The choice seems surprising, for he had from childhood displayed that propensity to fun in the form of parody and punning which afterwards made him a reputation. In 1813 he was ordained and took a country curacy; he married in the following year, and in 1821 removed to London on obtaining the appointment of minor canon of St. Paul's Cathedral. Three years later he became one of the priests in ordinary of his Majesty's chapel royal. In 1826 he first contributed to *Blackwood's Magazine;* and on the establishment of *Bentley's Miscellany* in 1837 he began to furnish the series of grotesque metrical tales known as *The Ingoldsby Legends*. These became very popular, were published in a collected form, and have since passed through numerous editions. In variety and whimsicality of rhymes these verses have hardly a rival since the days of *Hudibras*. But beneath this obvious popular quality there lies a store of solid antiquarian learning, the fruit of patient enthusiastic research by the light of the midnight lamp, in out-of-the-way old books, which few readers who laugh over his pages detect. If it were of any avail we might regret that a more active faculty of veneration did not keep him from writing some objectionable passages of the *Legends*. His life was grave, dignified, and highly honored. His sound judgment and his kind heart made him the trusted counsellor, the valued friend, and the frequent peacemaker; and he was intolerant of all that was mean, and base, and false. In politics he was a Tory of the old school; yet he was the life-long friend of the liberal Sydney Smith, whom in many respects he singularly resembled. Theodore Hook was one of his most intimate friends. Mr. Barham was a contributor to the *Edinburgh Review* and the *Literary Gazette;* published a novel in three volumes, entitled *My Cousin Nicholas;* and, strange to tell, wrote nearly a third of the articles in Gorton's *Biographical Dictionary.* His life was not without such changes and sorrows as make men grave. He had nine children, and six of them died in his lifetime. But he retained vigor and freshness of heart and mind to the last, and his latest verses show no signs of decay. He died in London after a long and painful illness, June 17, 1845.—*Encyclopædia Britannica.*

TO RICHARD BENTLEY, ESQ.

My dear Sir:—

You wish me to collect into a single volume certain rambling extracts from our family memoranda, many of which have already appeared in the pages of your Miscellany. At the same time you tell me that doubts are entertained in certain quarters as to the authenticity of their details.

Now with respect to their genuineness, the old oak chest, in which the originals are deposited, is not more familiar to my eyes than it is to your own; and if its contents have any value at all, it consists in the strict veracity of the facts they record.

To convince the most incredulous I can only add that should business—pleasure is out of the question—ever call them into the neighborhood of Folkestone, let them take the high road from Canterbury to Dover till they reach the eastern extremity of Barham Downs. Here a beautiful green lane diverging abruptly to the right will carry them through the Oxenden plantations and the unpretending village of Denton to the foot of a very respectable hill—as hills go in this part of Europe. On reaching its summit let them look straight before them,—and if, among the hanging woods which crown the opposite side of the valley, they cannot distinguish an antiquated Manor-house of Elizabethan architecture, with its gable ends, stone stanchions, and tortuous chimneys rising above the surrounding trees, why—the sooner they procure a pair of Dollond's patent spectacles the better.

If, on the contrary, they can manage to descry it, and, proceeding some five or six furlongs through the avenue, will ring at the Lodge gate,—they cannot mistake the stone lion with the Ingoldsby escutcheon (Ermine, a saltire engrailed Gules) in his paws,—they will be received with a hearty old English welcome.

The papers in question having been written by different parties, and at various periods, I have thought it advisable to reduce the more ancient of them into a comparatively modern phraseology, and to make my collateral ancestor, Father John, especially, "deliver himself like a man of this world;" Mr. Maguire, indeed, is the only Gentleman who, in his account of the late Coronation, retains his own rich vernacular.

As to arrangement, I shall adopt the sentiment expressed by the Constable of Bourbon four centuries ago, *teste* Shakspeare, one which seems to become more fashionable every day,

"The Devil take all order !!—I'll to the throng !"

Believe me to be,
My dear Sir,
Yours, most indubitably and immeasurably,

THOMAS INGOLDSBY.

TAPPINGTON EVERARD, *Jan.* 20, 1840.

PREFACE TO THE SECOND EDITION.

TO RICHARD BENTLEY, ESQ.

MY DEAR SIR:—

I should have replied sooner to your letter, but that the last three days in January are, as you are aware, always dedicated, at the Hall, to an especial *battue*, and the old house is full of shooting-jackets, shot-belts, and "double Joes." Even the women wear percussion caps, and your favorite (?) Rover, who, you may remember, examined the calves of your legs with such suspicious curiosity at Christmas, is as pheasant-mad as if he were a biped, instead of being a genuine four-legged scion of the Blenheim breed. I have managed, however, to avail myself of a lucid interval in the general hallucination (how the rain *did* come down on Monday!), and as you tell me the excellent friend whom you are in the habit of styling "a Generous and Enlightened Public" has emptied your shelves of the first edition, and "asks for more," why, I agree with you, it *would* be a want of *respect* to that very *respectable* personification, when furnishing him with a further supply, not to endeavor, at least, to amend my faults, which are few, and your own, which are more numerous. I have, therefore, gone to work *con amore*, supplying occasionally on my own part a deficient note or elucidatory stanza, and on yours knocking out, without remorse, your superfluous *i*'s, and now and then eviscerating your *colon*.

My duty to your illustrious friend thus performed, I have

a crow to pluck with him. Why will he persist—as you tell me he does persist—in calling me by all sorts of names but those to which I am entitled by birth and baptism—my "Sponsorial and Patronymic appellations," as Dr. Pangloss has it? Mrs. Malaprop complains, and with justice, of an "assault upon her parts of speech;" but to attack one's very existence—to deny that one *is* a person *in esse*, and scarcely to admit that one *may be* a person *in posse*—is tenfold cruelty;— "it is pressing to death, whipping, and hanging!" Let me entreat all such likewise to remember that, as Shakspeare beautifully expresses himself elsewhere—I give his words as quoted by a very worthy baronet in a neighboring county, when protesting against a defamatory placard at a general election—

> " Who steals my purse steals stuff!—
> 'Twas mine—'tisn't his—nor nobody else's!
> But he who runs away with my GOOD NAME,
> Robs me of what does not do him any good,
> And makes me deuced poor!!" *

In order utterly to squabash and demolish every gainsayer, I had thought, at one time, of asking my old and esteemed friend, Richard Lane, to crush them at once with his magic pencil, and to transmit my features to posterity, where all his works are sure to be "delivered according to the direction;" but somehow the noble-looking profiles which he has recently executed of the Kemble family put me a little out of conceit of my own; while the undisguised amusement which my "Mephistopheles eyebrow," as he termed it, afforded him in the "full face," induced me to lay aside the design. Besides, my dear sir, since, as has been well observed, "there never was a married man yet who had not somebody remarkably like him walking about town," it is a thousand to one but my lineaments might after all, out of sheer perverseness, be ascribed

---

* A reading which seems most unaccountably to have escaped the researches of all modern Shakspeareans, including the rival editors of the new and illustrated versions.

to any body rather than to the real owner. I have therefore
sent you, instead thereof, a fair sketch of Tappington, taken
from the Folkestone road (I tore it last night out of Julia
Simpkinson's *album*): get Gilks to make a woodcut of it.

And now, if any miscreant (I use the word only in its primary
and "Pickwickian" sense of "Unbeliever") ventures to throw
any further doubt upon the matter, why, as Jack Cade's friend
says in the play, "There are the chimneys in my father's house,
and the bricks are alive at this day to testify it!"

"Why, very well then—we hope here be truths!"

Heaven be with you, my dear sir!—I was getting a little
excited; but you, who are mild as the milk that dews the soft
whisker of the new-weaned kitten, will forgive me when, wiping
away the nascent moisture from my brow, I "pull in," and
subscribe myself,

Yours quite as much as his own,

THOMAS INGOLDSBY.

TAPPINGTON EVERARD, *Feb.* 2, 1843.

INGOLDSBY LEGENDS.

𝕮𝖍𝖊 𝕾𝖕𝖊𝖈𝖙𝖗𝖊 𝖔𝖋 𝕮𝖆𝖕𝖕𝖎𝖓𝖌𝖙𝖔𝖓.

"IT is very odd, though; what can have become of them?" said Charles Seaforth, as he peeped under the valance of an old-fashioned bedstead, in an old-fashioned apartment of a still more old-fashioned manor-house; "'tis confoundedly odd, and I can't make it out at all. Why, Barney, where are they? —and where the d—l are you?"

No answer was returned to this appeal; and the lieutenant, who was, in the main, a reasonable person—at least as reasonable a person as any young gentleman of twenty-two in "the service" can fairly be expected to be—cooled when he reflected that his servant could scarcely reply extempore to a summons which it was impossible he should hear.

An application to the bell was the considerate result; and the footsteps of as tight a lad as ever put pipe-clay to belt sounded along the gallery.

"Come in!" said his master. An ineffectual attempt upon the door reminded Mr. Seaforth that he had locked himself in. "By heaven! this is the oddest thing of all," said he, as he turned the key and admitted Mr. Maguire into his dormitory.

"Barney, where are my pantaloons?"

"Is it the breeches?" asked the valet, casting an inquiring eye round the apartment :—"is it the breeches, sir?"

"Yes; what have you done with them?"

"Sure then your honor had them on when you went to bed, and it's hereabout they'll be, I'll be bail;" and Barney lifted a fashionable tunic from a cane-backed arm-chair, proceeding in

2   (17)

his examination. But the search was vain : there was the tunic aforesaid ; there was a smart-looking kerseymere waistcoat ; but the most important article of all in a gentleman's wardrobe was still wanting.

"Where *can* they be?" asked the master, with a strong accent on the auxiliary verb.

"Sorrow a know I knows," said the man.

"It *must* have been the devil, then, after all, who has been here and carried them off!" cried Seaforth, staring full into Barney's face.

Mr. Maguire was not devoid of the superstition of his countrymen, still he looked as if he did not quite subscribe to the *sequitur*.

His master read incredulity in his countenance. "Why, I tell you, Barney, I put them there, on that arm-chair, when I got into bed ; and, by heaven! I distinctly saw the ghost of the old fellow they told me of come in at midnight, put on my pantaloons, and walk away with them."

"May be so," was the cautious reply.

"I thought, of course, it was a dream ; but then—where the d—l are the breeches?"

The question was more easily asked than answered. Barney renewed his search, while the lieutenant folded his arms, and, leaning against the toilet, sank into a reverie.

"After all, it must be some trick of my laughter-loving cousins," said Seaforth.

"Ah! then, the ladies!" chimed in Mr. Maguire, though the observation was not addressed to him ; "and will it be Miss Caroline or Miss Fanny that's stole your honor's things?"

"I hardly know what to think of it," pursued the bereaved lieutenant, still speaking in soliloquy, with his eye resting dubiously on the chamber-door. "I locked myself in, that's certain ; and—but there must be some other entrance to the room—pooh! I remember—the private staircase ; how could I be such a fool?" and he crossed the chamber to where a low oaken doorcase was dimly visible in a distant corner. He paused before it. Nothing now interfered to screen it from observation ; but it bore tokens of having been at some earlier period concealed by tapestry, remains of which yet clothed the walls on either side the portal.

"This way they must have come," said Seaforth; "I wish with all my heart I had caught them!"

"Och! the kittens!" sighed Mr. Barney Maguire.

But the mystery was yet as far from being solved as before. True, there *was* the "other door;" but then that, too, on examination, was even more firmly secured than the one which opened on the gallery,—two heavy bolts on the inside effectually prevented any *coup de main* on the lieutenant's *bivouac* from that quarter. He was more puzzled than ever; nor did the minutest inspection of the walls and floor throw any light upon the subject: one thing only was clear,—the breeches were gone! "It is *very* singular," said the lieutenant.

————

Tappington (generally called Tapton) Everard is an antiquated but commodious manor-house in the eastern division of the county of Kent. A former proprietor had been high-sheriff in the days of Elizabeth, and many a dark and dismal tradition was yet extant of the licentiousness of his life and the enormity of his offences. The Glen, which the keeper's daughter was seen to enter, but never known to quit, still frowns darkly as of yore; while an ineradicable bloodstain on the oaken stair yet bids defiance to the united energies of soap and sand. But it is with one particular apartment that a deed of more especial atrocity is said to be connected. A stranger guest—so runs the legend—arrived unexpectedly at the mansion of the "Bad Sir Giles." They met in apparent friendship; but the ill-concealed scowl on their master's brow told the domestics that the visit was not a welcome one; the banquet, however, was not spared; the wine cup circulated freely,—too freely, perhaps, for sounds of discord at length reached the ears of even the excluded serving-men, as they were doing their best to imitate their betters in the lower hall. Alarmed, some of them ventured to approach the parlor; one, an old and favored retainer of the house, went so far as to break in upon his master's privacy. Sir Giles, already high in oath, fiercely enjoined his absence, and he retired; not, however, before he had distinctly heard from the stranger's lips a menace that "there was that within his pocket which could disprove the knight's right to issue that or any other command within the walls of Tapton."

The intrusion, though momentary, seemed to have produced a beneficial effect; the voices of the disputants fell, and the conversation was carried on thenceforth in a more subdued tone, till, as evening closed in, the domestics, when summoned to attend with lights, found not only cordiality restored, but that a still deeper carouse was meditated. Fresh stoups, and from the choicest bins, were produced; nor was it till at a late, or rather early, hour that the revellers sought their chambers.

The one allotted to the stranger occupied the first floor of the eastern angle of the building, and had once been the favorite apartment of Sir Giles himself. Scandal ascribed this preference to the facility which a private staircase, communicating with the grounds, had afforded him, in the old knight's time, of following his wicked courses unchecked by parental observation; a consideration which ceased to be of weight when the death of his father left him uncontrolled master of his estate and actions. From that period Sir Giles had established himself in what were called the "state apartments," and the "oaken chamber" was rarely tenanted, save on occasions of extraordinary festivity, or when the yule log drew an unusually large accession of guests around the Christmas hearth.

On this eventful night it was prepared for the unknown visitor, who sought his couch heated and inflamed from his midnight orgies, and in the morning was found in his bed a swollen and blackened corpse. No marks of violence appeared upon the body; but the livid hue of the lips, and certain dark-colored spots visible on the skin, aroused suspicions which those who entertained them were too timid to express. Apoplexy, induced by the excesses of the preceding night, Sir Giles's confidential leech pronounced to be the cause of his sudden dissolution. The body was buried in peace; and though some shook their heads as they witnessed the haste with which the funeral rites were hurried on, none ventured to murmur. Other events arose to distract the attention of the retainers; men's minds became occupied by the stirring politics of the day; while the near approach of that formidable armada, so vainly arrogating to itself a title which the very elements joined with human valor to disprove, soon interfered to weaken, if not obliterate, all remembrance of the nameless stranger who had died within the walls of Tapton Everard.

Years rolled on : the " Bad Sir Giles " had himself long since gone to his account, the last, as it was believed, of his immediate line; though a few of the older tenants were sometimes heard to speak of an elder brother, who had disappeared in early life, and never inherited the estate. Rumors, too, of his having left a son in foreign lands were at one time rife; but they died away, nothing occurring to support them : the property passed unchallenged to a collateral branch of the family, and the secret, if secret there were, was buried in Denton churchyard, in the lonely grave of the mysterious stranger. One circumstance alone occurred, after a long intervening period, to revive the memory of these transactions. Some workmen employed in grubbing an old plantation, for the purpose of raising on its site a modern shrubbery, dug up, in the execution of their task, the mildewed remnants of what seemed to have been once a garment. On more minute inspection, enough remained of silken slashes and a coarse embroidery to identify the relics as having once formed part of a pair of trunk hose; while a few papers which fell from them, altogether illegible from damp and age, were by the unlearned rustics conveyed to the then owner of the estate.

Whether the squire was more successful in deciphering them was never known; he certainly never alluded to their contents; and little would have been thought of the matter but for the inconvenient memory of an old woman, who declared she heard her grandfather say that when the "stranger guest" was poisoned, though all the rest of his clothes were there, his breeches, the supposed repository of the supposed documents, could never be found. The master of Tapton Everard smiled when he heard Dame Jones's hint of deeds which might impeach the validity of his own title in favor of some unknown descendant of some unknown heir; and the story was rarely alluded to, save by one or two miracle-mongers, who had heard that others had seen the ghost of old Sir Giles, in his nightcap, issue from the postern, enter the adjoining copse, and wring his shadowy hands in agony, as he seemed to search vainly for something hidden among the evergreens. The stranger's death-room had, of course, been occasionally haunted from the time of his decease; but the periods of visitation had latterly become very rare—even Mrs. Botherby, the housekeeper, being forced to admit that during her long sojourn at the manor she had never "met with anything worse than herself;" though, as the old lady afterwards added upon more mature reflection, "I must say I think I saw the devil *once.*"

Such was the legend attached to Tapton Everard, and such the story which the lively Caroline Ingoldsby detailed to her equally mercurial cousin, Charles Seaforth, lieutenant in the Hon. East India Company's second regiment of Bombay Fencibles, as arm-in-arm they promenaded a gallery decked with some dozen grim-looking ancestral portraits, and, among others, with that of the redoubted Sir Giles himself. The gallant commander had that very morning paid his first visit to the house of his maternal uncle, after an absence of several years passed with his regiment on the arid plains of Hindostan, whence he was now returned on a three years' furlough. He had gone out a boy—he returned a man; but the impression made upon his youthful fancy by his favorite cousin remained unimpaired, and to Tapton he directed his steps, even before he sought the home of his widowed mother,—comforting himself in this breach of filial decorum by the reflection that, as the manor was so little out of his way, it would be unkind to pass, as it were, the door of his relatives, without just looking in for a few hours.

But he found his uncle as hospitable, and his cousin more charming than ever; and the looks of one, and the requests of the other, soon precluded the possibility of refusing to lengthen the "few hours" into a few days, though the house was at the moment full of visitors.

The Peterses were there from Ramsgate; and Mr., Mrs., and the two Miss Simpkinsons, from Bath, had come to pass a month with the family; and Tom Ingoldsby had brought down his college friend the Honorable Augustus Sucklethumbkin, with his groom and pointers, to take a fortnight's shooting. And then there was Mrs. Ogleton, the rich young widow, with her large black eyes, who, people did say, was setting her cap at the young squire, though Mrs. Botherby did not believe it; and, above all, there was Mademoiselle Pauline, her *femme de chambre*, who "*mon-Dieu'd*" everything and everybody, and cried "*Quel horreur!*" at Mrs. Botherby's cap. In short, to use the last-named and much-respected lady's own expression, the house was "choke-full" to the very attics,—all save the "oaken chamber," which, as the lieutenant expressed a most magnanimous disregard of ghosts, was forthwith appropriated to his particular accommodation. Mr. Maguire meanwhile was fain to share the apartment of Oliver Dobbs, the squire's own man: a jocular proposal of joint occupancy having been first indignantly rejected by "Mademoiselle," though preferred with the "laste taste in life" of Mr. Barney's most insinuating brogue.

"Come, Charles, the urn is absolutely getting cold; your breakfast will be quite spoiled: what can have made you so idle?" Such was the morning salutation of Miss Ingoldsby to the *militaire* as he entered the breakfast-room half an hour after the latest of the party.

"A pretty gentleman, truly, to make an appointment with!" chimed in Miss Frances. "What is become of our ramble to the rocks before breakfast?"

"Oh! the young men never think of keeping a promise now," said Mrs. Peters, a little ferret-faced woman with underdone eyes.

"When I was a young man," said Mr. Peters, "I remember I always made a point of——"

"Pray, how long ago was that?" asked Mr. Simpkinson from Bath.

"Why, sir, when I married Mrs. Peters, I was—let me see— I was——"

"Do pray hold your tongue, P., and eat your breakfast!" interrupted his better half, who had a mortal horror of chronological references; "it's very rude to tease people with your family affairs."

The lieutenant had by this time taken his seat in silence—a good-humored nod, and a glance, half-smiling, half-inquisitive, being the extent of his salutation. Smitten as he was, and in the immediate presence of her who had made so large a hole in his heart, his manner was evidently *distrait*, which the fair Caroline in her secret soul attributed to his being solely occupied by her *agrémens:* how would she have bridled had she known that they only shared his meditations with a pair of breeches!

Charles drank his coffee and spiked some half-dozen eggs, darting occasionally a penetrating glance at the ladies, in hope of detecting the supposed waggery by the evidence of some furtive smile or conscious look. But in vain; not a dimple moved indicative of roguery, nor did the slightest elevation of eyebrow rise confirmative of his suspicions. Hints and insinuations passed unheeded—more particular inquiries were out of the question:—the subject was unapproachable.

In the meantime, "patent cords" were just the thing for a morning's ride; and, breakfast ended, away cantered the party over the downs, till, every faculty absorbed by the beauties, animate and inanimate, which surrounded him, Lieutenant Seaforth of the Bombay Fencibles bestowed no more thought upon his breeches than if he had been born on the top of Ben Lomond.

―――――

Another night had passed away; the sun rose brilliantly, forming with his level beams a splendid rainbow in the far-off west, whither the heavy cloud, which for the last two hours had been pouring its waters on the earth, was now flying before him.

"Ah! then, and it's little good it'll be the claning of ye," apostrophized Mr. Barney Maguire, as he deposited in front of his master's toilet a pair of "bran new" jockey boots, one of Hoby's primest fits, which the lieutenant had purchased in his way through town. On that very morning had they come for the first time under the valet's depurating hand, so little soiled, indeed, from the turfy ride of the preceding day, that a less scrupulous domestic might, perhaps, have considered the application of "Warren's Matchless," or oxalic acid, altogether superfluous. Not so Barney: with the nicest care had he removed the slightest impurity from each polished surface, and there they stood, rejoicing in their sable radiance. No wonder a pang shot across Mr. Maguire's breast as he thought on the

work now cut out for them, so different from the light labors
of the day before; no wonder he murmured with a sigh, as the
scarce-dried window-panes disclosed a road now inch deep in
mud, "Ah! then, it's little good the claning of ye!"—for well
had he learned in the hall below that eight miles of a stiff clay
soil lay between the manor and Bolsover Abbey, whose picturesque ruins,

> "Like ancient Rome, majestic in decay,"

the party had determined to explore. The master had already
commenced dressing, and the man was fitting straps upon a light
pair of crane-necked spurs, when his hand was arrested by the
old question—"Barney, where are the breeches?"

They were nowhere to be found!

Mr. Seaforth descended that morning, whip in hand, and
equipped in a handsome green riding-frock, but no "breeches
and boots to match" were there: loose jean trousers, surmount-
ing a pair of diminutive Wellingtons, embraced, somewhat incongruously, his nether man, *vice* the "patent cords," returned,
like yesterday's pantaloons, absent without leave. The "top-
boots" had a holiday.

"A fine morning after the rain," said Mr. Simpkinson from
Bath.

"Just the thing for the 'ops," said Mr. Peters. "I remember
when I was a boy——"

"Do hold your tongue, P.," said Mrs. Peters—advice which
that exemplary matron was in the constant habit of administering to "her P.," as she called him, whenever he prepared to
vent his reminiscences. Her precise reason for this it would be
difficult to determine, unless, indeed, the story be true which a
little bird had whispered into Mrs. Botherby's ear—Mr. Peters,
though now a wealthy man, had received a liberal education at
a charity school, and was apt to recur to the days of his muffin-
cap and leathers. As usual, he took his wife's hint in good
part, and "paused in his reply."

"A glorious day for the ruins!" said young Ingoldsby. "But,

Charles, what the deuce are you about? you don't mean to ride
through our lanes in such toggery as that?"

"Lassy me!" said Miss Julia Simpkinson, "won't you be very
wet?"

"You had better take Tom's cab," quoth the squire.

But this proposition was at once overruled; Mrs. Ogleton had
already nailed the cab, a vehicle of all others the best adapted
for a snug flirtation.

"Or drive Miss Julia in the phaeton?" No; that was the
post of Mr. Peters, who, indifferent as an equestrian, had acquired some fame as a whip while travelling through the mid-
land counties for the firm of Bagshaw, Snivelby, and Ghrimes.

"Thank you, I shall ride with my cousins," said Charles,
with as much *nonchalance* as he could assume—and he did so;
Mr. Ingoldsby, Mrs. Peters, Mr. Simpkinson from Bath, and his
eldest daughter with her *album*, following in the family coach.
The gentleman-commoner "voted the affair d—d slow," and
declined the party altogether in favor of the gamekeeper and a
cigar. "There was 'no fun' in looking at old houses!" Mrs.
Simpkinson preferred a short *séjour* in the still-room with Mrs.
Botherby, who had promised to initiate her in that grand *ar-
canum*, the transmutation of gooseberry jam into Guava jelly.

"Did you ever see an old abbey before, Mr. Peters?"

"Yes, miss, a French one; we have got one at Ramsgate; he
teaches the Miss Joneses to parley-voo, and is turned of sixty."

Miss Simpkinson closed her album with an air of ineffable
disdain.

Mr. Simpkinson from Bath was a professed antiquary, and
one of the first water; he was master of Gwillim's Heraldry
and Mills's History of the Crusades; knew every plate in the
Monasticon; had written an essay on the origin and dignity of
the office of overseer, and settled the date on a Queen Anne's
farthing. An influential member of the Antiquarian Society,
to whose "Beauties of Bagnigge Wells" he had been a liberal
subscriber, procured him a seat at the board of that learned
body, since which happy epoch Sylvanus Urban had not a more

indefatigable correspondent. His inaugural essay on the President's cocked hat was considered a miracle of erudition; and his account of the earliest application of gilding to gingerbread, a masterpiece of antiquarian research. His eldest daughter was of a kindred spirit: if her father's mantle had not fallen upon her, it was only because he had not thrown it off himself; she had caught hold of its tail, however, while it yet hung upon his honored shoulders. To souls so congenial, what a sight was the magnificent ruin of Bolsover! its broken arches, its mouldering pinnacles, and the airy tracery of its half-demolished windows. The party were in raptures; Mr. Simpkinson began to meditate an essay, and his daughter an ode: even Seaforth, as he gazed on these lonely relics of the olden time, was betrayed into a momentary forgetfulness of his love and losses: the widow's eye-glass turned from her *cicisbeo's* whiskers to the mantling ivy; Mrs. Peters wiped her spectacles; and "her P." supposed the central tower "had once been the county jail." The squire was a philosopher, and had been there often before, so he ordered out the cold tongue and chickens.

"Bolsover Priory," said Mr. Simpkinson, with the air of a connoisseur,—"Bolsover Priory was founded in the reign of Henry the Sixth, about the beginning of the eleventh century. Hugh de Bolsover had accompanied that monarch to the Holy Land in the expedition undertaken by way of penance for the murder of his young nephews in the Tower. Upon the dissolution of the monasteries, the veteran was enfeoffed in the lands and manor, to which he gave his own name of Bowlsover, or Bee-owls-over (by corruption Bolsover),—a Bee in chief, over three Owls, all proper, being the armorial ensigns borne by this distinguished crusader at the siege of Acre."

"Ah! that was Sir Sidney Smith," said Mr. Peters; "I've heard tell of him, and all about Mrs. Partington, and——"

"P., be quiet, and don't expose yourself!" sharply interrupted his lady. P. was silenced, and betook himself to the bottled stout.

"These lands," continued the antiquary, "were held in grand sergeantry by the presentation of three white owls and a pot of honey——"

"Lassy me! how nice!" said Miss Julia. Mr. Peters licked his lips.

"Pray give me leave, my dear—owls and honey, whenever the king should come a rat-catching into this part of the country."

"Rat-catching!" ejaculated the squire, pausing abruptly in the mastication of a drumstick.

"To be sure, my dear sir: don't you remember the rats once came under the forest laws—a minor species of venison? 'Rats, mice, and such small deer,' eh?—Shakspeare, you know. Our ancestors ate rats ('The nasty fellows!' shuddered Miss Julia, in a parenthesis); and owls, you know, are capital mousers——"

"I've seen a howl," said Mr. Peters; "there's one in the So-hological Gardens,—a little hook-nosed chap in a wig,—only its feathers and——"

Poor P. was destined never to finish a speech.

"*Do* be quiet!" cried the authoritative voice; and the would-be naturalist shrank into his shell, like a snail in the "Soho-logical Gardens."

"You should read Blount's 'Jocular Tenures,' Mr. Ingolds-by," pursued Simpkinson. "A learned man was Blount! Why, sir, His Royal Highness the Duke of York once paid a silver horse-shoe to Lord Ferrers——"

"I've heard of him," broke in the incorrigible Peters; "he was hanged at the Old Bailey in a silk rope for shooting Dr. Johnson."

The antiquary vouchsafed no notice of the interruption; but, taking a pinch of snuff, continued his harangue.

"A silver horse-shoe, sir, which is due from every scion of royalty who rides across one of his manors; and, if you look into the penny county histories, now publishing by an eminent friend of mine, you will find that Langhale in Co. Norf. was held by one Baldwin *per saltum, sufflatum, et pettum;* that is, he was to come every Christmas into Westminster Hall, there to take a leap, cry hem! and——"

"Mr. Simpkinson, a glass of sherry?" cried Tom Ingoldsby, hastily.

"Not any, thank you, sir. This Baldwin, surnamed *Le*——"

"Mrs. Ogleton challenges you, sir; she insists upon it," said Tom, still more rapidly, at the same time filling a glass and forcing it on the *savant*, who, thus arrested in the very crisis of his narrative, received and swallowed the potation as if it had been physic.

"What on earth has Miss Simpkinson discovered there?" continued Tom; "something of interest. See how fast she is writing."

The diversion was effectual; every one looked towards Miss Simpkinson, who, far too ethereal for "creature comforts," was seated apart on the dilapidated remains of an altar-tomb, committing eagerly to paper something that had strongly impressed her; the air—the eye in a "fine frenzy rolling,"—all betokened that the divine *afflatus* was come. Her father rose and stole silently towards her.

"What an old boar!" muttered young Ingoldsby; alluding perhaps to a slice of brawn which he had just begun to operate upon, but which, from the celerity with which it disappeared, did not seem so very difficult of mastication.

But what had become of Seaforth and his fair Caroline all this while? Why, it so happened that they had been simultaneously stricken with the picturesque appearance of one of those high and pointed arches which that eminent antiquary, Mr. Horseley Curties, has described in his "Ancient Records" as "a *Gothic* window of the *Saxon* order;" and then the ivy clustered so thickly and so beautifully on the other side that they went round to look at that; and then their proximity deprived it of half its effect, and so they walked across to a little knoll, a hundred yards off, and in crossing a small ravine they came to what in Ireland they call "a bad step," and Charles had to carry his cousin over it; and then when they had to come back, she would not give him the trouble again for the world, so they followed a better but more circuitous route, and there were hedges and ditches in the way, and stiles to get over and gates to get through, so that an hour or more had elapsed before they were able to rejoin the party.

"Lassy me!" said Miss Julia Simpkinson, "how long you have been gone!"

And so they had. The remark was a very just as well as a very natural one. They were gone a long while, and a nice cosy chat they had; and what do you think it was all about, my dear miss?

"Oh, lassy me! love, no doubt, and the moon, and eyes, and nightingales, and——"

Stay, stay, my sweet young lady; do not let the fervor of your feelings run away with you! I do not pretend to say, indeed, that one or more of these pretty subjects might not have been introduced; but the most important and leading topic of the conference was—Lieutenant Seaforth's breeches.

"Caroline," said Charles, "I have had some very odd dreams since I have been at Tappington."

"Dreams, have you?" smiled the young lady, arching her taper neck like a swan in pluming. "Dreams, have you?"

"Ay, dreams,—or dream, perhaps, I should say; for, though repeated, it was still the same. And what do you imagine was its subject?"

"It is impossible for me to divine," said the tongue;—"I have not the least difficulty in guessing," said the eye, as plainly as ever eye spoke.

"I dreamt—of your great-grandfather!"

There was a change in the glance—"My great-grandfather?"

"Yes, the old Sir Giles, or Sir John, you told me about the other day: he walked into my bedroom in his short cloak of murrey-colored velvet, his long rapier, and his Raleigh-looking hat and feather, just as the picture represents him; but with one exception."

"And what was that?"

"Why, his lower extremities, which were visible, were those of a skeleton."

"Well?"

"Well, after taking a turn or two about the room, and looking round him with a wistful air, he came to the bed's foot, stared at me in a manner impossible to describe,—and then he—he laid hold of my pantaloons; whipped his long bony legs into them in a twinkling; and strutting up to the glass, seemed to view himself in it with great complacency. I tried to speak, but in vain. The effort, however, seemed to excite his attention; for, wheeling about, he showed me the grimmest-looking death's head you can well imagine, and with an indescribable grin strutted out of the room."

"Absurd! Charles. How can you talk such nonsense?"
"But, Caroline,—the breeches are really gone."

On the following morning, contrary to his usual custom, Sea-forth was the first person in the breakfast parlor. As no one else was present, he did precisely what nine young men out of ten so situated would have done; he walked up to the mantle-piece, established himself upon the rug, and, subducting his coat-tails one under each arm, turned towards the fire that portion of the human frame which it is considered equally indecorous to present to a friend or an enemy. A serious, not to say anxious, expression was visible upon his good-humored countenance, and his mouth was fast buttoning itself up for an incipient whistle, when little Floy, a tiny spaniel of the Blenheim breed,—the pet object of Miss Julia Simpkinson's affections,—bounced out from beneath a sofa, and began to bark at—his pantaloons.

They were cleverly "built," of a light-gray mixture, a broad stripe of the most vivid scarlet traversing each seam in a perpendicular direction from hip to ankle—in short, the regimental costume of the Royal Bombay Fencibles. The animal, educated in the country, had never seen such a pair of breeches in her life—*Omne ignotum pro magnifico!* The scarlet streak, inflamed as it was by the reflection of the fire, seemed to act on Flora's nerves as the same color does on those of bulls and turkeys; she advanced at the *pas de charge*, and her vociferation, like her amazement, was unbounded. A sound kick from the disgusted officer changed its character, and induced a retreat at the very moment when the mistress of the pugnacious quadruped entered to the rescue.

"Lassy me! Flo, what *is* the matter?" cried the sympathizing lady, with a scrutinizing glance levelled at the gentleman.

It might as well have lighted on a feather bed. His air of imperturbable unconsciousness defied examination; and as he would not, and Flora could not, expound, that injured individual was compelled to pocket up her wrongs. Others of the household soon dropped in, and clustered round the board dedicated to the most sociable of meals; the urn was paraded "hissing

hot," and the cups which "cheer, but not inebriate," steamed
redolent of hyson and pekoe; muffins and marmalade, newspapers and Finnon haddies, left little room for observation on
the character of Charles's warlike "turn-out." At length a
look from Caroline, followed by a smile that nearly ripened to
a titter, caused him to turn abruptly and address his neighbor.
It was Miss Simpkinson, who, deeply engaged in sipping her tea
and turning over her album, seemed, like a female Chrouono-
tonthologos, "immersed in cogibundity of cogitation." An
interrogatory on the subject of her studies drew from her the
confession that she was at that moment employed in putting the
finishing touches to a poem inspired by the romantic shades of
Bolsover. The entreaties of the company were of course urgent.
Mr. Peters, "who liked verses," was especially persevering, and
Sappho at length compliant. After a preparatory hem! and a
glance at the mirror to ascertain that her look was sufficiently
sentimental, the poetess began :—

> " There is a calm, a holy feeling,
>   Vulgar minds can never know,
> O'er the bosom softly stealing,—
>   Chasten'd grief, delicious woe!
> Oh! how sweet at eve regaining
>   Yon lone tower's sequester'd shade—
> Sadly mute and uncomplaining——"

—Yow!—yeough!—yeough!—yow!—yow! yelled a hapless sufferer from beneath the table. It was an unlucky hour for
quadrupeds; and if "every dog will have his day," he could
not have selected a more unpropitious one than this. Mrs.
Ogleton, too, had a pet,—a favorite pug,—whose squab figure,
black muzzle, and tortuosity of tail, that curled like a head
of celery in a salad-bowl, bespoke his Dutch extraction. Yow!
yow! yow! continued the brute,—a chorus in which Flo instantly joined. Sooth to say, pug had more reason to express
his dissatisfaction than was given him by the muse of Simpkinson; the other only barked for company. Scarcely had the
poetess got through her first stanza, when Tom Ingoldsby, in
the enthusiasm of the moment, became so lost in the material
world, that, in his abstraction, he unwarily laid his hand on the
cock of the urn. Quivering with emotion, he gave it such an

unlucky twist that the full stream of its scalding contents descended on the gingerbread hide of the unlucky Cupid. The confusion was complete; the whole economy of the table disarranged—the company broke up in most admired disorder—and "vulgar minds will never know" anything more of Miss Simpkinson's ode till they peruse it in some forthcoming Annual.

Seaforth profited by the confusion to take the delinquent who had caused this "stramash" by the arm, and to lead him to the lawn, where he had a word or two for his private ear. The conference between the young gentlemen was neither brief in its duration nor unimportant in its result. The subject was what the lawyers call tripartite, embracing the information that Charles Seaforth was over head and ears in love with Tom Ingoldsby's sister; secondly, that the lady had referred him to "papa" for his sanction; thirdly and lastly, his nightly visitations, and consequent bereavement. At the two first items Tom smiled auspiciously—at the last he burst out into an absolute "guffaw."

"Steal your breeches! Miss Bailey over again, by Jove," shouted Ingoldsby. "But a gentleman, you say,—and Sir Giles too. I am not sure, Charles, whether I ought not to call you out for aspersing the honor of the family."

"Laugh as you will, Tom,—be as incredulous as you please. One fact is incontestable—the breeches are gone! Look here— I am reduced to my regimentals; and if these go, to-morrow I must borrow of you!"

Rochefoucauld says there is something in the misfortunes of our very best friends that does not displease us; assuredly we can, most of us, laugh at their petty inconveniences, till called upon to supply them. Tom composed his features on the instant, and replied with more gravity, as well as with an expletive which, if my Lord Mayor had been within hearing, might have cost him five shillings.

"There is something very queer in this, after all. The clothes, you say, have positively disappeared. Somebody is playing you a trick; and, ten to one, your servant has a hand in it. By the way, I heard something yesterday of his kicking up a bobbery in the kitchen, and seeing a ghost, or something of that kind, himself. Depend upon it, Barney is in the plot."

3

It now struck the lieutenant at once that the usually buoyant spirits of his attendant had of late been materially sobered down, his loquacity obviously circumscribed, and that he, the said lieutenant, had actually rung his bell three several times that very morning before he could procure his attendance. Mr. Maguire was forthwith summoned, and underwent a close examination. The "bobbery" was easily explained. Mr. Oliver Dobbs had hinted his disapprobation of a flirtation carrying on between the gentleman from Munster and the lady from the Rue St. Honoré. Mademoiselle had boxed Mr. Maguire's ears, and Mr. Maguire had pulled Mademoiselle upon his knee, and the lady had *not* cried *Mon Dieu!* And Mr. Oliver Dobbs said it was very wrong; and Mrs. Botherby said it was "scandalous," and what ought not to be done in any moral kitchen; and Mr. Maguire had got hold of the Honorable Augustus Sucklethumbkin's powder-flask, and had put large pinches of the best Double Dartford into Mr. Dobbs's tobacco-box; and Mr. Dobbs's pipe had exploded, and set fire to Mrs. Botherby's Sunday cap; and Mr. Maguire had put it out with the slop-basin, "barring the wig;" and then they were all so "cantankerous" that Barney had gone to take a walk in the garden; and then—then Mr. Barney had seen a ghost.

"A what? you blockhead!" asked Tom Ingoldsby.

"Sure then, and it's meself will tell your honor the rights of it," said the ghost-seer. "Meself and Miss Pauline, sir,—or Miss Pauline and meself, for the ladies comes first anyhow,—we got tired of the hobstroppylous scrimmaging among the ould servants, that didn't know a joke when they seen one: and we went out to look at the comet,—that's the rorybory-alehouse, they calls him in this country,—and we walked upon the lawn, —and divil of any alehouse there was there at all; and Miss Pauline said it was bekase of the shrubbery maybe, and why wouldn't we see it better beyonst the trees? and so we went to the trees, but sorrow a comet did meself see there, barring a big ghost instead of it."

"A ghost? And what sort of a ghost, Barney?"

"Och, then, divil a lie I'll tell your honor. A tall ould gentleman he was, all in white, with a shovel on the shoulder of him, and a big torch in his fist,—though what he wanted with

that it's meself can't tell, for his eyes were like gig-lamps, let
alone the moon and the comet, which wasn't there at all :—and
' Barney,' says he to me,—'cause why he knew me,—' Barney,'
says he, ' what is it you're doing with the *colleen* there, Barney ?'
Divil a word did I say. Miss Pauline screeched, and cried
murther in French, and ran off with herself; and of course
meself was in a mighty hurry after the lady, and had no time
to stop palavering with him any way: so I dispersed at once, and
the ghost vanished in a flame of fire !"

Mr. Maguire's account was received with avowed incredulity
by both gentlemen ; but Barney stuck to his text with unflinch-
ing pertinacity. A reference to Mademoiselle was suggested,
but abandoned, as neither party had a taste for delicate inves-
tigations.

" I'll tell you what, Seaforth," said Ingoldsby, after Barney
had received his dismissal, " that there is a trick here is evident ;
and Barney's vision may possibly be a part of it. Whether he
is most knave or fool you best know. At all events, I will sit
up with you to-night, and see if I can convert my ancestor into
a visiting acquaintance. Meanwhile your finger on your lip !"

" 'Twas now the very witching time of night,
    When churchyards yawn, and graves give up their dead."

Gladly would I grace my tale with decent horror, and therefore I do beseech the " gentle reader" to believe that if all the
succedanea to this mysterious narrative are not in strict keeping,
he will ascribe it only to the disgraceful innovations of modern
degeneracy upon the sober and dignified habits of our ancestors.
I can introduce him, it is true, into an old and high-roof chamber, its walls covered on three sides with black oak wainscoting,
adorned with carvings of fruit and flowers long anterior to those of
Grinling Gibbons ; the fourth side is clothed with a curious rem-
nant of dingy tapestry, once elucidatory of some Scriptural history, but of *which* not even Mrs. Botherby could determine. Mr.
Simpkinson, who had examined it carefully, inclined to believe
the principal figure to be either Bathsheba, or Daniel in the

lions' den; while Tom Ingoldsby decided in favor of the King of
Bashan. All, however, was conjecture, tradition being silent on
the subject. A lofty arched portal led into, and a little arched
portal led out of, this apartment; they were opposite each other,
and each possessed the security of massy bolts on its interior.
The bedstead, too, was not one of yesterday, but manifestly
coeval with days ere Seddons was, and when a good four-post
"article" was deemed worthy of being a royal bequest. The
bed itself, with all the appurtenances of palliasse, mattresses,
etc., was of far later date, and looked most incongruously com-
fortable; the casements, too, with their little diamond-shaped
panes and iron binding, had given way to the modern hetero-
doxy of the sash-window. Nor was this all that conspired to
ruin the costume, and render the room a meet haunt for such
"mixed spirits" only as could condescend to don at the same
time an Elizabethan doublet and Bond-Street inexpressibles.

With their green morocco slippers on a modern fender, in
front of a disgracefully modern grate, sat two young gentlemen,
clad in "shawl-pattern" dressing-gowns and black silk stocks,
much at variance with the high cane-backed chairs which supported them. A bunch of abomination, called a cigar, reeked
in the left-hand corner of the mouth of one, and in the right-
hand corner of the mouth of the other—an arrangement happily adapted for the escape of the noxious fumes up the chimney without that unmerciful "funking" each other which a
less scientific disposition of the weed would have induced. A
small pembroke table filled up the intervening space between
them, sustaining, at each extremity, an elbow and a glass of
toddy—thus in "lonely pensive contemplation" were the two
worthies occupied, when the "iron tongue of midnight had
tolled twelve."

"Ghost-time's come!" said Ingoldsby, taking from his waistcoat pocket a watch like a gold half-crown, and consulting it
as though he suspected the turret-clock over the stables of men-
dacity.

"Hush!" said Charles; "did I not hear a footstep?"

There was a pause:—there *was* a footstep—it sounded distinctly—it reached the door—it hesitated, stopped, and—passed
on.

Tom darted across the room, threw open the door, and became aware of Mrs. Botherby toddling to her chamber, at the other end of the gallery, after dosing one of the housemaids with an approved julep from the Countess of Kent's *Choice Manual.*

"Good-night, sir!" said Mrs. Botherby.

"Go to the d—l!" said the disappointed ghost-hunter.

An hour—two—rolled on, and still no spectral visitation, nor did aught intervene to make night hideous; and when the turret-clock sounded at length the hour of three, Ingoldsby, whose patience and grog were alike exhausted, sprang from his chair, saying—

"This is all infernal nonsense, my good fellow. Deuce of any ghost shall we see to-night; it's long past the canonical hour. I'm off to bed; and as to your breeches, I'll insure them for the next twenty-four hours at least, at the price of the buckram."

"Certainly.—Oh! thank'ee—to be sure!" stammered Charles, rousing himself from a reverie which had degenerated into an absolute snooze.

"Good-night, my boy! Bolt the door behind me; and defy the Pope, the Devil, and the Pretender!"

Seaforth followed his friend's advice, and the next morning came down to breakfast dressed in the habiliments of the preceding day. The charm was broken, the demon defeated; the light grays with the red stripe down the seams were yet *in rerum naturâ,* and adorned the person of their lawful proprietor.

Tom felicitated himself and his partner of the watch on the result of their vigilance; but there is a rustic adage which warns us against self-gratulation before we are quite "out of the wood."—Seaforth was yet within its verge.

———

A rap at Tom Ingoldsby's door the following morning startled him as he was shaving—he cut his chin.

"Come in, and be d—d to you!" said the martyr, pressing his thumb on the scarified epidermis. The door opened, and exhibited Mr. Barney Maguire.

"Well, Barney, what is it?" quoth the sufferer, adopting the vernacular of his visitant.

"The master, sir——"

"Well, what does he want?"

"The loanst of a breeches, plase your honor."

"Why, you don't mean to tell me——By Heaven, this is too good!" shouted Tom, bursting into a fit of uncontrollable laughter. "Why, Barney, you don't mean to say the ghost has got them again?"

Mr. Maguire did not respond to the young squire's risibility; the cast of his countenance was decidedly serious.

"Faith, then, it's gone they are, sure enough! Hasn't meself been looking over the bed, and under the bed, and *in* the bed, for the matter of that, and divil a ha'p'orth of breeches is there to the fore at all :—I'm bothered entirely!"

"Hark'ee! Mr. Barney," said Tom, incautiously removing his thumb and letting a crimson stream "incarnadine the multitudinous" lather that plastered his throat—"this may be all very well with your master, but you don't humbug *me*, sir :— tell me instantly what have you done with the clothes?"

This abrupt transition from "lively to severe" certainly took Maguire by surprise, and he seemed for an instant as much disconcerted as it is possible to disconcert an Irish gentleman's gentleman.

"Me? is it meself, then, that's the ghost to your honor's thinking?" said he after a moment's pause, and with a slight shade of indignation in his tones: "is it I would stale the master's things—and what would I do with them?"

"That you best know :—what your purpose is I can't guess, for I don't think you mean to 'stale' them, as you call it; but that you are concerned in their disappearance, I am satisfied. Confound this blood!—give me a towel, Barney."

Maguire acquitted himself of the commission. "As I've a sowl, your honor," said he, solemnly, "little it is meself knows of the matter: and after what I seen——"

"What you've seen! Why, what *have* you seen?—Barney, I don't want to inquire into your flirtations; but don't suppose you can palm off your saucer eyes and gig-lamps upon me!"

"Then, as sure as your honor's standing there, I saw him:

and why wouldn't I, when Miss Pauline was to the fore as well as meself, and——"

"Get along with your nonsense—leave the room, sir!"

"But the master?" said Barney, imploringly; "and without a breeches?—sure he'll be catching cowld!——"

"Take that, rascal!" replied Ingoldsby, throwing a pair of pantaloons at, rather than to, him: "but don't suppose, sir, you shall carry on your tricks here with impunity; recollect there is such a thing as a treadmill, and that my father is a county magistrate."

Barney's eye flashed fire—he stood erect, and was about to speak; but, mastering himself, not without an effort, he took up the garment, and left the room as perpendicular as a Quaker.

———————

"Ingoldsby," said Charles Seaforth, after breakfast, "this is now past a joke; to-day is the last of my stay; for, notwithstanding the ties which detain me, common decency obliges me to visit home after so long an absence. I shall come to an immediate explanation with your father on the subject nearest my heart, and depart while I have a change of dress left. On his answer will my return depend! In the meantime tell me candidly,—I ask it in all seriousness, and as a friend,—am I not a dupe to your well-known propensity to hoaxing? have you not a hand in——"

"No, by heaven, Seaforth; I see what you mean: on my honor, I am as much mystified as yourself; and if your servant——"

"Not he:—if there be a trick, he at least is not privy to it."

"If there *be* a trick? why, Charles, do you think——"

"I know not *what* to think, Tom. As surely as you are a living man, so surely did that spectral anatomy visit my room again last night, grin in my face, and walk away with my trousers: nor was I able to spring from my bed, or break the chain which seemed to bind me to my pillow."

"Seaforth!" said Ingoldsby, after a short pause, "I will—— But hush! here are the girls and my father.—I will carry off the females, and leave you a clear field with the governor: carry your point with him, and we will talk about your breeches afterwards."

Tom's diversion was successful; he carried off the ladies *en masse* to look at a remarkable specimen of the class *Dodecandria Monogynia*,—which they could not find;—while Seaforth marched boldly up to the encounter, and carried "the governor's" outworks by a *coup de main*. I shall not stop to describe the progress of the attack; suffice it that it was as successful as could have been wished, and that Seaforth was referred back again to the lady. The happy lover was off at a tangent; the botanical party was soon overtaken; and the arm of Caroline, whom a vain endeavor to spell out the Linnæan name of a daffy-down-dilly had detained a little in the rear of the others, was soon firmly locked in his own.

> " What was the world to them,
> Its noise, its nonsense, and its ' breeches,' all?"

Seaforth was in the seventh heaven; he retired to his room that night as happy as if no such thing as a goblin had ever been heard of, and personal chattels were as well fenced in by law as real property. Not so Tom Ingoldsby: the mystery,—for mystery there evidently was,—had not only piqued his curiosity, but ruffled his temper. The watch of the previous night had been unsuccessful, probably because it was undisguised. To-night he would "ensconce himself," not indeed "behind the arras,"—for the little that remained was, as we have seen, nailed to the wall,—but in a small closet which opened from one corner of the room, and, by leaving the door ajar, would give to its occupant a view of all that might pass in the apartment. Here did the young ghost-hunter take up a position, with a good stout sapling under his arm, a full half-hour before Seaforth retired for the night. Not even his friend did he let into his confidence, fully determined that if his plan did not succeed, the failure should be attributed to himself alone.

At the usual hour of separation for the night, Tom saw, from his concealment, the lieutenant enter his room, and after taking a few turns in it, with an expression so joyous as to betoken that his thoughts were mainly occupied by his approaching happiness, proceed slowly to disrobe himself. The coat, the waistcoat, the black silk stock, were gradually discarded; the green morocco slippers were kicked off, and then—ay, and then—his countenance grew grave; it seemed to occur to him all at once that this was his last stake,—nay, that the very breeches he had on were not his own,—that to-morrow morning was his last, and that if he lost *them*——. A glance showed that his mind was made up; he replaced the single button he had just subducted, and threw himself upon the bed in a state of transition,—half chrysalis, half grub.

Wearily did Tom Ingoldsby watch the sleeper by the flickering light of the night-lamp, till the clock striking one induced him to increase the narrow opening which he had left for the purpose of observation. The motion, slight as it was, seemed to attract Charles's attention; for he raised himself suddenly to a sitting posture, listened for a moment, and then stood upright upon the floor. Ingoldsby was on the point of discovering himself, when, the light flashing full upon his friend's countenance, he perceived that, though his eyes were open, "their sense was shut,"—that he was yet under the influence of sleep. Seaforth advanced slowly to the toilet, lit his candle at the lamp that stood on it, then, going back to the bed's foot, appeared to search eagerly for something which he could not find. For a few moments he seemed restless and uneasy, walking round the apartment and examining the chairs, till, coming fully in front of a large swing glass that flanked the dressing-table, he paused as if contemplating his figure in it. He now returned towards the bed; put on his slippers, and with cautious and stealthy steps proceeded towards the little arched doorway that opened on the private staircase.

As he drew the bolt, Tom Ingoldsby emerged from his hiding-place; but the sleep-walker heard him not; he proceeded softly down stairs, followed at a due distance by his friend; opened the door which led out upon the gardens; and stood at once among the thickest of the shrubs, which there clustered round the base of a corner turret, and screened the postern from common observation. At this moment Ingoldsby had nearly spoiled all by making a false step: the sound attracted Seaforth's attention,—he paused and turned; and, as the full moon shed her light directly upon his pale and troubled features, Tom marked, almost with dismay, the fixed and rayless appearance of his eyes :—

"There was no speculation in those orbs
    That he did glare withal."

The perfect stillness preserved by his follower seemed to reassure him ; he turned aside, and from the midst of a thickset laurustinus drew forth a gardener's spade, shouldering which he proceeded with greater rapidity into the midst of the shrubbery. Arrived at a certain point where the earth seemed to have been recently disturbed, he set himself heartily to the task of digging, till, having thrown up several shovelfuls of mould, he stopped, flung down his tool, and very composedly began to disencumber himself of his pantaloons.

Up to this moment Tom had watched him with a wary eye : he now advanced cautiously, and, as his friend was busily engaged in disentangling himself from his garment, made himself master of the spade. Seaforth, meanwhile, had accomplished his purpose : he stood for a moment with

"His streamers waving in the wind,"

occupied in carefully rolling up the small-clothes into as compact a form as possible, and all heedless of the breath of heaven, which might certainly be supposed at such a moment, and in such a plight, to "visit his frame too roughly."

He was in the act of stooping low to deposit the pantaloons in the grave which he had been digging for them, when Tom Ingoldsby came close behind him, and with the flat side of the spade——

The shock was effectual ;—never again was Lieutenant Seaforth known to act the part of a somnambulist. One by one, his breeches,—his trousers,—his pantaloons,—his silk-net tights, —his patent cords,—his showy grays with the broad red stripe of the Bombay Fencibles, were brought to light,—rescued from the grave in which they had been buried, like the strata of a

Christmas pie; and after having been well aired by Mrs. Botherby, became once again effective.

The family, the ladies especially, laughed;—the Peterses
laughed;—the Simpkinsons laughed;—Barney Maguire cried
"Botheration!" and Mam'selle Pauline, "*Mon Dieu!*"

Charles Seaforth, unable to face the quizzing which awaited
him on all sides, started off two hours earlier than he had proposed:—he soon returned, however; and having, at his father-
in-law's request, given up the occupation of Rajah-hunting and
shooting Nabobs, led his blushing bride to the altar.

Mr. Simpkinson from Bath did not attend the ceremony, being
engaged at the grand Junction meeting of *savans*, then congre-
gating from all parts of the known world in the city of Dublin.
His essay, demonstrating that the globe is a great custard,
whipped into coagulation by whirlwinds, and cooked by elec-
tricity,—a little too much baked in the Isle of Portland, and a
thought underdone about the Bog of Allen,—was highly spoken
of, and narrowly escaped obtaining a Bridgewater prize.

Miss Simpkinson and her sister acted as bridesmaids on the
occasion; the former wrote an *epithalamium*, and the latter cried
"Lassy me!" at the clergyman's wig. Some years have since
rolled on; the union has been crowned with two or three tidy
little offshoots from the family tree, of whom Master Neddy is
"grandpapa's darling," and Mary Anne mamma's particular
"Sock." I shall only add, that Mr. and Mrs. Seaforth are living
together quite as happily as two good-hearted, good-tempered
bodies, very fond of each other, can possibly do; and that,
since the day of his marriage, Charles has shown no disposition to jump out of bed, or ramble out of doors o'nights,—
though from his entire devotion to every wish and whim of his
young wife, Tom insinuates that the fair Caroline does still
occasionally take advantage of it so far as to "slip on the
breeches."

————

It was not till some years after the events just recorded that
Miss Mary Anne, the "pet Sock" before alluded to, was made
acquainted with the following piece of family biography. It was
communicated to her in strict confidence by Nurse Botherby, a

maiden niece of the old lady's, then recently promoted from the ranks in the still-room, to be second in command in the nursery department.

The story is connected with a dingy wizen-faced portrait, in an oval frame, generally known by the name of "Uncle Stephen," though from the style of his cut-velvet it is evident that some generations must have passed away since any living being could have stood towards him in that degree of consanguinity.

THE NURSE'S STORY.

The Hand of Glory.

"Malefica quædam auguriatrix in Angliâ fuit, quam demones horribiliter extraxerunt, et imponentes super equum terribilem, per aera rapuerunt; Clamoresque terribiles (ut ferunt) per quatuor fermè miliaria audiebantur."—*Nuremb. Chron.*

ON the lone bleak moor,   At the midnight hour,
    Beneath the Gallows Tree,
Hand in hand   The Murderers stand
By one, by two, by three!
   And the Moon that night   With a gray, cold light
Each baleful object tips;
   One half of her form   Is seen through the storm,
The other half's hid in Eclipse!
   And the cold Wind howls,   And the Thunder growls,
And the Lightning is broad and bright;
   And altogether   It's very bad weather,
And an unpleasant sort of a night!
   "Now mount who list,   And close by the wrist
Sever me quickly the Dead Man's fist!—
   Now climb who dare   Where he swings in air,
And pluck me five locks of the Dead Man's hair!"

There's an old woman dwells upon Tappington Moor,
She hath years on her back at the least fourscore,
And some people fancy a great many more;
  Her nose it is hook'd, Her back it is crook'd,
  Her eyes blear and red: On the top of her head
  Is a mutch, and on that A shocking bad hat,
Extinguisher-shaped, the brim narrow and flat!
Then,—my gracious!—her beard!—it would sadly perplex
A spectator at first to distinguish her sex;
Nor, I'll venture to say, without scrutiny could he
Pronounce her, off-handed, a Punch or a Judy.
Did you see her, in short, that mud-hovel within,
With her knees to her nose, and her nose to her chin,
Leering up with that queer, indescribable grin,
You'd lift up your hands in amazement, and cry,
"—Well!—I never *did* see such a regular Guy!"

  And now before That Old Woman's door,
  Where nought that's good may be,
  Hand in hand The Murderers stand
  By one, by two, by three!
Oh! 'tis a horrible sight to view,
In that horrible hovel, that horrible crew,
By the pale blue glare of that flickering flame,
Doing the deed that hath never a name!
  'Tis awful to hear Those words of fear!
The prayer mutter'd backwards and said with a sneer!
(Matthew Hopkins himself has assured us that when
A witch says her prayers, she begins with "Amen.")—
  —'Tis awful to see On that Old Woman's knee
The dead, shrivell'd hand, as she clasps it with glee!—
  And now with care, The five locks of hair
From the skull of the Gentleman dangling up there,
  With the grease and the fat Of a black Tom Cat
  She hastens to mix, And to twist into wicks,
And one on the thumb and each finger to fix.—
(For another receipt the same charm to prepare,
Consult Mr. Ainsworth and *Petit Albert*.)

" Now open lock   To the Dead Man's knock!
  Fly bolt, and bar, and band!—
    Nor move, nor swerve   Joint, muscle, or nerve,
At the spell of the Dead Man's hand!
Sleep all who sleep!—Wake all who wake!—
But be as the Dead for the Dead Man's sake!"

———

All is silent! all is still,
Save the ceaseless moan of the bubbling rill
As it wells from the bosom of Tappington Hill,
    And in Tappington Hall   Great and Small,
Gentle and Simple, Squire and Groom,
Each one hath sought his separate room,
And Sleep her dark mantle hath o'er them cast,
For the midnight hour hath long been past!
All is darksome in earth and sky,
Save, from yon casement, narrow and high,
    A quivering beam   On the tiny stream
Plays, like some taper's fitful gleam
By one that is watching wearily.

Within that casement, narrow and high,
In his secret lair, where none may spy,
Sits one whose brow is wrinkled with care,
And the thin gray locks of his failing hair
Have left his little bald pate all bare;
    For his full-bottom'd wig   Hangs, bushy and big,
On the top of his old-fashion'd, high-back'd chair.
    Unbraced are his clothes,   Ungarter'd his hose,
His gown is bedizen'd with tulip and rose,
Flowers of remarkable size and hue,
Flowers such as Eden never knew;
—And there by many a sparkling heap
    Of the good red gold,   The tale is told
What powerful spell avails to keep
That careworn man from his needful sleep!
Haply he deems no eye can see
As he gloats on his treasure greedily,—

The shining store   Of glittering ore,
The fair rose-noble, the bright moidore,
And the broad Double-Joe from ayont the sea,—
But there's one that watches as well as he;
   For, wakeful and sly,   In a closet hard by,
On his truckle bed lieth a little Foot-page,
A boy who's uncommonly sharp of his age,
   Like young Master Horner,   Who erst in a corner
   Sat eating a Christmas pie:
And, while that Old Gentleman's counting his hoards,
Little Hugh peeps through a crack in the boards!

––––––

   There's a voice in the air,   There's a step on the stair,
The old man starts in his cane-back'd chair;
   At the first faint sound   He gazes around,
And holds up his dip of sixteen to the pound.
   Then half arose   From beside his toes
His little pug-dog with his little pug nose,
But, ere he can vent one inquisitive sniff,
That little pug-dog stands stark and stiff,
   For low, yet clear,   Now fall on the ear,
—Where once pronounced for ever they dwell—
The unholy words of the Dead Man's spell!

   " Open lock   To the Dead Man's knock!
   Fly bolt, and bar, and band!—
   Nor move, nor swerve   Joint, muscle, or nerve,
At the spell of the Dead Man's hand!
Sleep all who sleep!—Wake all who wake!—
But be as the Dead for the Dead Man's sake!"

Now lock, nor bolt, nor bar avails,
Nor stout oak panel thick-studded with nails.
Heavy and harsh the hinges creak,
Though they had been oil'd in the course of the week;
The door opens wide as wide may be,
   And there they stand,   That murderous band,
   Lit by the light of the GLORIOUS HAND,
   By one!—by two!—by three!

They have pass'd through the porch, they have pass'd through
 the hall,
Where the Porter sat snoring against the wall;
 The very snore froze In his very snub nose,
You'd have verily deem'd he had snored his last
When the GLORIOUS HAND by the side of him pass'd!
E'en the little wee mouse, as it ran o'er the mat
At the top of its speed to escape from the cat,
 Though half dead with affright, Paused in its flight;
And the cat that was chasing that little wee thing
Lay couch'd as a statue in act to spring!
 And now they are there, On the head of the stair,
And the long crooked whittle is gleaming and bare!
—I really don't think any money would bribe
Me the horrible scene that ensued to describe,
 Or the wild, wild glare Of that old man's eye,
 His dumb despair, and deep agony.

The kid from the pen, and the lamb from the fold,
Unmoved may the blade of the butcher behold;
They dream not—ah, happier they!—that the knife,
Though uplifted, can menace their innocent life;
It falls;—the frail thread of their being is riven,
They dread not, suspect not, the blow till 'tis given.—
But, oh! what a thing 'tis to see and to know
That the bare knife is raised in the hand of the foe,
Without hope to repel, or to ward off the blow!—
—Enough!—let's pass over as fast as we can
The fate of that gray, that unhappy old man!

 But fancy poor Hugh, Aghast at the view,
 Powerless alike to speak or to do!
 In vain doth he try To open the eye
That is shut, or close that which is clapt to the chink,
Though he'd give all the world to be able to wink!—
No!—for all that this world can give or refuse,
I would not be now in that little boy's shoes,
Or indeed any garment at all that is Hugh's!

—'Tis lucky for him that the chink in the wall
He has peep'd through so long, is so narrow and small!

    Wailing voices, sounds of woe
      Such as follow departing friends,
    That fatal night round Tappington go,
      Its long-drawn roofs and its gable ends:
    Ethereal Spirits, gentle and good,
      Aye weep and lament o'er a deed of blood.

'Tis early dawn—the morn is gray,
And the clouds and the tempest have pass'd away,
And all things betoken a very fine day;
But, while the lark her carol is singing,
Shrieks and screams are through Tappington ringing.
    Upstarting all,   Great and small,
Each one who's found within Tappington Hall,
Gentle and Simple, Squire or Groom,
All seek at once that Old Gentleman's room;
    And there, on the floor,   Drench'd in its gore,
A ghastly corpse lies exposed to the view,
Carotid and jugular both cut through!
    And there, by its side,   'Mid the crimson tide,
Kneels a little Foot-page of tenderest years;
Adown his pale cheek the fast-falling tears
Are coursing each other round and big,
And he's stanching the blood with a full-bottom'd wig.
Alas! and alack for his stanching!—'tis plain,
As anatomists tell us, that never again
Shall life revisit the foully slain,
When once they've been cut through the jugular vein.

There's a hue and a cry through the County of Kent,
And in chase of the cut-throats a Constable's sent,
But no one can tell the man which way they went:
There's a little Foot-page with that Constable goes,
And a little pug-dog with a little pug nose.
  4

In Rochester town, At the sign of the Crown,
Three shabby-genteel men are just sitting down
To a fat stubble-goose, with potatoes done brown;
  When a little Foot-page Rushes in, in a rage,
Upsetting the apple-sauce, onions, and sage.
That little Foot-page takes the first by the throat,
And a little pug-dog takes the next by the coat,
And a Constable seizes the one more remote;
And fair rose-nobles and broad moidores
The Waiter pulls out of their pockets by scores,
And the Boots and the Chambermaids run in and stare;
And the Constable says, with a dignified air,
" You're *wanted*, Gen'lemen, one and all,
For that 'ere precious lark at Tappington Hall!"

There's a black gibbet frowns upon Tappington Moor,
Where a former black gibbet has frowned before:
  It is as black as black may be,
    And murderers there Are dangling in air,
By one!—by two!—by three!

There's a horrid old hag in a steeple-crowned hat,
Round her neck they have tied to a hempen cravat
A Dead Man's hand, and a dead Tom Cat!
They have tied up her thumbs, they have tied up her toes,
  They have tied up her eyes, they have tied up her limbs;
Into Tappington mill-dam souse she goes,
  With a whoop and a halloo!—" She swims!—She swims!"
    They have dragged her to land, And every one's hand
  Is grasping a fagot, a billet, or brand,
When a queer-looking horseman, drest all in black,
Snatches up that old harridan just like a sack
To the crupper behind him, puts spurs to his hack,
Makes a dash through the crowd, and is off in a crack!
  No one can tell, Though they guess pretty well,
Which way that grim rider and old woman go,
For all see he's a sort of infernal Ducrow;
And she screamed so, and cried, We may fairly decide
That the old woman did not much relish her ride!

MORAL.

This truest of stories confirms beyond doubt
That truest of adages—" Murder will out!"
In vain may the blood-spiller " double" and fly,
In vain even witchcraft and sorcery try:
Although for a time he may 'scape, by-and-by
He'll be sure to be caught by a Hugh and a Cry!

ONE marvel follows another as naturally as one "shoulder
of mutton" is said "to drive another down." A little Welsh
girl, who sometimes makes her way from the kitchen into the
nursery, after listening with intense interest to this tale, immediately started off at score with the sum and substance of what,
in due reverence for such authority, I shall call

PATTY MORGAN THE MILKMAID'S STORY.

"𝕷ook at the 𝕮lock."

FYTTE I.

" LOOK at the clock!" quoth Winifred Pryce,
     As she opened the door to her husband's knock,
Then paused to give him a piece of advice,
     "You nasty Warmint, look at the Clock!
     Is this the way, you   Wretch, every day you
Treat her who vowed to love and obey you?—
     Out all night!   Me in a fright;
Staggering home as it's just getting light!
You intoxified brute!—you insensible block!—
Look at the Clock!—Do!—Look at the Clock!"

Winifred Pryce was tidy and clean,
Her gown was a flowered one, her petticoat green,

Her buckles were bright as her milking cans,
And her hat was a beaver, and made like a man's;
Her little red eyes were deep set in their socket-holes,
Her gown-tail was turned up, and tucked through the pocket-
     holes;
    A face like a ferret   Betokened her spirit:
To conclude, Mrs. Pryce was not over young,
Had very short legs, and a very long tongue.

    Now David Pryce   Had one darling vice;
Remarkably partial to anything nice,
Nought that was good to him came amiss,
Whether to eat, or to drink, or to kiss!
    Especially ale—   If it was not too stale
I really believe he'd have emptied a pail;
    Not that in Wales   They talk of their Ales;
To pronounce the word they make use of might trouble you,
Being spelt with a C, two Rs, and a W.

    That particular day,   As I've heard people say,
Mr. David Pryce had been soaking his clay,
And amusing himself with his pipe and cheroots,
The whole afternoon, at the Goat-in-Boots,
    With a couple more soakers,   Thoroughbred smokers,
Both, like himself, prime singers and jokers;
And long after day had drawn to a close,
And the rest of the world was wrapp'd in repose,
They were roaring out "Shenkin!" and "Ar hydd y nos;"
While David himself, to a Sassenach tune,
Sang, "We've drunk down the Sun, boys! let's drink down
    the Moon!
    What have we with day to do?
    Mrs. Winifred Price, 'twas made for you;"
At length, when they couldn't well drink any more,
Old "Goat-in-Boots" show'd them the door:
    And then came that knock,   And the sensible shock
David felt when his wife cried, "Look at the Clock!"
For the hands stood as crooked as crooked might be,
The long at the Twelve, and the short at the Three!

That self-same clock had long been a bone
Of contention between this Darby and Joan,
And often, among their pother and rout,
When this otherwise amiable couple fell out,
  Pryce would drop a cool hint, With an ominous squint
At its case, of an " Uncle" of his, who'd a "Spout."
  That horrid word "Spout" No sooner came out
Than Winifred Pryce would turn her about,
  And with scorn on her lip, And a hand on each hip,
"Spout" herself till her nose grew red at the tip.
  " You thundering willin, I know you'd be killing
Your wife—ay, a dozen of wives—for a shilling!
  You may do what you please, You may sell my chemise
(Mrs. P. was too well-bred to mention her smock),
But I never will part with my Grandmother's Clock!"

Mrs. Pryce's tongue ran long and ran fast;
But patience is apt to wear out at last,
And David Pryce in temper was quick,
So he stretch'd out his hand and caught hold of a stick;
Perhaps in its use he might mean to be lenient,
But walking just then wasn't very convenient.
  So he threw it, instead, Direct at her head;
  It knock'd off her hat; Down she fell flat;
Her case, perhaps, was not much mended by that:
But whatever it was,—whether rage and pain
Produced apoplexy, or burst a vein,
Or her tumble produced a concussion of brain,
I can't say for certain,—but *this* I can,
When, sober'd by fright, to assist her he ran,
Mrs. Winifred Pryce was as dead as Queen Anne!

  The fearful catastrophe Named in my last strophe
As adding to grim Death's exploits such a vast trophy,
Made a great noise; and the shocking fatality
Ran over, like wildfire, the whole Principality.
And then came Mr. Ap Thomas, the Coroner,
With his jury to sit, some dozen or more, on her.
  Mr. Pryce, to commence His "ingenious defence,"
Made a "powerful appeal" to the jury's "good sense:"

"The world he must defy Ever to justify
Any presumption of ' Malice Prepense.' "
   The unlucky lick From the end of his stick
He " deplored,"—he was " apt to be rather too quick ;"—
   But, really, her prating Was so aggravating:
Some trifling correction was just what he meant :—all
The rest, he assured them, was " quite accidental!"

   Then he calls Mr. Jones, Who depones to her tones,
And her gestures, and hints about " breaking his bones ;"
While Mr. Ap Morgan and Mr. Ap Rhys
   Declare the deceased Had styled him " a Beast,"
And swear they had witness'd, with grief and surprise,
The allusion she made to his limbs and his eyes.

The jury, in fine, having sat on the body
The whole day, discussing the case, and gin toddy,
Return'd about half-past eleven at night
The following verdict, " We find, *Sarve her right !*"

Mr. Pryce, Mrs. Winifred Pryce being dead,
Felt lonely, and moped ; and one evening he said
He would marry Miss Davis at once in her stead.

   Not far from his dwelling, From the vale proudly swelling,
Rose a mountain ; its name you'll excuse me from telling,
For the vowels made use of in Welsh are so few,
That the A and the E, the I, O, and the U,
Have really but little or nothing to do ;
And the duty, of course, falls the heavier by far
On the L, and the H, and the N, and the R.
   Its first syllable, " PEN," Is pronounceable ;—then
Come two L Ls, and two H Hs, two F Fs, and an N,
About half a score Rs, and some Ws follow,
Beating all my best efforts at euphony hollow:
But we shan't have to mention it often, so when
We do, with your leave, we'll curtail it to " PEN."

Well—the moon shone bright Upon " Pen," that night,
When Pryce, being quit of his fuss and his fright,

Was scaling its side   With that sort of stride
A man puts out when walking in search of a bride.
      Mounting higher and higher,   He began to perspire,
Till, finding his legs were beginning to tire,
      And feeling opprest   By a pain in his chest,
He paused, and turned round to take breath and to rest:
A walk all up hill is apt, we know,
To make one, however robust, puff and blow,
So he stopped and looked down on the valley below.

      O'er fell and o'er fen,   Over mountain and glen,
All bright in the moonshine, his eye roved, and then
All the Patriot rose in his soul, and he thought
Upon Wales, and her glories, and all he'd been taught
      Of her Heroes of old,   So brave and so bold,—
Of her Bards with long beards, and harps mounted in gold:
      Of King Edward the First,   Of memory accurst;
And the scandalous manner in which he behaved,
      Killing poets by dozens   With their uncles and cousins,
Of whom not one in fifty had ever been shaved—
Of the Court Ball, at which, by a lucky mishap,
Owen Tudor fell into Queen Katherine's lap;
      And how Mr. Tudor   Successfully wooed her,
Till the Dowager put on a new wedding ring,
And so made him Father-in-law to the King.

He thought upon Arthur and Merlin of yore,
On Gryffith ap Conau and Owen Glendour;
On Pendragon, and Heaven knows how many more.
He thought of all this, as he gazed, in a trice,
And on all things, in short, but the late Mrs. Pryce;
When a lumbering noise from behind made him start,
And sent the blood back in full tide to his heart,
      Which went pit-a-pat,   As he cried out, "What's that?"—
      That very queer sound?—   Does it come from the ground?
Or the air,—from above,—or below,—or around?—
      It is not like Talking,   It is not like Walking,
It's not like the clattering of pot or of pan,
Or the tramp of a horse,—or the tread of a man,—

Or the hum of a crowd, or the shouting of boys,—
It's really a deuced odd sort of a noise !
Not unlike a cart's,—but that can't be ; for when
Could "all the King's horses, and all the King's men,"
With Old Nick for a wagoner, drive one up "PEN"?

Pryce, usually brimful of valor when drunk,
Now experienced what schoolboys denominate "funk."
   In vain he looked back   On the whole of the track
He had traversed ; a thick cloud, uncommonly black,
At this moment obscured the broad disk of the moon,
And did not seem likely to pass away soon ;
   While clearer and clearer,   'Twas plain to the hearer,
Be the noise what it might, it drew nearer and nearer,
And sounded, as Pryce to this moment declares,
Very much "like a Coffin a-walking up stairs."

   Mr. Pryce had begun   To "make up" for a run,
As in such a companion he saw no great fun,
   When a single bright ray   Shone out on the way
He had passed, and he saw, with no little dismay,
Coming after him, bounding o'er crag and o'er rock,
The deceased Mrs. Winifred's "Grandmother's Clock ! !"
'Twas so !—it had certainly moved from its place,
And come lumbering on thus, to hold him in chase ;
'Twas the very same Head, and the very same Case,
And nothing was altered at all—but the Face !
In that he perceived, with no little surprise,
The two little winder-holes turned into eyes
   Blazing with ire,   Like two coals of fire ;
And the "Name of the Maker" was changed to a Lip,
And the Hands to a Nose with a very red tip.
No !—he could not mistake it,—'twas SHE to the life !
The identical face of his poor defunct wife !

   One glance was enough,   Completely "*Quant. suff.*,"
As the doctors write down when they send you their "stuff."
Like a Weather-cock whirled by a vehement puff,

David turned himself round; Ten feet of ground
He cleared, in his start, at the very first bound!
I've seen people run at West-End Fair for cheeses—
I've seen ladies run at Bow Fair for chemises—
At Greenwich Fair twenty men run for a hat,
And one from a Bailiff much faster than that:
At foot-ball I've seen lads run after the bladder—
I've seen Irish bricklayers run up a ladder—
I've seen little boys run away from a cane—
And I've seen (that is, *read of*) good running in Spain;*
    But I never did read Of, or witness, such speed
As David exerted that evening.—Indeed
All I have ever heard of boys, women, or men,
Falls far short of Pryce, as he ran over PEN!

He reaches its brow,— He has past it, and now,
Having once gained the summit, and managed to cross it, he
Rolls down the side with uncommon velocity;
    But run as he will, Or roll down the hill,
The bugbear behind him is after him still!
And close at his heels, not at all to his liking,
The terrible clock keeps on ticking and striking,
    Till, exhausted and sore, He can't run any more,
But falls as he reaches Miss Davis's door,
And screams when they rush out, alarmed at his knock,
" Oh! Look at the Clock!—Do!—Look at the Clock!!"

Miss Davis looked up, Miss Davis looked down,
She saw nothing there to alarm her;—a frown
    Came o'er her white forehead; She said, " it was horrid
A man should come knocking at that time of night,
And give her Mamma and herself such a fright;—
    To squall and to bawl About nothing at all!"
She begged " he'd not think of repeating his call:
    His late wife's disaster By no means had past her;"
She'd " have him to know she was meat for his Master!"
Then regardless alike of his love and his woes,
She turned on her heel and she turned up her nose.

* I-run is a town said to have been so named from something of this sort.

Poor David in vain   Implored to remain;
He "dared not," he said, "cross the mountain again."
    Why the fair was obdurate   None knows,—to be sure, it
Was said she was setting her cap at the Curate.
Be that as it may, it is certain the sole hole
Pryce found to creep into that night was the Coal-hole!
    In that shady retreat,   With nothing to eat,
And with very bruised limbs, and with very sore feet,
    All night close he kept;   I can't say he slept;
But he sighed, and he sobbed, and he groaned, and he wept;
    Lamenting his sins,   And his two broken shins,
Bewailing his fate with contortions and grins,
And her he once thought a complete *Rara Avis*,
Consigning to Satan,—viz., cruel Miss Davis!

Mr. David has since had a "serious call,"
He never drinks ale, wine, or spirits, at all,
And they say he is going to Exeter Hall
    To make a grand speech,   And to preach, and to teach
People that "they can't brew their malt liquor too small."
That an ancient Welsh Poet, one PYNDAR AP TUDOR,
Was right in proclaiming "ARISTON MEN UDOR!"
    Which means "The pure Element   Is for Man's belly
        meant!"
And that *Gin's* but a *Snare* of Old Nick the deluder!

And "still on each evening when pleasure fills up,"
At the old Goat-in-Boots, with Metheglin, each cup,
    Mr. Pryce, if he's there,   Will get into "The Chair,"
And make all his *quondam* associates stare
By calling aloud to the Landlady's daughter,
"Patty, bring a cigar, and a glass of Spring Water!"
The dial he constantly watches; and when
The long hand's at the "XII.," and the short at the "X.,"
    He gets on his legs,   Drains his glass to the dregs,
Takes his hat and great-coat off their several pegs,
With his President's hammer bestows his last knock,
And says solemnly—"Gentlemen!
                LOOK AT THE CLOCK!!!"

THE succeeding Legend has long been an established favorite with all of us, as containing much of the personal history of one of the greatest ornaments of the family tree.

To the wedding between the sole heiress of this redoubted hero and a direct ancestor is it owing that the Lioncels of Shurland hang so lovingly parallel with the Saltire of the Ingoldsbys, and now form as cherished a quartering in their escutcheon as the "dozen white lowses" in the "old coat" of Shallow.

Gray Dolphin.

A LEGEND OF SHEPPEY.

"HE won't—won't he? Then bring me my boots!" said the Baron.

Consternation was at its height in the castle of Shurland—a caitiff had dared to disobey the Baron! and—the Baron had called for his boots!

A thunderbolt in the great hall had been a *bagatelle* to it.

A few days before a notable miracle had been wrought in the neighborhood; and in those times miracles were not so common as they are now; no royal balloons, no steam, no railroads,—while the few Saints who took the trouble to walk with their heads under their arms, or to pull the devil by the nose, scarcely appeared above once in a century;—so the affair made the greater sensation.

The clock had done striking twelve, and the Clerk of Chatham was untrussing his points preparatory to seeking his truckle-bed; a half-emptied tankard of mild ale stood at his elbow, the roasted crab yet floating on its surface. Midnight had surprised the worthy functionary while occupied in discussing it, and with his task yet unaccomplished. He meditated a mighty draft: one hand was fumbling with his tags, while the other was extended in the act of grasping the jorum, when a knock on the portal, solemn and sonorous, arrested his fingers. It was repeated thrice ere Emmanuel Saddleton had presence

of mind sufficient to inquire who sought admittance at that un-
timeous hour.

"Open! open! good Clerk of St. Bridget's," said a female
voice, small yet distinct and sweet,—an excellent thing in
woman.

The Clerk arose, crossed to the doorway, and undid the
latchet.

On the threshold stood a Lady of surpassing beauty: her
robes were rich, and large, and full; and a diadem, sparkling
with gems that shed a halo around, crowned her brow: she
beckoned the Clerk as he stood in astonishment before her.

"Emmanuel!" said the Lady; and her tones sounded like
those of a silver flute. "Emmanuel Saddleton, truss up your
points, and follow me!"

The worthy Clerk stared aghast at the vision; the purple
robe, the cymar, the coronet,—above all, the smile; no, there
was no mistaking her; it was the blessed St. Bridget herself!

And what could have brought the sainted lady out of her
warm shrine at such a time of night? and on such a night? for
it was as dark as pitch, and, metaphorically speaking, "rained
cats and dogs."

Emmanuel could not speak, so he looked the question.

"No matter for that," said the Saint, answering to his thought.
"No matter for that, Emmanuel Saddleton; only follow me,
and you'll see!"

The Clerk turned a wistful eye at the corner cupboard.

"Oh! never mind the lantern, Emmanuel: you'll not want
it: but you may bring a mattock and a shovel." As she spoke,
the beautiful apparition held up her delicate hand. From the
tip of each of her long taper fingers issued a lambent flame of
such surpassing brilliancy as would have plunged a whole gas
company into despair—it was a "Hand of Glory,"* such a one
as tradition tells us yet burns in Rochester Castle every St.
Mark's Eve. Many are the daring individuals who have
watched in Gundulph's Tower, hoping to find it, and the treasure it guards;—but none of them ever did.

"This way, Emmanuel!" and a flame of peculiar radiance

---

* One of the uses to which this mystic chandelier was put was the protection of
secreted treasure. Blow out all the fingers at one puff and you had the money.

streamed from her little finger, as it pointed to the pathway leading to the churchyard.

Saddleton shouldered his tools, and followed in silence.

The cemetery of St. Bridget's was some half-mile distant from the Clerk's domicile, and adjoined a chapel dedicated to that illustrious lady, who, after leading but a so-so life, had died in the odor of sanctity. Emmanuel Saddleton was fat and scant of breath, the mattock was heavy, and the Saint walked too fast for him: he paused to take second wind at the end of the first furlong.

· "Emmanuel," said the holy lady, good-humoredly, for she heard him puffing; "rest awhile, Emmanuel, and I'll tell you what I want with you."

Her auditor wiped his brow with the back of his hand, and looked all attention and obedience.

"Emmanuel," continued she, "what did you and Father Fothergill, and the rest of you, mean yesterday by burying that drowned man so close to me? He died in mortal sin, Emmanuel; no shrift, no unction, no absolution: why he might as well have been excommunicated. He plagues me with his grinning, and I can't have any peace in my shrine. You must howk him up again, Emmanuel!"

"To be sure, madam,—my lady,—that is, your holiness," stammered Saddleton, trembling at the thought of the task assigned him. "To be sure, your ladyship; only—that is——"

"Emmanuel," said the Saint, "you'll do my bidding, or it would be better you had!" and her eye changed from a dove's eye to that of a hawk, and a flash came from it as bright as the one from her little finger. The Clerk shook in his shoes; and, again dashing the cold perspiration from his brow, followed the footsteps of his mysterious guide.

———

The next morning all Chatham was in an uproar. The Clerk of St. Bridget's had found himself at home at daybreak, seated in his own arm-chair, the fire out, and—the tankard of ale out too! Who had drunk it?—where had he been?—how had he got home?—all was a mystery!—he remembered a "mass of things, but nothing distinctly;" all was fog and fantasy. What he could clearly recollect was that he had dug up the Grinning Sailor, and that the Saint had helped to throw him into the river again. All was thenceforth wonderment and devotion. Masses were sung, tapers were kindled, bells were tolled; the monks of St. Romuald had a solemn procession, the abbot at their head, the sacristan at their tail, and the holy breeches of St. Thomas à Becket in the centre;—Father Fothergill brewed a XXX puncheon of holy water. The rood of Gillingham was deserted; the chapel of Rainham forsaken; every one who had a soul to be saved flocked with his offering to St. Bridget's shrine, and Emmanuel Saddleton gathered more fees from the promiscuous piety of that one week than he had pocketed during the twelve preceding months.

Meanwhile the corpse of the ejected reprobate oscillated like a pendulum between Sheerness and Gillingham Reach. Now borne by the Medway into the Western Swale, now carried by the refluent tide back to the vicinity of its old quarters,—it seemed as though the River god and Neptune were amusing themselves with a game of subaqueous battledore, and had chosen this unfortunate carcass as a marine shuttlecock. For some time the alternation was kept up with great spirit, till Boreas, interfering in the shape of a stiffish "Nor'wester," drifted the bone (and.flesh) of contention ashore on the Shurland domain, where it lay in all the majesty of mud. It was soon discovered by the retainers, and dragged from its oozy bed, grinning worse than ever. Tidings of the godsend were of course carried instantly to the castle; for the Baron was a very great man; and if a dun cow had flown across his property unannounced by the warder, the Baron would have kicked him, the said warder, from the topmost battlement into the bottommost ditch,—a descent of peril, and one which "Ludwig the Leaper," or the illustrious Trenck himself, might well have shrunk from encountering.

"An't please your lordship——" said Peter Periwinkle.

"No, villain! it does not please me!" roared the Baron.

His lordship was deeply engaged with a peck of Feversham oysters: he doted on shellfish, hated interruption at meals, and had not yet despatched more than twenty dozen of the "natives."

" There's a body, my lord, washed ashore in the lower creek," said the seneschal.

The Baron was going to throw the shells at his head; but paused in the act, and said, with much dignity,—

" Turn out the fellow's pockets!"

But the defunct had before been subjected to the double scrutiny of Father Fothergill and the Clerk of St. Bridget's. It was ill gleaning after such hands; there was not a single maravedi.

We have already said that Sir Robert de Shurland, Lord of the Isle of Sheppey, and of many a fair manor on the mainland, was a man of worship. He had rights of freewarren, saccage and sockage, cuisage and jambage, fosse and fork, infang theofe and outfang theof; and all waifs and strays belonged to him in fee simple.

" Turn out his pockets!" said the knight.

" An't please you, my lord, I must say as how they was turned out afore, and the devil a rap's left."

" Then bury the blackguard!"

" Please your lordship, he has been buried once."

" Then bury him again, and be —— !" The Baron bestowed a benediction.

The seneschal bowed low as he left the room, and the Baron went on with his oysters.

Scarcely ten dozen more had vanished when Periwinkle reappeared.

" An't please you, my lord, Father Fothergill says as how that it's the Grinning Sailor, and he won't bury him anyhow."

" Oh! he won't—won't he?" said the Baron. Can it be wondered at that he called for his boots?

Sir Robert de Shurland, Lord of Shurland and Minster, Baron of Sheppey *in comitatu* Kent, was, as has been before hinted, a very great man. He was also a very little man; that is, he was relatively great, and relatively little—or physically little, and metaphorically great—like Sir Sidney Smith and the late Mr. Buonaparte. To the frame of a dwarf he united the soul of a giant and the valor of a gamecock. Then, for so small a man, his strength was prodigious; his fist would fell an ox, and his kick—oh! his kick was tremendous, and, when he had his boots on, would—to use an expression of his own, which he had picked up in the holy wars—would "send a man from Jericho to June." He was bull-necked and bandy-legged; his chest was broad and deep, his head large and uncommonly thick, his eyes a little bloodshot, and his nose *retroussé*, with a remarkably red tip. Strictly speaking, the Baron could not be called handsome; but his *tout ensemble* was singularly impressive; and when he called for his boots everybody trembled, and dreaded the worst.

"Periwinkle," said the Baron, as he encased his better leg, "let the grave be twenty feet deep!"

"Your lordship's command is law."

"And, Periwinkle"—Sir Robert stamped his left heel into its receptacle—"and, Periwinkle, see that it be wide enough to hold not exceeding two!"

"Ye—ye—yes, my lord."

"And, Periwinkle—tell Father Fothergill I would fain speak with his Reverence."

"Ye—ye—yes, my lord."

The Baron's beard was peaked: and his moustaches, stiff and stumpy, projected horizontally, like those of a Tom Cat; he twirled the one, he stroked the other, he drew the buckle of his surcingle a thought tighter, and strode down the great staircase three steps at a stride.

The vassals were assembled in the great hall of Shurland Castle; every check was pale, every tongue was mute: expectation and perplexity were visible on every brow. What would his lordship do? Were the recusant anybody else, gyves to the heels and hemp to the throat were but too good for him; but it was Father Fothergill who had said "I won't;" and though the Baron was a very great man, the Pope was a greater, and the Pope was Father Fothergill's great friend—some people said he was his uncle.

Father Fothergill was busy in the refectory trying conclusions with a venison pasty, when he received the summons of his patron to attend him in the chapel cemetery. Of course he lost no time in obeying it, for obedience was the general rule in Shurland Castle. If anybody ever said "I won't," it was the exception; and, like all other exceptions, only proved the rule the stronger. The Father was a friar of the Augustine persuasion; a brotherhood which, having been planted in Kent some few centuries earlier, had taken very kindly to the soil, and overspread the county much as hops did some few centuries later. He was plump and portly, a little thick-winded, especially after dinner, stood five feet four in his sandals, and weighed hard upon eighteen stone. He was, moreover, a personage of singular piety; and the iron girdle, which, he said, he wore under his cassock to mortify withal, might have been well mistaken for the tire of a cart-wheel. When he arrived, Sir Robert was pacing up and down by the side of a newly-opened grave.

"*Benedicite!* fair son" (the Baron was as brown as a cigar)— "*Benedicite!*" said the Chaplain.

The Baron was too angry to stand upon compliment. "Bury me that grinning caitiff there!" quoth he, pointing to the defunct.

"It may not be, fair son," said the Friar; "he hath perished without absolution."

"Bury the body!" roared Sir Robert.

"Water and earth alike reject him," returned the Chaplain; "holy St. Bridget herself——"

"Bridget me no Bridgets!—do me thine office quickly, Sir Shaveling! or, by the Piper that played before Moses——" The oath was a fearful one; and whenever the Baron swore to do mischief he was never known to perjure himself. He was playing with the hilt of his sword. "Do me thine office, I say. Give him his passport to Heaven."

"He is already gone to Hell!" stammered the Friar.

"Then do you go after him!" thundered the Lord of Shurland.

His sword half leaped from its scabbard. No!—the trenchant blade, that had cut Sulciman Ben Malck Ben Buckskin from helmet to chine, disdained to daub itself with the cerebellum of a miserable monk;—it leaped back again;—and as the Chaplain, scared at its flash, turned him in terror, the Baron gave him a kick!—one kick!—it was but one!—but such a one! Despite its obesity, up flew his holy body in an angle of forty-five degrees; then, having reached its highest point of elevation, sank headlong into the open grave that yawned to receive it.

5

If the reverend gentleman had possessed such a thing as a neck, he had infallibly broken it! as he did not, he only dislocated his vertebræ—but that did quite as well. He was as dead as ditch-water!

"In with the other rascal!" said the Baron—and he was obeyed; for there he stood in his boots. Mattock and shovel made short work of it; twenty feet of superincumbent mold pressed down alike the saint and the sinner. "Now sing a requiem who list!" said the Baron, and his lordship went back to his oysters.

The vassals at Castle Shurland were astounded, or, as the Seneschal Hugh better expressed it, "perfectly conglomerated," by this event. What! murder a monk in the odor of sanctity— and on consecrated ground too! They trembled for the health of the Baron's soul. To the unsophisticated many it seemed that matters could not have been much worse had he shot a bishop's coach-horse—all looked for some signal judgment. The melancholy catastrophe of their neighbors at Canterbury was yet rife in their memories: not two centuries had elapsed since those miserable sinners had cut off the tail of the blessed St. Thomas's mule. The tail of the mule, it was well known, had been forthwith affixed to that of the Mayor; and rumor said it had since been hereditary in the corporation. The least that could be expected was that Sir Robert should have a friar tacked on to his for the term of his natural life! Some bolder spirits there were, 'tis true, who viewed the matter in various lights, according to their different temperaments and dispositions; for perfect unanimity existed not even in the good old times. The verderer, roistering Hob Roebuck, swore roundly, "'Twere as good a deed as eat to kick down the chapel as well as the monk." Hob had stood there in a white sheet for kissing Giles Miller's daughter. On the other hand, Simpkin Agnew, the bell-ringer, doubted if the devil's cellar, which runs under the bottomless abyss, were quite deep enough for the delinquent, and speculated on the probability of a hole being dug in it for his especial accommodation. The philosophers and economists thought, with Saunders McBullock, the Baron's bagpiper, that a "feckless monk more or less was nae great subject for a clam-jamphry," especially as "the supply considerably exceeded the

demand;" while Malthouse, the tapster, was arguing to Dame
Martin that a murder now and then was a seasonable check to
population, without which the Isle of Sheppey would in time
be devoured, like a mouldy cheese, by inhabitants of its own
producing. Meanwhile, the Baron ate his oysters and thought
no more of the matter.

But this tranquillity of his lordship was not to last. A
couple of Saints had been seriously offended; and we have all
of us read at school that celestial minds are by no means insensible to the provocations of anger. There were those who
expected that St. Bridget would come in person, and have the
friar up again, as she did the sailor; but perhaps her ladyship
did not care to trust herself within the walls of Shurland Castle.
To say the truth, it was scarcely a decent house for a female
Saint to be seen in. The Baron's gallantries, since he became
a widower, had been but too notorious; and her own reputation
was a little blown upon in the earlier days of her earthly pil-
grimage: then things were so apt to be misrepresented—in
short, she would leave the whole affair to St. Austin, who, being
a gentleman, could interfere with propriety, avenge her affront
as well as his own, and leave no loophole for scandal. St.
Austin himself seems to have had his scruples, though of their
precise nature it would be difficult to determine, for it were idle
to suppose him at all afraid of the Baron's boots. Be this as it
may, the mode which he adopted was at once prudent and effi-
cacious. As an ecclesiastic, he could not well call the Baron
out—had his boots been out of the question; so he resolved to
have recourse to the law. Instead of Shurland Castle, therefore, he repaired forthwith to his own magnificent monastery,
situate just within the walls of Canterbury, and presented himself in a vision to its abbot. No one who has ever visited that
ancient city can fail to recollect the splendid gateway which
terminates the vista of St. Paul's Street, and stands there yet in
all its pristine beauty. The tiny train of miniature artillery
which now adorns its battlements is, it is true, an ornament of
a later date; and is said to have been added some centuries
after by a learned but jealous proprietor, for the purpose of
shooting any wiser man than himself who might chance to come
that way. Tradition is silent as to any discharge having taken

place, nor can the oldest inhabitant of modern days recollect any such occurrence.* Here it was, in a handsome chamber, immediately over the lofty archway, that the Superior of the monastery lay buried in a brief slumber, snatched from his accustomed vigils. His mitre—for he was a mitred Abbot, and had a seat in parliament—rested on a table beside him; near it stood a silver flagon of Gascony wine, ready, no doubt, for the pious uses of the morrow. Fasting and watching had made him more than usually somnolent, than which nothing could have been better for the purpose of the Saint, who now appeared to him radiant in all the colors of the rainbow.

"Anselm!" said the beatific vision,—"Anselm! are you not a pretty fellow to lie snoring there when your brethren are being knocked at head, and Mother Church herself is menaced?—It is a sin and a shame, Anselm!"

"What's the matter?—Who are you?" cried the Abbot, rubbing his eyes, which the celestial splendor of his visitor had set a winking. "Ave Maria! St. Austin himself! Speak, *Beatissime!* what would you with the humblest of your votaries?"

"Anselm!" said the Saint, "a brother of our order, whose soul Heaven assoilzie! hath been foully murdered. He hath been ignominiously kicked to the death, Anselm; and there he lieth cheek-by-jowl with a wretched carcass, which our sister Bridget has turned out of her cemetery for unseemly grinning. Arouse thee, Anselm!"

"Ay, so please you, *Sanctissime!*" said the Abbot. "I will order forthwith that thirty masses be said, thirty *Paters*, and thirty *Aves*."

"Thirty fools' heads!" interrupted his patron, who was a little peppery.

"I will send for bell, book, and candle——"

"Send for an inkhorn, Anselm. Write me now a letter to his Holiness the Pope in good round terms, and another to the Coroner, and another to the Sheriff, and seize me the never-enough-to-be-anathematized villain who hath done this deed! Hang him as high as Haman, Anselm!—up with him!—down with his dwelling-place, root and branch, hearth-stone and roof-

---

* Since the appearance of the first edition of this Legend "the guns" have been dismounted. Rumor hints at some alarm on the part of the Town Council.

tree,—down with it all, and sow the site with salt and saw-dust!"

St. Austin, it will be perceived, was a radical reformer.

"Marry will I," quoth the Abbot, warming with the Saint's eloquence; "ay, marry will I, and that *instanter*. But there is one thing you have forgotten, most Beatified—the name of the culprit."

"Robert de Shurland."

"The Lord of Sheppey! Bless me!" said the Abbot, cross-ing himself, "won't that be rather inconvenient? Sir Robert is a bold baron, and a powerful; blows will come and go, and crowns will be cracked, and——"

"What is that to you, since yours will not be of the number?"

"Very true, *Beatissime!*—I will don me with speed, and do your bidding."

"Do so, Anselm!—fail not to hang the Baron, burn his castle, confiscate his estate, and buy me two large wax candles for my own particular shrine out of your share of the property."

With this solemn injunction the vision began to fade.

"One thing more!" cried the Abbot, grasping his rosary.

"What is that?" asked the Saint.

"*O Beate Augustine, ora pro nobis!*"

"Of course I shall," said St. Austin. "*Pax vobiscum!*"—and Abbot Anselm was left alone.

Within an hour all Canterbury was in commotion. A friar had been murdered,—two friars—ten—twenty; a whole convent had been assaulted, sacked, burnt,—all the monks had been killed, and all the nuns had been kissed! Murder! fire! sacri-lege! Never was city in such an uproar. From St. George's gate to St. Dunstan's suburb, from the Donjon to the borough of Staplegate, all was noise and hubbub. "Where was it?"—"When was it?"—"How was it?" The Mayor caught up his chain, the Aldermen donned their furred gowns, the Town Clerk put on his spectacles. "Who was he?"—"What was he?"—"Where was he?"—He should be hanged,—he should be burned,—he should be broiled,—he should be fried,—he should be scraped to death with red-hot oyster shells! "Who was he?"—"What was his name?"

The Abbot's Apparitor drew forth his roll and read aloud:—

"Sir Robert de Shurland, Knight banneret, Baron of Shurland and Minster, and Lord of Sheppey."

The Mayor put his chain in his pocket, the Aldermen took off their gowns, the Town Clerk put his pen behind his ear. It was a county business altogether :—the Sheriff had better call out the *posse comitatus.*

While saints and sinners were thus leaguing against him, the Baron de Shurland was quietly eating his breakfast. He had passed a tranquil night, undisturbed by dreams of cowl or capuchin; nor was his appetite more affected than his conscience. On the contrary, he sat rather longer over his meal than usual: luncheon time came, and he was ready as ever for his oysters; but scarcely had Dame Martin opened his first half-dozen when the warder's horn was heard from the barbican.

"Who the devil's that?" said Sir Robert. "I'm not at home, Periwinkle. I hate to be disturbed at meals, and I won't be at home to anybody."

"An't please your lordship," answered the Seneschal, " Paul Prior hath given notice that there is a body——"

"Another body!" roared the Baron. "Am I to be everlastingly plagued with bodies—no time allowed me to swallow a morsel? Throw it into the moat!"

"So please you, my lord, it is a body of horse,—and—and Paul says there is a still larger body of foot behind it; and he thinks, my lord—that is, he does not know, but he thinks—and we all think, my lord—that they are coming to—to besiege the castle!"

"Besiege the castle! Who? What? What for?"

"Paul says, my lord, that he can see the banner of St. Austin, and the bleeding heart of Hamo de Crevecœur, the Abbot's chief vassal; and there is John de Northwood, the sheriff, with his red cross engrailed; and Hever, and Leybourne, and Heaven knows how many more; and they are all coming on as fast as ever they can."

"Periwinkle," said the Baron, "up with the drawbridge; down with the portcullis. Bring me a cup of canary and my nightcap. I won't be bothered with them: I shall go to bed."

"To bed, my lord!" cried Periwinkle, with a look that seemed to say, "He's crazy!"

At this moment the shrill tones of a trumpet were heard to sound thrice from the champaign. It was the signal for parley. The Baron changed his mind: instead of going to bed, he went to the ramparts.

"Well, rapscallions! and what now?" said the Baron.

A herald, two pursuivants, and a trumpeter, occupied the foreground of the scene; behind them, some three hundred paces off, upon a rising ground, was drawn up in battle array the main body of the ecclesiastical forces.

"Hear you, Robert de Shurland, Knight, Baron of Shurland and Minster, and Lord of Sheppey, and know all men by these presents, that I do hereby attach you, the said Robert, of murder and sacrilege, now or of late done and committed by you, the said Robert, contrary to the peace of our Sovereign Lord the King, his crown and dignity; and I do hereby require and charge you, the said Robert, to forthwith surrender and give up your own proper person, together with the castle of Shurland aforesaid, in order that the same may be duly dealt with according to law. And here standeth John de Northwood, Esquire, good man and true, sheriff of this his Majesty's most loyal county of Kent, to enforce the same, if need be, with his *posse comitatus*——"

"His what?" said the Baron.

"His *posse comitatus*, and——"

"Go to Bath!" said the Baron.

A defiance so contemptuous roused the ire of the adverse commanders. A volley of missiles rattled about the Baron's ears. Nightcaps avail little against contusions. He left the walls and returned to the great hall.

"Let them pelt away," quoth the Baron: "there are no windows to break, and they can't get in." So he took his afternoon nap, and the siege went on.

Towards evening his lordship awoke, and grew tired of the din. Guy Pearson, too, had got a black eye from a brickbat, and the assailants were clambering over the outer wall. So the Baron called for his Sunday hauberk of Milan steel and his great two-handed sword with the terrible name. It was the fashion in feudal times to give names to swords: King Arthur's was christened Excalibar; the Baron called his Tickletoby, and whenever he took it in hand it was no joke.

"Up with the portcullis! down with the bridge!" said Sir Robert; and out he sallied, followed by the *élite* of his retainers. Then there was a pretty to-do. Heads flew one way, arms and legs another. Round went Tickletoby; and wherever it alighted, down came horse and man. The Baron excelled himself that day. All that he had done in Palestine faded in the comparison; he had fought for fun there, but now it was for life and lands. Away went John de Northwood; away went William of Hever and Roger of Leybourne. Hamo de Crevecœur, with the church vassals and the banner of St. Austin, had been gone some time. The siege was raised, and the Lord of Sheppey was left alone in his glory.

But, brave as the Baron undoubtedly was, and total as had been the defeat of his enemies, it cannot be supposed that *La Stoccata* would be allowed to carry it away thus. It has before been hinted that Abbot Anselm had written to the Pope, and Boniface the Eighth piqued himself on his punctuality as a correspondent in all matters connected with church discipline. He sent back an answer by return of post; and by it all Christian people were strictly enjoined to aid in exterminating the offender, on pain of the greater excommunication in this world, and a million of years of purgatory in the next. But then, again, Boniface the Eighth was rather at a discount in England just then. He had affronted Longshanks, as the royal lieges had nicknamed their monarch; and Longshanks had been rather sharp upon the clergy in consequence. If the Baron de Shurland could but get the King's pardon for what, in his cooler moments, he admitted to be a peccadillo, he might sniff at the Pope, and bid him "do his devilmost."

Fortune, who, as the poet says, delights to favor the bold, stood his friend on this occasion. Edward had been for some time collecting a large force on the coast of Kent, to carry on his French wars for the recovery of Guienne; he was expected shortly to review it in person; but, then, the troops lay principally in cantonments about the mouth of the Thames, and his Majesty was to come down by water. What was to be done?— the royal barge was in sight, and John de Northwood and Hamo de Crevecœur had broken up all the boats to boil their camp-kettles. A truly great mind is never without resources.

"Bring me my boots!" said the Baron.

They brought him his boots, and his dapple-gray steed along with them. Such a courser! all blood and bone, short-backed, broad-chested, and—but that he was a little ewe-necked—fault-less in form and figure. The Baron sprang upon his back, and dashed at once into the river.

The barge which carried Edward Longshanks and his for-tunes had by this time nearly reached the Nore; the stream was broad and the current strong, but Sir Robert and his steed were almost as broad, and a great deal stronger. After breast-ing the tide gallantly for a couple of miles, the knight was near enough to hail the steersman.

"What have we got here?" said the King. "It's a mer-maid," said one. "It's a grampus," said another. "It's the devil," said a third. But they were all wrong; it was only Robert de Shurland. "Grammercy," said the King, "that fellow was never born to be drowned!"

It has been said before that the Baron had fought in the Holy Wars; in fact, he had accompanied Longshanks, when only heir apparent, in his expedition twenty-five years before, although his name is unaccountably omitted by Sir Harris Nicolas in his list of crusaders. He had been present at Acre when Amirand of Joppa stabbed the prince with a poisoned dagger, and had lent Princess Eleanor his own tooth-brush after she had sucked out the venom from the wound. He had slain certain Saracens, contented himself with his own plunder, and never dunned the commissariat for arrears of pay. Of course he ranked high in Edward's good graces, and had received the honor of knight-hood at his hands on the field of battle.

In one so circumstanced it cannot be supposed that such a trifle as the killing of a frowzy friar would be much resented, even had he not taken so bold a measure to obtain his pardon. His petition was granted, of course, as soon as asked; and so it would have been had the indictment drawn up by the Canter-bury town-clerk, viz., "That he, the said Robert de Shurland, etc., had then and there, with several, to wit, one thousand, pairs of boots, given sundry, to wit, two thousand, kicks, and therewith and thereby killed divers, to wit, ten thousand, Austin Friars," been true to the letter.

Thrice did the gallant gray circumnavigate the barge, while Robert de Winchelsey, the chancellor and archbishop to boot, was making out, albeit with great reluctance, the royal pardon. The interval was sufficiently long to enable his Majesty, who, gracious as he was, had always an eye to business, just to hint that the gratitude he felt towards the Baron was not unmixed with a lively sense of services to come; and that, if life were now spared him, common decency must oblige him to make himself useful. Before the archbishop, who had scalded his fingers with the wax in affixing the great seal, had time to take them out of his mouth, all was settled, and the Baron de Shurland had pledged himself to be forthwith in readiness, *cum suis*, to accompany his liege lord to Guienne.

With the royal pardon secured in his vest, boldly did his lordship turn again to the shore; and as boldly did his courser oppose his breadth of chest to the stream. It was a work of no common difficulty or danger; a steed of less "mettle and bone" had long since sunk in the effort: as it was, the Baron's boots were full of water, and Gray Dolphin's chamfrain more than once dipped beneath the wave. The convulsive snorts of the noble animal showed his distress; each instant they became more loud and frequent; when his hoof touched the strand, and "the horse and his rider" stood once again in safety on the shore.

Rapidly dismounting, the Baron was loosening the girths of his demi-pique, to give the panting animal breath, when he was aware of as ugly an old woman as he had ever clapped eyes upon, peeping at him under the horse's belly.

"Make much of your steed, Robert Shurland! Make much of your steed!" cried the hag, shaking at him her long and bony finger. "Groom to the hide, and corn to the manger! He has saved your life, Robert Shurland, for the nonce; but he shall yet be the means of your losing it for all that!"

The Baron started: "What's that you say, you old fagot?" He ran round by his horse's tail; the woman was gone!

The Baron paused; his great soul was not to be shaken by trifles; he looked around him, and solemnly ejaculated the word "Humbug!" then, slinging the bridle across his arm, walked slowly on in the direction of the castle.

The appearance, and still more the disappearance, of the crone had, however, made an impression; every step he took he became more thoughtful. "'Twould be deuced provoking, though, if he *should* break my neck after all." He turned and gazed at Dolphin with the scrutinizing eye of a veterinary surgeon. "I'll be shot if he is not groggy!" said the Baron.

With his lordship, like another great commander, "Once to be in doubt, was once to be resolved:" it would never do to go to the wars on a rickety prad. He dropped the rein, drew forth Tickletoby, and, as the enfranchised Dolphin, good easy horse, stretched out his ewe-neck to the herbage, struck off his head at a single blow. "There, you lying old beldame!" said the Baron; "now take him away to the knacker's."

Three years were come and gone. King Edward's French wars were over; both parties having fought till they came to a stand-still, shook hands, and the quarrel, as usual, was patched up by a royal marriage. This happy event gave his Majesty leisure to turn his attention to Scotland, where things, through the intervention of William Wallace, were looking rather queerish. As his reconciliation with Philip now allowed of his fighting the Scotch in peace and quietness, the monarch lost no time in marching his long legs across the border, and the short ones of the Baron followed him of course. At Falkirk, Tickletoby was in great request; and in the year following, we find a contemporary poet hinting at his master's prowess under the walls of Caerlaverock—

> Obec eus fu athimines
> Li beau Robert de Shurland
> Iti kant seoit sur le thebal
> Ne sembloit home ke someille.

A quatrain which Mr. Simpkinson translates,

> "With them was marching
> The good Robert de Shurland,
> Who, when seated on horseback,
> Does not resemble a man asleep!"

So thoroughly awake, indeed, does he seem to have proved

himself, that the bard subsequently exclaims in an ecstasy of admiration,

> Si ie estoie une pucelette
> Je li donrie ceur et cors
> Tant est de lu bons li recors.

> "If I were a young maiden,
> I would give my heart and person,
> So great is his fame!"

Fortunately the poet was a tough old monk of Exeter; since such a present to a nobleman, now in his grand climacteric, would hardly have been worth the carriage. With the reduction of this stronghold of the Maxwells seem to have concluded the Baron's military services; as on the very first day of the fourteenth century we find him once more landed on his native shore, and marching, with such of his retainers as the wars had left him, towards the hospitable shelter of Shurland Castle. It was then, upon that very beach, some hundred yards distant from high-water mark, that his eye fell upon something like an ugly old woman in a red cloak. She was seated on what seemed to be a large stone, in an interesting attitude, with her elbows resting upon her knees, and her chin upon her thumbs. The Baron started: the remembrance of his interview with a similar personage in the same place, some three years since, flashed upon his recollection. He rushed towards the spot, but the form was gone;—nothing remained but the seat it had appeared to occupy. This, on examination, turned out to be no stone, but the whitened skull of a dead horse! A tender remembrance of the deceased Gray Dolphin shot a momentary pang into the Baron's bosom; he drew the back of his hand across his face; the thought of the hag's prediction in an instant rose, and banished all softer emotions. In utter contempt of his own weakness, yet with a tremor that deprived his redoubtable kick of half its wonted force, he spurned the relic with his foot. One word alone issued from his lips, elucidatory of what was passing in his mind—it long remained imprinted on the memory of his faithful followers—that word was "Gammon!" The skull bounded across the beach till it reached the very margin of the stream;—one instant more and it would be engulfed for ever. At that moment a loud "Ha! ha! ha!" was distinctly heard by the whole train to issue from its bleached and toothless jaws: it sank beneath the flood in a horse laugh.

Meanwhile Sir Robert de Shurland felt an odd sort of sensation in his right foot. His boots had suffered in the wars. Great pains had been taken for their preservation. They had been "soled" and "heeled" more than once;—had they been "goloshed," their owner might have defied Fate! Well has it been said that "there is no such thing as a trifle." A nobleman's life depended upon a question of ninepence.

The Baron marched on; the uneasiness in his foot increased. He plucked off his boot;—a horse's tooth was sticking in his great toe!

The result may be anticipated. Lame as he was, his lordship, with characteristic decision, would hobble on to Shurland; his walk increased the inflammation; a flagon of *aqua vitæ* did not mend matters. He was in a high fever; he took to his bed. Next morning the toe presented the appearance of a Bedford-shire carrot; by dinner-time it had deepened to a beet-root; and when Bargrave, the leech, at last sliced it off, the gangrene was too confirmed to admit of remedy. Dame Martin thought it high time to send for Miss Margaret, who, ever since her mother's death, had been living with her maternal aunt, the abbess, in the Ursuline convent at Greenwich. The young lady came, and with her came one Master Ingoldsby, her cousin-german by the mother's side; but the Baron was too far gone in the dead-thraw to recognize either. He died as he lived, unconquered and unconquerable. His last words were—"Tell the old hag she may go to——." Whither remains a secret. He expired without fully articulating the place of her destination.

But who and what *was* the crone who prophesied the catastrophe? Ay, "that is the mystery of this wonderful history." Some say it was Dame Fothergill, the late confessor's mamma; others, St. Bridget herself; others thought it was nobody at all, but only a phantom conjured up by conscience. As we do not know, we decline giving an opinion.

And what became of the Clerk of Chatham?—Mr. Simpkinson avers that he lived to a good old age, and was at last hanged by Jack Cade, with his inkhorn about his neck, for "setting boys copies." In support of this he adduces his name "Emmanuel," and refers to the historian Shakspeare. Mr. Peters, on the contrary, considers this to be what he calls one of Mr. Simpkinson's "Anacreonisms," inasmuch as, at the introduction of Mr. Cade's reform measure, the Clerk, if alive, would have been hard upon two hundred years old. The probability is that the unfortunate alluded to was his great-grandson.

Margaret Shurland in due course became Margaret Ingoldsby: her portrait still hangs in the gallery at Tappington. The features are handsome, but shrewish, betraying, as it were, a touch of the old Baron's temperament; but we never could learn that she actually kicked her husband. She brought him a very pretty fortune in chains, owches, and Saracen ear-rings; the barony, being a male fief, reverted to the Crown.

In the abbey-church at Minster may yet be seen the tomb of a recumbent warrior, clad in the chain-mail of the thirteenth century.* His hands are clasped in prayer; his legs, crossed in that position so prized by Templars in ancient and tailors in modern days, bespeak him a soldier of the faith in Palestine. Close behind his dexter calf lies, sculptured in bold relief, a horse's head: and a respectable elderly lady, as she shows the monument, fails not to read her auditors a fine moral lesson on the sin of ingratitude, or to claim a sympathizing tear to the memory of poor "Gray Dolphin!"

---

* Subsequent to the first appearance of the foregoing narrative, the tomb alluded to has been opened during the course of certain repairs which the church has undergone. Mr. Simpkinson, who was present at the exhumation of the body within, and has enriched his collection with three of its grinders, says the bones of one of the great toes were wanting. He speaks in terms of great admiration at the thickness of the skull, and is of opinion that the skeleton is that of a great patriot much addicted to Lundyfoot.

IT is on my own personal reminiscences that I draw for the
following story : the scene of its leading event was most familiar
to me in early life.   If the principal actor in it be yet living,
he must have reached a very advanced age.   He was often
at the Hall, in my infancy, on professional visits.   It is, however, only from those who " prated of his whereabouts " that I
learned the history of this adventure with

The Ghost.

THERE stands a City,—neither large nor small,—
　　Its air and situation sweet and pretty ;
It matters very little—if at all—
　　Whether its denizens are dull or witty,
Whether the ladies there are short or tall,
　　Brunettes or blondes, only, there stands a city !—
Perhaps 'tis also requisite to minute
That there's a Castle and a Cobbler in it.

A fair Cathedral, too, the story goes,
　　And kings and heroes lie entombed within her ;
There pious Saints in marble pomp repose,
　　Whose shrines are worn by knees of many a sinner ;
There, too, full many an Aldermanic nose
　　Rolled its loud diapason after dinner ;
And there stood high the holy sconce of Becket,
—Till four assassins came from France to crack it.

The Castle was a huge and antique mound,
　　Proof against all th' artillery of the quiver,
Ere those abominable guns were found,
　　To send cold lead through gallant warrior's liver.
It stands upon a gently rising ground,
　　Sloping down gradually to the river,
Resembling (to compare great things with smaller)
A well-scooped, mouldy Stilton cheese—but taller.

The Keep, I find, 's been sadly altered lately,
 And 'stead of mail-clad knights, of honor jealous,
In martial panoply so grand and stately,
 Its walls are filled with money-making fellows,
And stuffed, unless I'm misinformed greatly,
 With leaden pipes, and coke, and coals, and bellows;
In short, so great a change has come to pass,
'Tis now a manufactory of Gas.

But to my tale.—Before this profanation,
 And ere its ancient glories were cut short all,
A poor hard-working Cobbler took his station
 In a small house, just opposite the portal;
His birth, his parentage, and education,
 I know but little of—a strange, odd mortal;
His aspect, air, and gait, were all ridiculous;
His name was Mason—he'd been christened Nicholas.

Nick had a wife possessed of many a charm,
 And of the Lady Huntingdon persuasion;
But, spite of all her piety, her arm
 She'd sometimes exercise when in a passion;
And, being of a temper somewhat warm,
 Would now and then seize, upon small occasion,
A stick, or stool, or anything that round did lie,
And baste her lord and master most confoundedly.

No matter!—'tis a thing that's not uncommon,
 'Tis what we all have heard and most have read of—
I mean a bruising, pugilistic woman,
 Such as I own I entertain a dread of,
—And so did Nick, whom sometimes there would come on
 A sort of fear his Spouse might knock his head off,
Demolish half his teeth, or drive a rib in,
She shone so much in "facers" and in "fibbing."

"There's time and place for all things," said a sage
 (King Solomon, I think), and this I can say,
Within a well-roped ring, or on a stage,
 Boxing may be a very pretty *Fancy*,

When Messrs. Burke or Bendigo engage ;
   —'Tis not so well in Susan, Jane, or Nancy :—
To get well milled by any one's an evil,
But by a lady—'tis the very devil.

And so thought Nicholas, whose only trouble
   (At least his worst) was this his rib's propensity ;
For sometimes from the alehouse he would hobble,
   His senses lost in a sublime immensity
Of cogitation ; then he couldn't cobble—
   And then his wife would often try the density
Of his poor skull, and strike with all her might,
As fast as kitchen-wenches strike a light.

Mason, meek soul, who ever hated strife,
   Of this same striking had a morbid dread ;
He hated it like poison—or his wife—
   A vast antipathy !—but so he said ;
And very often, for a quiet life,
   On these occasions he'd sneak up to bed,
Grope darkling in, and, soon as at the door
He heard his lady, he'd pretend to snore.

One night, then, ever partial to society,
   Nick, with a friend (another jovial fellow),
Went to a Club—I should have said Society—
   At the " City Arms," once called the Porto Bello ;
A Spouting party, which, though some decry it, I
   Consider no bad lounge when one is mellow ;
There they discuss the tax on salt and leather,
And change of ministers and change of weather.

In short, it was a kind of British Forum,
   Like John Gale Jones's, erst in Piccadilly,
Only they managed things with more decorum,
   And the orations were not *quite* so silly ;
Far different questions, too, would come before 'em,
   Not always politics, which, will ye nill ye,
Their London prototypes were always willing
To give one *quantum suff.* of—for a shilling.

6

It more resembled one of later date,
   And tenfold talent, as I'm told, in Bow Street,
Where kindlier-natured souls do congregate;
   And, though there are who deem that same a low street,
Yet, I'm assured, for frolicsome debate
   And genuine humor, it's surpassed by no street,
When the "Chief Baron" enters, and assumes
To "rule" o'er mimic "Thesigers" and "Broughams."

Here they would oft forget their Rulers' faults,
   And waste in ancient lore the midnight taper;
Inquire if Orpheus first produced the Waltz,
   How Gaslights differ from the Delphic Vapor,
Whether Hippocrates gave Glauber's Salts,
   And what the Romans wrote on ere they'd paper.
This night the subject of their disquisitions
Was Ghosts, Hobgoblins, Sprites, and Apparitions.

One learned gentleman, "a sage, grave man,"
   Talked of the Ghost in Hamlet, "sheathed in steel;"
His well-read friend, who next to speak began,
   Said "That was Poetry, and nothing real;"
A third, of more extensive learning, ran
   To Sir George Villiers' Ghost, and Mrs. Veal,—
Of sheeted spectres spoke with shortened breath,
And thrice he quoted "Drelincourt on Death."

Nick smoked and smoked, and trembled as he heard
   The point discussed, and all they said upon it:
How, frequently, some murdered man appeared,
   To tell his wife and children who had done it;
Or how a Miser's ghost, with grisly beard,
   And pale lean visage, in an old Scotch bonnet,
Wandered about to watch his buried money!
When all at once Nick heard the clock strike One,—he

Sprang from his seat, not doubting but a lecture
   Impended from his fond and faithful She;
Nor could he well to pardon him expect her,
   For he had promised to "be home to tea;"

But having luckily the key o' the back door,
    He fondly hoped that, unperceived, he
Might creep up stairs again, pretend to doze,
And hoax his spouse with music from his nose.

Vain, fruitless hope!—The wearied sentinel
    At eve may overlook the crouching foe,
Till, ere his hand can sound the alarum-bell,
    He sinks beneath the unexpected blow;
Before the whiskers of Grimalkin fell,
    When slumbering on her post, the mouse may go—
But woman, wakeful woman, 's never weary,
—Above all, when she waits to thump her deary.

Soon Mrs. Mason heard the well-known tread;
    She heard the key slow creaking in the door,
Spied, through the gloom obscure, towards the bed
    Nick creeping soft, as oft he had crept before;
When, bang, she threw a something at his head,
    And Nick at once lay prostrate on the floor;
While she exclaimed, with her indignant face on—
" How dare you use your wife so, Mr. Mason?"

Spare we to tell how fiercely she debated,
    Especially the length of her oration—
Spare we to tell how Nick expostulated,
    Roused by the bump into a good set passion,
So great that more than once he execrated,
    Ere he crawled into bed in his usual fashion;
—The Muses hate brawls; suffice it then to say,
He ducked below the clothes—and there he lay!

'Twas now the very witching time of night,
    When churchyards groan, and graves give up their dead,
And many a mischievous, enfranchised Sprite
    Had long since burst his bonds of stone or lead,
And hurried off, with schoolboy-like delight,
    To play his pranks near some poor wretch's bed,
Sleeping, perhaps serenely as a porpoise,
Nor dreaming of this fiendish Habeas Corpus.

Not so our Nicholas: his meditations
   Still to the same tremendous theme recurred,
The same dread subject of the dark narrations,
   Which, backed with such authority, he'd heard:
Lost in his own horrific contemplations,
   He pondered o'er each well-remembered word;
When at the bed's foot, close beside the post,
He verily believed he saw—a Ghost!

Plain, and more plain, the unsubstantial Sprite
   To his astonished gaze each moment grew;
Ghastly and gaunt, it reared its shadowy height,
   Of more than mortal seeming to the view,
And round its long, thin, bony fingers drew
   A tattered winding-sheet, of course *all white;*—
The moon that moment peeping through a cloud,
Nick very plainly saw it *through the shroud!*

And now those matted locks, which never yet
   Had yielded to the comb's unkind divorce,
Their long-contracted amity forget,
   And spring asunder with elastic force;
Nay, e'en the very cap, of texture coarse,
   Whose ruby cincture crowned that brow of jet,
Uprose in agony—the Gorgon's head
Was but a type of Nick's up-squatting in the bed.

From every pore distilled a clammy dew,
   Quaked every limb—the candle, too, no doubt,
En règle, would have burnt extremely blue,
   But Nick unluckily had put it out;
And he, though naturally bold and stout,
   In short, was in a most tremendous stew;—
The room was filled with a sulphureous smell,
But where that came from Mason could not tell.

All motionless the Spectre stood—and now
   Its rev'rend form more clearly shone confest.
From the pale cheek a beard of purest snow
   Descended o'er its venerable breast;

The thin gray hairs, that crowned its furrowed brow,
  Told of years long gone by.—An awful guest
It stood, and with an action of command,
Beckoned the Cobbler with its wan right hand.

" Whence and what art thou, Execrable Shape ?"
  Nick *might* have cried, could he have found a tongue,
But his distended jaws could only gape,
  And not a sound upon the welkin rung ;
His gooseberry orbs seemed as they would have sprung
  Forth from their sockets—like a frightened Ape
He sat upon his haunches, bolt upright,
And shook, and grinned, and chattered with affright.

And still the shadowy finger, long and lean,
  Now beckoned Nick, now pointed to the door ;
And many an ireful glance, and frown, between,
  The angry visage of the Phantom wore,
As if quite vexed that Nick would do no more
  Than stare, without e'en asking, " What d' ye mean ?"
Because, as we are told—a sad old joke, too—
Ghosts, like the ladies, " never speak till spoke to."

Cowards, 'tis said, in certain situations,
  Derive a sort of courage from despair,
And then perform, from downright desperation,
  Much more than many a bolder man would dare.
Nick saw the Ghost was getting in a passion,
  And therefore, groping till he found the chair,
Seized on his awl, crept softly out of bed,
And followed, quaking, where the Spectre led.

And down the winding stair, with noiseless tread,
  The tenant of the tomb passed slowly on ;
Each mazy turning of the humble shed
  Seemed to his step at once familiar grown,
So safe and sure the labyrinth did he tread
  As though the domicile had been his own,
Though Nick himself, in passing through the shop,
Had almost broke his nose against the mop.

Despite its wooden bolt, with jarring sound
　　The door upon its hinges open flew;
And forth the Spirit issued—yet around
　　It turned, as if its follower's fears it knew,
And, once more beckoning, pointed to the mound,
　　The antique Keep, on which the bright moon threw
With such effulgence her mild silvery gleam,
The visionary form seemed melting in her beam.

Beneath a pond'rous archway's sombre shade,
　　Where once the huge portcullis swung sublime,
'Mid ivied battlements in ruin laid,
　　Sole, sad memorials of the olden time,
The Phantom held its way—and though afraid
　　Even of the owls that sung their vesper chime,
Pale Nicholas pursued, its steps attending,
And wondering what on earth it all would end in.

Within the mouldering fabric's deep recess
　　At length they reached a court obscure and lone—
It seemed a drear and desolate wilderness,
　　The blackened walls with ivy all o'ergrown;
The night-bird shrieked her note of wild distress,
　　Disturbed upon her solitary throne,
As though indignant mortal step should dare,
So led, at such an hour, to venture there!

—The apparition paused, and would have spoke,
　　Pointing to what Nick thought an iron ring,
But then a neighboring chanticleer awoke,
　　And loudly 'gan his early matins sing;
And then "it started like a guilty thing,"
　　As that shrill clarion the silence broke.
—We know how much dead gentlefolks eschew
The appalling sound of "Cock-a-doodle-do!"

The vision was no more—and Nick alone—
　　"His streamers waving" in the midnight wind,
Which through the ruins ceased not to groan;
　　—His garment, too, was somewhat short behind,—

And, worst of all, he knew not where to find
   The ring,—which made him most his fate bemoan—
The iron ring,—no doubt of some trap-door,
'Neath which the old dead Miser kept his store.

"What's to be done?" he cried; " 'Twere vain to stay
   Here in the dark without a single clue—
Oh, for a candle now, or moonlight ray!
   'Fore George, I'm vastly puzzled what to do"
(Then clapped his hand behind),—" 'Tis chilly, too—
   I'll mark the spot, and come again by day.
What can I mark it by?—Oh, here's the wall—
The mortar's yielding—here I'll stick my awl!"

Then rose from earth to sky a withering shriek,
   A loud, a long-protracted note of woe,
Such as when tempests roar, and timbers creak,
   And o'er the side the masts in thunder go;
While on the deck resistless billows break,
   · And drag their victims to the gulfs below ;—
Such was the scream when, for the want of candle,
Nick Mason drove his awl in up to the handle.

Scared by his Lady's heart-appalling cry,
   Vanished at once poor Mason's golden dream—
For dream it was ;—and all his visions high,
   Of wealth and grandeur, fled before that scream—
And still he listens with averted eye,
   When gibing neighbors make "the Ghost" their theme ;
While ever from that hour they all declare
That Mrs. Mason used a cushion in her chair!

CONFOUND not, I beseech thee, reader, the subject of the following monody with the hapless hero of the tea-urn, Cupid, of "Yow-Yow-ing" memory. Tray was an attached favorite of many years' standing. Most people worth loving have had a friend of this kind; Lord Byron says he "never had but one, and here he (the dog, not the nobleman) lies!"

𝕮𝖍𝖊 𝕮𝖞𝖓𝖔𝖙𝖆𝖕𝖍.

> Poor Tray charmant!
> Poor Tray de mon ami!
> Dog-bury and Vergers.

OH! where shall I bury my poor dog Tray,
  Now his fleeting breath has passed away?—
Seventeen years, I can venture to say,
Have I seen him gambol, and frolic, and play,
Evermore happy, and frisky, and gay,
As though every one of his months was May,
And the whole of his life one long holiday—
Now he's a lifeless lump of clay,
Oh! where shall I bury my faithful Tray?

I am almost tempted to think it hard
That it may not be there, in yon sunny churchyard,
  Where the green willows wave   O'er the peaceful grave,
Which holds all that once was honest and brave,
Kind, and courteous, and faithful, and true;
Qualities, Tray, that were found in you.
But it may not be—yon sacred ground,
By holiest feelings fenced around,
May ne'er within its hallowed bound
Receive the dust of a soulless hound.

I would not place him in yonder fane,
Where the midday sun through the storied pane
Throws on the pavement a crimson stain;
Where the banners of chivalry heavily swing
O'er the pinnacled tomb of the Warrior King,
With helmet and shield, and all that sort of thing.

No!—come what may,   My gentle Tray
Shan't be an intruder on bluff Harry Tudor,
Or panoplied monarchs yet earlier and ruder
      Whom you see on their backs,   In stone or in wax,
Though the Sacristans now are "forbidden to ax"
For what Mr. Hume calls "a scandalous tax;"
While the Chartists insist they've a right to go snacks—
No!—Tray's humble tomb would look but shabby
'Mid the sculptured shrines of that gorgeous Abbey.

      Besides, in the place   They say there's not space
To bury what wet-nurses call a "Babby."
Even "Rare Ben Jonson," that famous wight,
I am told, is interred there bolt upright,
In just such a posture, beneath his bust,
As Tray used to sit in to beg for a crust.

      The epitaph, too,   Would scarcely do:
For what could it say, but "Here lies Tray,
A very good kind of a dog in his day!"
And satirical folks might be apt to imagine it
Meant as a quiz on the House of Plantagenet.

No! no!—The Abbey may do very well
For a feudal "Nob," or poetical "Swell,"
"Crusaders," or "Poets," or "Knights of St. John,"
Or Knights of St. John's Wood, who once went on
To the 𝕮astle of 𝕲oode 𝕷orde 𝕰glintoune.
Count Fiddle-fumkin, and Lord Fiddle-faddle,
"Sir Cravan," "Sir Gael," and "Sir Campbell of Saddell"
(Who, as poor Hook said, when he heard of the feat,
"Was somehow knocked out of his family-seat");
      The Esquires of the body   To my Lord Tomnoddy;
"Sir Fairlie," "Sir Lambe,"
And the "Knight of the Ram,"
The "Knight of the Rose," and the "Knight of the Dragon,"
      Who, save at the flagon,   And prog in the wagon,
The newspapers tell us did little "to brag on;"

And more, though the Muse knows but little concerning 'em,
"Sir Hopkins," "Sir Popkins," "Sir Gage," and "Sir Jerning-
      ham,"—

All *Preux Chevaliers,* in friendly rivalry
Who should best bring back the glory of Chi-valry.—
—(Pray be so good, for the sake of my song,
To pronounce here the ante-penultimate long;
Or some hyper-critic will certainly cry,
"The word 'Chivalry' is but a rhyme to the eye."

    And I own it is clear   A fastidious ear
Will be, more or less, always annoyed with you when you
Insert any rhyme that's not perfectly genuine.

    As to pleasing the "eye," 'Tisn't worth while to try,
Since Moore and Tom Campbell themselves admit "Spinach"
Is perfectly antiphonetic to "Greenwich.")—
But stay!—I say!
Let me pause while I may—
This digression is leading me sadly astray
From my object—a grave for my poor dog Tray!

I would not place him beneath thy walls,
And proud o'ershadowing dome, St. Paul's!
Though I've always considered Sir Christopher Wren,
As an architect, one of the greatest of men;
And, talking of Epitaphs,—much I admire his,
"*Circumspice si Monumentum requiris;*"
Which an erudite Verger translated to me,
"If you ask for his monument, *Sir-come-spy-see!*"—
    No!—I should not know where   To place him there;
I would not have him by surly Johnson be;—
Or that queer-looking horse that is rolling on Ponsonby;—
    Or those ugly minxes   The sister Sphynxes,
Mixed creatures, half lady, half lioness, *ergo*
(Denon says), the emblems of *Leo* and *Virgo;*
On one of the backs of which singular jumble,
Sir Ralph Abercrombie is going to tumble,
With a thump which alone were enough to despatch him,
If the Scotchman in front shouldn't happen to catch him.

No! I'd not have him there,—nor nearer the door,
Where the man and the Angel have got Sir John Moore,*

* See note at end of "The Cynotaph."

And are quietly letting him down through the floor,
By Gillespie, the one who escaped, at Vellore,
    Alone from the row ;— Neither he nor Lord Howe
Would like to be plagued with a little Bow-wow.
    No, Tray, we must yield, And go further a-field ;
To lay you by Nelson were downright effront'ry ;
—We'll be off from the City, and look at the country.

    It shall not be there, In that sepulchred square,
Where folks are interred for the sake of the air
(Though, pay but the dues, they could hardly refuse
To Tray what they grant to Thugs, and Hindoos,
Turks, Infidels, Heretics, Jumpers, and Jews),
    Where the tombstones are placed In the very *best taste*,
    At the feet and the head Of the elegant Dead,
And no one's received who's not " buried in lead :"
For, there lie the bones of Deputy Jones,
Whom the widow's tears and the orphan's groans
Affected as much as they do the stones
His executors laid on the Deputy's bones ;
    Little rest, poor knave ! Would Tray have in his grave ;
    Since Spirits, 'tis plain, Are sent back again,
To roam round their bodies,—the bad ones in pain,—
Dragging after them sometimes a heavy jack-chain ;
Whenever they met, alarmed by its groans, his
Ghost all night long would be barking at Jones's.

    Nor shall he be laid By that cross old maid,
Miss Penelope Bird,—of whom it is said
All the dogs in the parish were ever afraid.
    He must not be placed By one so strait-laced
In her temper, her taste, her morals, and waist.
For 'tis said, when she went up to Heaven, and St. Peter,
    Who happened to meet her, Came forward to greet her,
She pursed up with scorn every vinegar feature,
And bade him " Get out for a horrid Male Creature !"
So the Saint, after looking as if he could eat her,
Not knowing, perhaps, very well how to treat her,

And not being willing,—or able,—to beat her,
Sent her back to her grave till her temper grew sweeter,
With an epithet which I decline to repeat here.

　　No,—if Tray were interred　By Penelope Bird,
No dog would be e'er so be-" whelp "ed and be-" cur "red—
All the night long her cantankerous Sprite
Would be running about in the pale moonlight,
Chasing him round, and attempting to lick
The ghost of poor Tray with the ghost of a stick.

　　Stay!—let me see!—　Ay—here it shall be
At the root of this gnarled and time-worn tree,
　　Where Tray and I　Would often lie,
And watch the bright clouds as they floated by
In the broad expanse of the clear blue sky,
When the sun was bidding the world good-bye;
And the plaintive Nightingale, warbling nigh,
Poured forth her mournful melody;
While the tender Wood-pigeon's cooing cry
Has made me say to myself, with a sigh,
"How nice you would eat with a steak in a pie!"

Ay, here it shall be!—far, far from the view
Of the noisy world and its maddening crew;
　　Simple and few,　Tender and true,
The lines o'er his grave.—They have, some of them, too,
The advantage of being remarkably new.

Epitaph.

　　Affliction sore　Long time he bore,
Physicians were in vain!—
　　Grown blind, alas! he'd　Some Prussic Acid,
And that put him out of his pain!

NOTE, PAGE 90.

　In the autumn of 1824, Captain Medwin having hinted that certain beautiful lines on the burial of this gallant officer might have been the production of Lord Byron's Muse, the late Mr. Sydney Taylor, some-

what indignantly, claimed them for their rightful owner, the Rev.
Charles Wolfe. During the controversy a third claimant started up in
the person of a *soi-disant* "Doctor Marshall," who turned out to be a
Durham blacksmith, and his pretensions a hoax. It was then that a
certain "Doctor Peppercorn" put forth *his* pretensions, to what he
averred was the only "true and original" version, viz.—

Not a *sous* had he got,—not a guinea or note,
  And he looked confoundedly flurried,
As he bolted away without paying his shot,
  And the Landlady after him hurried.

We saw him again at dead of night,
  When home from the Club returning;
We twigged the Doctor beneath the light
  Of the gas-lamp brilliantly burning.

All bare, and exposed to the midnight dews,
  Reclined in the gutter we found him:
And he looked like a gentleman taking a snooze,
  With his *Marshall* cloak around him.

"The Doctor's as drunk as the devil," we said,
  And we managed a shutter to borrow;
We raised him, and sighed at the thought that his head
  Would "consumedly ache" on the morrow.

We bore him home, and we put him to bed,
  And we told his wife and his daughter
To give him, next morning, a couple of red
  Herrings, with soda-water.—

Loudly they talked of his money that's gone,
  And his Lady began to upbraid him;
But little he reck'd, so they let him snore on
  'Neath the counterpane just as we laid him.

We tuck'd him in, and had hardly done
  When, beneath the window calling,
We heard the rough voice of a son of a gun
  Of a watchman "One o'clock!" bawling.

Slowly and sadly we all walked down
  From his room in the uppermost story;
A rushlight we placed on the cold hearth-stone,
  And we left him alone in his glory.

Hos ego versiculos feci, tulit alter honores.—VIRGIL.
I wrote the lines—* * owned them—he told stories!
                                    THOMAS INGOLDSBY.

MRS. BOTHERBY'S STORY.

The Leech of Folkestone.

READER, were you ever bewitched?—I do not mean by a
"white wench's black eye," or by love-potions imbibed
from a ruby lip;—but, were you ever really and *bona fide*
bewitched, in the true Matthew Hopkins sense of the word?
Did you ever, for instance, find yourself from head to heel one
vast complication of cramps?—or burst out into sudorific exu-
dation like a cold thaw, with the thermometer at zero? Were
your eyes ever turned upside down, exhibiting nothing but
their whites? Did you ever vomit a paper of crooked pins?
or expectorate Whitechapel needles? These are genuine and
undoubted marks of possession; and if you never experienced
any of them,—why, "happy man be his dole!"

Yet such things have been : yea, we are assured, and that on
no mean authority, still are.

The World, according to the best geographers, is divided into
Europe, Asia, Africa, America, and Romney Marsh. In this
last-named and fifth quarter of the globe, a witch may still be
occasionally discovered in favorable, *i. e.*, stormy, seasons,
weathering Dungeness Point in an eggshell, or careering on her
broomstick over Dymchurch wall. A cow may yet be sometimes seen galloping like mad, with tail erect, and an old pair
of breeches on her horns, an unerring guide to the door of the
crone whose magic arts have drained her udder. I do not,
however, remember to have heard that any Conjurer has of
late been detected in the district.

Not many miles removed from the verge of this recondite
region stands a collection of houses, which its maligners call a
fishing-town, and its well-wishers a Watering-place. A limb of
one of the Cinque Ports, it has (or lately had) a corporation of
its own, and has been thought considerable enough to give a
second title to a noble family. Rome stood on seven hills;

Folkestone seems to have been built upon seventy. Its streets, lanes, and alleys,—fanciful distinctions without much real difference,—are agreeable enough to persons who do not mind running up and down stairs; and the only inconvenience at all felt by such of its inhabitants as are not asthmatic, is when some heedless urchin tumbles down a chimney, or an impertinent pedestrian peeps into a garret window.

At the eastern extremity of the town, on the sea-beach, and scarcely above high-water mark, stood, in the good old times, a row of houses then denominated "Frog-hole." Modern refinement subsequently euphonized the name into "East Street;" but "what's in a name?" the encroachments of Ocean have long since levelled all in one common ruin.

Here, in the early part of the seventeenth century, flourished in somewhat doubtful reputation, but comparative opulence, a compounder of medicines, one Master Erasmus Buckthorne,— the effluvia of whose drugs from within, mingling agreeably with the "ancient and fish-like smells" from without, wafted a delicious perfume throughout the neighborhood.

At seven of the clock on the morning when Mrs. Botherby's narrative commences, a stout Suffolk "punch," about thirteen hands and a half in height, was slowly led up and down before the door of the pharmacopolist by a lean and withered lad, whose appearance warranted an opinion, pretty generally expressed, that his master found him as useful in experimentalizing as in household drudgery; and that, for every pound avoirdupois of solid meat, he swallowed at the least two pounds troy weight of chemicals and galenicals. As the town clock struck the quarter, Master Buckthorne emerged from his laboratory, and, putting the key carefully into his pocket, mounted the sure-footed cob aforesaid, and proceeded up and down the acclivities and declivities of the town with the gravity due to his station and profession. When he reached the open country his pace was increased to a sedate canter, which, in somewhat more than half an hour, brought "the horse and his rider" in front of a handsome and substantial mansion, the numerous gable ends and bayed windows of which bespoke the owner a man of worship, and one well to do in the world.

"How now, Hodge Gardener?" quoth the Leech, scarcely

drawing bit; for Punch seemed to be aware that he had reached his destination, and paused of his own accord. "How now, man? How fares thine employer, worthy Master Marsh? How hath he done? How hath he slept? My potion hath done its office? Ha!"

"Alack! ill at ease, worthy sir, ill at ease," returned the hind. "His honor is up and stirring; but he hath rested none, and complaineth that the same gnawing pain devoureth, as it were, his very vitals. In sooth he is ill at ease."

"Morrow, doctor!" interrupted a voice from a casement opening on the lawn. "Good morrow! I have looked for, longed for, thy coming this hour and more. Enter at once: the pastry and tankard are impatient for thine attack."

"Marry, Heaven forbid that I should balk their fancy!" quoth the Leech *sotto voce*, as, abandoning the bridle to honest Hodge, he dismounted and followed a buxom-looking hand-maiden into the breakfast parlor.

There, at the head of his well-furnished board, sat Master Thomas Marsh, of Marston Hall, a yeoman well respected in his degree: one of that sturdy and sterling class which, taking rank immediately below the Esquire (a title in its origin purely military), occupied, in the wealthier counties, the position in society now filled by the Country Gentleman. He was one of those of whom the proverb ran:—

> "A Knight of Cales,
>   A Gentleman of Wales,
>   And a Laird of the North Countree,—
>   A Yeoman of Kent,
>   With his yearly rent,
>   Will buy them out all three!"

A cold sirloin, big enough to frighten a Frenchman, filled the place of honor, counterchecked by a game-pie of no stinted dimensions; while a silver flagon of "humming-bub"—viz., ale strong enough to blow a man's beaver off—smiled opposite in treacherous amenity. The sideboard groaned beneath sundry massive cups and waiters of the purest silver; while the huge skull of a fallow-deer, with its branching horns, frowned majestically above. All spoke of affluence, of comfort; all save the master, whose restless eye and feverish look hinted but too plainly the severest mental or bodily disorder. By the side of the proprietor of the mansion sat his consort, a lady now past the bloom of youth, yet still retaining many of its charms. The clear olive of her complexion, and "the darkness of her Andalusian eye," at once betrayed her foreign origin; in fact, her "lord and master," as husbands were even then, by a legal fiction, denominated, had taken her to his bosom in a foreign country. The cadet of his family, Master Thomas Marsh had early in life been engaged in commerce. In the pursuit of his vocation he had visited Antwerp, Hamburg, and most of the Hanse Towns; and had already formed a tender connection with the orphan offspring of one of old Alva's officers, when the unexpected deaths of one immediate and two presumptive heirs placed him next in succession to the family acres. He married, and brought home his bride: who, by the decease of the venerable possessor, heart-broken at the loss of his elder children, became eventually lady of Marston Hall. It has been said that she was beautiful, yet was her beauty of a character that operates on the fancy more than the affections; she was one to be admired rather than loved. The proud curl of her lip, the firmness of her tread, her arched brow and stately carriage, showed the decision, not to say haughtiness, of her soul; while her glances, whether lightening with anger or melting in extreme softness, betrayed the existence of passions as intense in kind as opposite in quality. She rose as Erasmus entered the parlor, and, bestowing on him a look fraught with meaning, quitted the room, leaving him in unrestrained communication with his patient.

"'Fore George, Master Buckthorne!" exclaimed the latter, as the Leech drew near, "I will no more of your pharmacy;—burn, burn, gnaw, gnaw,—I had as lief the foul fiend were in my gizzard as one of your drugs. Tell me, in the devil's name, what is the matter with me!"

Thus conjured, the practitioner paused, and even turned somewhat pale. There was a perceptible faltering in his voice as, evading the question, he asked, "What say your other physicians?"

"Doctor Phiz says it is wind,—Doctor Fuz says it is water,—and Doctor Buz says it is something between wind and water."

7

"They are all of them wrong," said Erasmus Buckthorne.

"Truly, I think so," returned the patient. "They are manifest asses; but you, good Leech, you are a horse of another color. The world talks loudly of your learning, your skill, and cunning in arts the most abstruse; nay, sooth to say, some look coldly on you therefor, and stickle not to aver that you are cater-cousin with Beelzebub himself."

"It is ever the fate of science," murmured the professor, "to be maligned by the ignorant and superstitious. But a truce with such folly;—let me examine your palate."

Master Marsh thrust out a tongue long, clear, and red as a beet-root. "There is nothing wrong there," said the Leech. "Your wrist:—no;—the pulse is firm and regular, the skin cool and temperate. Sir, there is nothing the matter with you."

"Nothing the matter with me, Sir 'Potecary?—But I tell you there is the matter with me,—much the matter with me. Why is it that something seems ever gnawing at my heart-strings?—Whence this pain in the region of the liver?—Why is it that I sleep not o' nights,—rest not o' days? Why——"

"You are fidgety, Master Marsh," said the doctor.

Master Marsh's brow grew dark: he half rose from his seat, supported himself by both hands on the arms of his elbow chair, and, in accents of mingled anger and astonishment, repeated the word "Fidgety!"

"Ay, fidgety," returned the doctor, calmly. "Tut, man, there is nought ails thee save thine own overweening fancies. Take less of food, more air, put aside thy flagon, call for thy horse; be boot and saddle the word! Why, hast thou not youth?"

"I have," said the patient.

"Wealth and a fair domain?"

"Granted," quoth Marsh, cheerily.

"And a fair wife?"

"Yea," was the response, but in a tone something less satisfied.

"Then arouse thee, man, shake off this fantasy, betake thyself to thy lawful occasions—use thy good hap,—follow thy pleasures, and think no more of these fancied ailments."

"But I tell you, master mine, these ailments are not fancied. I lose my rest, I loathe my food, my doublet sits loosely on me,—these racking pains. My wife, too, when I meet her gaze, the cold sweat stands on my forehead, and I could almost think——" Marsh paused abruptly, mused a while, then added, looking steadily at his visitor, "These things are not right; they pass the common, Master Erasmus Buckthorne."

A slight shade crossed the brow of the Leech, but its passage was momentary; his features softened to a smile, in which pity seemed slightly blended with contempt. "Have done with such follies, Master Marsh! You are well, an you would but think so. Ride, I say, hunt, shoot, do anything,—disperse these melancholic humors, and become yourself again."

"Well, I will do your bidding," said Marsh, thoughtfully. "It may be so; and yet,—but I will do your bidding. Master Cobb of Brenzet writes me that he hath a score or two of fat ewes to be sold a pennyworth; I had thought to have sent Ralph Looker, but I will essay to go myself. Ho, there!—saddle me the brown mare, and bid Ralph be ready to attend me on the gelding."

An expression of pain contracted the features of Master Marsh as he rose and slowly quitted the apartment to prepare for his journey; while the Leech, having bidden him farewell, vanished through an opposite door, and betook himself to the private boudoir of the fair mistress of Marston, muttering as he went a quotation from a then newly-published play,—

> "Not poppy, nor mandragora,
> Nor all the drowsy syrups of the world,
> Shall ever medicine thee to that sweet sleep
> Which thou ownedst yesterday."

*   *   *   *   *   *   *

Of what passed at this interview between the Folkestone doctor and the fair Spaniard, Mrs. Botherby declares she could never obtain any satisfactory elucidation. Not that tradition is silent on the subject,—quite the contrary; it is the abundance, not paucity, of the materials she supplies, and the consequent embarrassment of selection, that makes the difficulty. Some have averred that the Leech, whose character, as has been before hinted, was more than threadbare, employed his time in teaching her the mode of administering certain noxious compounds, the unconscious partaker whereof would pine and die so slowly and gradually as to defy suspicion. Others there were who affirmed that Lucifer himself was then and there raised *in propriâ personâ*, with all his terrible attributes of horn and hoof. In support of this assertion, they adduce the testimony of the aforesaid buxom housemaid, who protested that the Hall smelt that evening like a manufactory of matches. All, however, seemed to agree that the confabulation, whether human or infernal, was conducted with profound secrecy, and protracted to a considerable length; that its object, as far as could be divined, meant anything but good to the head of the family; that the lady, moreover, was heartily tired of her husband; and that, in the event of his removal by disease or casualty, Master Erasmus Buckthorne, albeit a great philosophist, would have no violent objection to "throw physic to the dogs," and exchange his laboratory for the estate of Marston, its live stock included. Some, too, have inferred that to him did Madame Isabel seriously incline; while others have thought, induced perhaps by subsequent events, that she was merely using him for her purposes; that one José, a tall, bright-eyed, hook-nosed stripling from her native land, was a personage not unlikely to put a spoke in the doctor's wheel; and that, should such a chance arise, the Sage, wise as he was, would, after all, run no slight risk of being "bamboozled."

Master José was a youth well-favored and comely to look upon. His office was that of page to the dame; an office which, after long remaining in abeyance, has been of late years revived, as may well be seen in the persons of sundry smart hobbledehoys, now constantly to be met with on staircases and in boudoirs, clad, for the most part, in garments fitted tightly to the shape, the lower moiety adorned with a broad stripe of crimson or silver lace, and the upper with what the first Wit of our times has described as "a favorable eruption of buttons." The precise duties of this employment have never, as far as we have heard, been accurately defined. The perfuming a handkerchief, the combing a lap-dog, and the occasional presentation of a sippet-shaped *billet doux*, are, and always have been, among them; but these a young gentleman standing five foot ten, and aged nineteen "last grass," might well be supposed to have outgrown. José, however, kept his place, perhaps because he was

not fit for any other. To the conference between his mistress
and the physician he had not been admitted; his post was to
keep watch and ward in the ante-room; and, when the interview was concluded, he attended the lady and her visitor as far
as the courtyard, where he held, with all due respect, the stirrup
for the latter, as he once more resumed his position on the back
of Punch.

Who is it that says, "little pitchers have large ears"? Some
deep metaphysician of the potteries, who might have added that
they have also quick eyes, and sometimes silent tongues. There
was a little metaphorical piece of crockery of this class, who,
screened by a huge elbow-chair, had sat a quiet and unobserved
spectator of the whole proceedings between her mamma and
Master Erasmus Buckthorne. This was Miss Marian Marsh,
a rosy-cheeked, laughter-loving imp of some six years old, but
one who could be mute as a mouse when the fit was on her. A
handsome and highly-polished cabinet, of the darkest ebony,
occupied a recess at one end of the apartment; this had long
been a great subject of speculation to little Miss. Her curiosity,
however, had always been repelled; nor had all her coaxing
even won her an inspection of the thousand and one pretty
things which its recesses no doubt contained. On this occasion
it was unlocked, and Marian was about to rush forward in eager
anticipation of a peep at its interior, when, child as she was,
the reflection struck her that she would stand a better chance
of carrying her point by remaining *perdue*. Fortune for once
favored her: she crouched closer than before, and saw her
mother take something from one of the drawers, which she
handed over to the Leech. Strange mutterings followed, and
words whose sound was foreign to her youthful ears. Had she
been older, their import, perhaps, might have been equally unknown. After a while there was a pause; and then the lady,
as in answer to a requisition from the gentleman, placed in his
hand a something which she took from her toilet. The transaction, whatever its nature, seemed now to be complete, and the
article was carefully replaced in the drawer from which it had
been taken. A long and apparently interesting conversation
then took place between the parties, carried on in a low tone.
At its termination, Mistress Marsh and Master Erasmus Buck-

thorne quitted the boudoir together. But the cabinet!—ay, that was left unfastened; the folding doors still remained invitingly expanded, the bunch of keys dangling from the lock. In an instant the spoiled child was in a chair; the drawer so recently closed yielded at once to her hand, and her hurried researches were rewarded by the prettiest little waxen doll imaginable. It was a first-rate prize, and Miss lost no time in appropriating it to herself. Long before Madame Marsh had returned to her *Sanctum* Marian was seated under a laurustinus in the garden, nursing her new baby with the most affectionate solicitude.

*   *   *   *   *   *   *   *

"Susan, look here; see what a nasty scratch I have got upon my hand," said the young lady, when routed at length from her hiding-place to her noontide meal.

"Yes, Miss, this is always the way with you! mend, mend, mend,—nothing but mend! Scrambling about among the bushes, and tearing your clothes to rags. What with you, and with madam's farthingales and kirtles, a poor bower-maiden has a fine time of it!"

"But I have not torn my clothes, Susan, and it was not the bushes; it was the doll: only see what a great ugly pin I have pulled out of it! and look, here is another!" As she spoke, Marian drew forth one of those extended pieces of black pointed wire with which, in the days of toupees and pompoons, our foremothers were wont to secure their fly caps and head-gear from the impertinent assaults of "Zephyrus and the Little Breezes."

"And pray, Miss, where did you get this pretty doll, as you call it?" asked Susan, turning over the puppet, and viewing it with a scrutinizing eye.

"Mamma gave it me," said the child.—This was a fib.

"Indeed!" quoth the girl thoughtfully; and then, in a half soliloquy, and a lower key, "Well! I wish I may die if it doesn't look like master! But come to your dinner, Miss! Hark! the *bell is striking One!*"

Meanwhile Master Thomas Marsh and his man Ralph were threading the devious paths, then, as now, most pseudonymously dignified with the name of roads, that wound between Marston Hall and the frontier of Romney Marsh. Their progress was

comparatively slow; for though the brown mare was as good a
roadster as man might back, and the gelding no mean nag of
his hands, yet the tracts, rarely traversed save by the rude
wains of the day, miry in the "bottoms," and covered with
loose and rolling stones on the higher grounds, rendered barely
passable the perpetual alternation of hill and valley.

The master rode on in pain, and the man in listlessness;
although the intercourse between two individuals so situated
was much less restrained in those days than might suit the refinement of a later age, little passed approximating to conversation beyond an occasional and half-stifled groan from the
one, or a vacant whistle from the other. An hour's riding had
brought them among the woods of Acryse; and they were
about to descend one of those green and leafy lanes, rendered
by matted and overarching branches alike impervious to shower
or sunbeam, when a sudden and violent spasm seized on Master
Marsh, and nearly caused him to fall from his horse. With
some difficulty he succeeded in dismounting and seating himself by the roadside. Here he remained for a full half-hour
in great apparent agony; the cold sweat rolled in large round
drops adown his clammy forehead, a universal shivering palsied
every limb, his eyeballs appeared to be starting from their
sockets, and to his attached though dull and heavy serving-
man he seemed as one struggling in the pangs of impending
dissolution. His groans rose thick and frequent; and the
alarmed Ralph was hesitating between his disinclination to
leave him and his desire to procure such assistance as one of
the few cottages, rarely sprinkled in that wild country, might
afford, when, after a long-drawn sigh, his master's features as
suddenly relaxed; he declared himself better, the pang had
passed away, and, to use his own expression, he "felt as if a
knife had been drawn from out his very heart." With Ralph's
assistance, after a while he again reached his saddle; and
though still ill at ease, from a deep-seated and gnawing pain,
which ceased not, as he averred, to torment him, the violence
of the paroxysm was spent, and it returned no more.

Master and man pursued their way with increased speed as,
emerging from the wooded defiles, they at length neared the
coast; then, leaving the romantic castle of Saltwood, with its

neighboring town of Hithe, a little on their left, they proceeded along the ancient paved causeway, and, crossing the old Roman road, or Watling, plunged again into the woods that stretched between Lympne and Ostenhanger.

The sun rode high in the heavens, and its meridian blaze was powerfully felt by man and horse, when, again quitting their leafy covert, the travellers debouched on the open plain of Aldington Frith, a wide tract of unenclosed country stretching down to the very borders of "the Marsh" itself.

Here it was, in the neighboring chapelry, the site of which may yet be traced by the curious antiquary, that Elizabeth Barton, the "Holy Maid of Kent," had, something less than a hundred years previous to the period of our narrative, commenced that series of supernatural pranks which eventually procured for her head an unenvied elevation upon London Bridge; and though the parish had since enjoyed the benefit of the incumbency of Master Erasmus's illustrious and enlightened Namesake, still, truth to tell, some of the old leaven was even yet supposed to be at work. The place had, in fact, an ill name; and, though Popish miracles had ceased to electrify its denizens, spells and charms, operating by a no less wondrous agency, were said to have taken their place. Warlocks and other unholy subjects of Satan were reported to make its wild recesses their favorite rendezvous, and that to an extent which eventually attracted the notice of no less a person than the sagacious Matthew Hopkins himself, Witchfinder-General to the British Government.

A great portion of the Frith, or Fright, as the name was then, and is still, pronounced, had formerly been a Chase, with rights of Free-warren, etc., appertaining to the Archbishops of the Province. Since the Reformation, however, it had been disparked; and when Master Thomas Marsh and his man Ralph entered upon its confines, the open greensward exhibited a lively scene, sufficiently explanatory of certain sounds that had already reached their ears while yet within the sylvan screen that concealed their origin.

It was Fair-day; booths, stalls, and all the rude *paraphernalia* of an assembly that then met as much for the purposes of traffic as festivity, were scattered irregularly over the turf;

peddlers with their packs, horse-croupers, pig-merchants, itin-
erant vendors of crockery and cutlery, wandered promiscuously
among the mingled groups, exposing their several wares and
commodities, and soliciting custom. On one side was the gaudy
ribbon, making its mute appeal to rustic gallantry; on the
other the delicious brandy-ball and alluring lollipop, com-
pounded after the most approved receipt in the "True Gentle-
woman's Garland," and "raising the waters" in the mouth of
many an expectant urchin.

Nor were rural sports wanting to those whom pleasure, rather
than business, had drawn from their humble homes. Here was
the tall and slippery pole, glittering in its grease, and crowned
with the ample cheese that mocked the hopes of the discomfited
climber. There the fugitive pippin, swimming in water not of
the purest, and bobbing from the expanded lips of the juvenile
Tantalus. In this quarter the ear was pierced by squeaks from
some beleaguered porker, whisking his well-soaped tail from the
grasp of one already in fancy his captor. In that the eye rested, with undisguised delight, upon the grimaces of grinning
candidates for the honors of the horse-collar. All was fun,
frolic, courtship, junketing, and jollity.

Maid Marian, indeed, with her lieges, Robin Hood, Scarlet,
and Little John, was wanting; Friar Tuck was absent; even
the Hobby-horse had disappeared: but the agile Morris-dancers
yet were there, and jingled their bells merrily among stalls well
stored with gingerbread, tops, whips, whistles, and all those
noisy instruments of domestic torture in which scenes like these
are even now so fertile. Had I a foe whom I held at deadliest
feud, I would entice his favorite child to a Fair, and buy him
a Whistle and a Penny-trumpet.

In one corner of the green, a little apart from the thickest of
the throng, stood a small square stage, nearly level with the
chins of the spectators, whose repeated bursts of laughter seemed
to intimate the presence of something more than usually amusing. The platform was divided into two unequal portions; the
smaller of which, surrounded by curtains of a coarse canvas,
veiled from the eyes of the profane the *penetralia* of this
movable temple of Esculapius, for such it was. Within its
interior, and secure from vulgar curiosity, the Quack-salver

had hitherto kept himself ensconced; occupied, no doubt, in
the preparation and arrangement of that wonderful *panacea*
which was hereafter to shed the blessings of health among the
admiring crowd.   Meanwhile his attendant Jack-pudding was
busily employed on the *proscenium*, doing his best to attract
attention by a practical facetiousness which took wonderfully
with the spectators, interspersing it with the melodious notes of
a huge cow's horn.   The fellow's costume varied but little in
character from that in which the late (alas! that we should
have to write the word—late!) Mr. Joseph Grimaldi was accustomed to present himself before "a generous and enlightened
public;" the principal difference consisted in this, that the upper
garment was a long white tunic, of a coarse linen, surmounted
by a caricature of the ruff then fast falling into disuse, and was
secured from the throat downwards by a single row of broad
white metal buttons; and his legs were cased in loose wide
trousers of the same material; while his sleeves, prolonged to a
most disproportionate extent, descended far below the fingers,
and acted as flappers in the somersets and caracoles with which
he diversified and enlivened his antics.   Consummate impu-
dence, not altogether unmixed with a certain sly humor, sparkled in his eye through the chalk and ochre with which his
features were plentifully bedaubed; and especially displayed
itself in a succession of jokes, the coarseness of which did not
seem to detract from their merit in the eyes of his applauding
audience.

He was in the midst of a long and animated harangue explanatory of his master's high pretensions; he had informed
his gaping auditors that the latter was the seventh son of a
seventh son, and of course, as they very well knew, an Unborn
Doctor; that to this happy accident of birth he added the
advantage of most extensive travel; that in his search after
science he had not only perambulated the whole of this world,
but had trespassed on the boundaries of the next; that the
depths of the Ocean and the bowels of the Earth were alike
familiar to him; that besides salves and cataplasms of sovereign
virtue, by combining sundry mosses, gathered many thousand
fathoms below the surface of the sea, with certain unknown
drugs found in an undiscovered island, and boiling the whole

in the lava of Vesuvius, he had succeeded in producing his celebrated balsam of Crackapanoko, the never-failing remedy for all human disorders, and which, a proper trial allowed, would go near to reanimate the dead. " Draw near!" continued the worthy, "draw near, my masters! and you, my good mistresses, draw near, every one of you. Fear not high and haughty carriage: though greater than King or Kaiser, yet is the mighty Aldrovando milder than mother's milk; flint to the proud, to the humble he is as melting wax; he asks not your disorders, he sees them himself at a glance—nay, without a glance; he tells your ailments with his eyes shut!—Draw near! draw near! the more incurable the better! List to the illustrious Doctor Aldrovando, first physician to Prester John, Leech to the Grand Llama, and Hakim in Ordinary to Mustapha Muley Bey!"

"Hath your master ever a charm for the toothache, an't please you?" asked an elderly countryman, whose swollen cheek bespoke his interest in the question.

" A charm!—a thousand, and every one of them infallible. Toothache, quotha! I had hoped you had come with every bone in your body fractured or out of joint. A toothache!— propound a tester, master o' mine—we ask not more for such trifles: do my bidding, and thy jaws, even with the word, shall cease to trouble thee!"

The clown, fumbling a while in a deep leathern purse, at length produced a sixpence, which he tendered to the jester. " Now to thy master, and bring me the charm forthwith."

" Nay, honest man; to disturb the mighty Aldrovando on such slight occasion were pity of my life: arced my counsel aright, and I will warrant thee for the nonce. Hie thee home, friend; infuse this powder in cold spring-water, fill thy mouth with the mixture, and sit upon the fire till it boils!"

" Out on thee for a pestilent knave!" cried the cozened countryman; but the roar of merriment around bespoke the bystanders well pleased with the jape put upon him. He retired, venting his spleen in audible murmurs; and the mountebank, finding the feelings of the mob enlisted on his side, waxed more impudent every instant, filling up the intervals between his fooleries with sundry capers and contortions and discordant notes from the cow's horn.

"Draw near, draw near, my masters! Here have ye a remedy for every evil under the sun, moral, physical, natural, and supernatural! Hath any man a termagant wife?—here is that will tame her presently! Hath any one a smoky chimney?—here is an incontinent cure!"

To the first infliction no man ventured to plead guilty, though there were those standing by who thought their neighbors might have profited withal. For the last-named recipe started forth at least half a dozen candidates. With the greatest gravity imaginable, Pierrot, having pocketed their groats, delivered to each a small packet curiously folded and closely sealed, containing, as he averred, directions which, if truly observed, would preclude any chimney from smoking for a whole year. They whose curiosity led them to dive into the mystery found that a sprig of mountain ash culled by moonlight was the charm recommended, coupled, however, with the proviso that no fire should be lighted on the hearth during its exercise.

The frequent bursts of merriment proceeding from this quarter at length attracted the attention of Master Marsh, whose line of road necessarily brought him near this end of the fair; he drew bit in front of the stage just as its noisy occupant, having laid aside his formidable horn, was drawing still more largely on the amazement of "the public" by a feat of especial wonder,—he was eating fire! Curiosity mingled with astonishment was at its height; and feelings not unallied to alarm were beginning to manifest themselves, among the softer sex especially, as they gazed on the flames that issued from the mouth of the living volcano. All eyes, indeed, were fixed upon the fire-eater with an intentness that left no room for observing another worthy who had now emerged upon the scene. This was, however, no less a personage than the *Deus ex machinâ*,— the illustrious Aldrovando himself.

Short in stature and spare in form, the sage had somewhat increased the former by a steeple-crowned hat adorned with a cock's feather; while the thick shoulder-padding of a quilted doublet, surmounted by a falling band, added a little to his personal importance in point of breadth. His habit was composed throughout of black serge, relieved with scarlet slashes in the sleeves and trunks; red was the feather in his hat, red were the roses in his shoes, which rejoiced, moreover, in a pair of red heels. The lining of a short cloak of faded velvet, that hung transversely over his left shoulder, was also red. Indeed, from all that we could ever see or hear, this agreeable alternation of red and black appears to be the mixture of colors most approved at the court of Beelzebub, and the one most generally adopted by his friends and favorites. His features were sharp and shrewd, and a fire sparkled in his keen gray eye, much at variance with the wrinkles that ran their irregular furrows above his prominent and bushy brows. He had advanced slowly from behind his screen while the attention of the multitude was absorbed by the pyrotechnics of Mr. Merryman, and stationing himself at the extreme corner of the stage, stood quietly leaning on a crutch-handle walking-staff of blackest ebony, his glance steadily fixed on the face of Marsh, from whose countenance the amusement he had insensibly begun to derive had not succeeded in removing all traces of bodily pain.

For a while the latter was unobservant of the inquisitorial survey with which he was regarded; the eyes of the parties, however, at length met. The brown mare had a fine shoulder; she stood pretty nearly sixteen hands. Marsh himself, though slightly bowed by ill-health and the "coming autumn" of life, was full six feet in height. His elevation giving him an unobstructed view over the heads of the pedestrians, he had naturally fallen into the rear of the assembly, which brought him close to the diminutive Doctor, with whose face, despite the red heels, his own was about upon a level.

"And what makes Master Marsh here? what sees he in the mummeries of a miserable buffoon to divert him when his life is in jeopardy?" said a shrill cracked voice that sounded as in his very ear. It was the Doctor who spoke.

"Knowest thou me, friend?" said Marsh, scanning with awakened interest the figure of his questioner: "I call thee not to mind; and yet—stay, where have we met?"

"It skills not to declare," was the answer; "suffice it we *have* met—in other climes perchance—and now meet happily again— happily at least for thee."

"Why, truly the trick of thy countenance reminds me of

somewhat I have seen before; where or when I know not: but what wouldst thou with me?"

"Nay, rather what wouldst thou here, Thomas Marsh? What wouldst thou on the Frith of Aldington? Is it a score or two of paltry sheep? or is it something *nearer to thy heart?*"

Marsh started as the last words were pronounced with more than common significance: a pang shot through him at the moment, and the vinegar aspect of the charlatan seemed to relax into a smile half compassionate, half sardonic.

"Grammercy," quoth Marsh, after a long-drawn breath, "what knowest thou of me, fellow, or of my concerns? What knowest thou——"

"This know I, Master Thomas Marsh," said the stranger gravely, "that thy life is even now perilled, evil practices are against thee; but no matter, thou art quit for the nonce—other hands than mine have saved thee! Thy pains are over. Hark! *the clock strikes One!*" As he spoke, a single toll from the bell-tower of Bilsington came, wafted by the western breeze, over the thick-set and lofty oaks which intervened between the Frith and what had once been a priory. Doctor Aldrovando turned as the sound came floating on the wind, and was moving, as if half in anger, towards the other side of the stage, where the mountebank, his fires extinct, was now disgorging to the admiring crowd yard after yard of gaudy-colored ribbon.

"Stay! Nay, prithee stay!" cried Marsh, eagerly. "I was wrong; in faith I was. A change, and that a sudden and most marvellous, hath indeed come over me; I am free; I breathe again; I feel as though a load of years had been removed; and, is it possible?—hast thou done this?"

"Thomas Marsh!" said the Doctor, pausing, and turning for the moment on his heel, "I have *not:* I repeat, that other and more innocent hands than mine have done this deed. Nevertheless, heed my counsel well! Thou art parlously encompassed; I, and I only, have the means of relieving thee. Follow thy courses; pursue thy journey; but as thou valuest life and more than life, be at the foot of yonder woody knoll what time the rising moon throws her first beam upon the bare and blighted summit that towers above its trees."

He crossed abruptly to the opposite quarter of the scaffolding,

and was in an instant deeply engaged in listening to those whom
the cow's horn had attracted, and in prescribing for their real
or fancied ailments. Vain were all Marsh's efforts again to
attract his notice; it was evident that he studiously avoided
him; and when, after an hour or more spent in useless endeavor, he saw the object of his anxiety seclude himself once
more within his canvas screen, he rode slowly and thoughtfully
off the field.

What should he do? Was the man a mere quack? an im-
postor? His name thus obtained! that might be easily done.
But then, his secret griefs; the Doctor's knowledge of them;
their cure: for he felt that his pains were gone, his healthful
feelings restored!

True, Aldrovando, if that were his name, had disclaimed
all co-operation in his recovery; but he knew, or he at least announced it. Nay, more; he had hinted that he was yet in jeopardy; that practices—and the chord sounded strangely in
unison with one that had before vibrated within him—that
practices were in operation against his life! It was enough!
He would keep tryst with the Conjurer, if conjurer he were;
and, at least, ascertain who and what he was, and how he had
become acquainted with his own person and secret afflictions.

When the late Mr. Pitt was determined to keep out Buonaparte, and prevent his gaining a settlement in the county of
Kent, among other ingenious devices adopted for that purpose,
he caused to be constructed what was then, and has ever since
been, conventionally termed a "Military Canal." This is a not
very practicable ditch, some thirty feet wide, and nearly nine
feet deep in the middle, extending from the town and port of
Hithe to within a mile of the town and port of Rye, a distance
of about twenty miles; and forming, as it were, the cord of a
bow, the arc of which constitutes that remote fifth quarter of
the globe spoken of by travellers. Trivial objections to the
plan were made at the time by cavillers; and an old gentleman
of the neighborhood, who proposed, as a cheap substitute, to
put down his own cocked hat upon a pole, was deservedly pooh-
poohed down; in fact, the job, though rather an expensive one,
was found to answer remarkably well. The French managed,
indeed, to scramble over the Rhine, and the Rhone, and other

insignificant currents; but they never did, or could, pass Mr.
Pitt's "Military Canal." At no great distance from the centre
of this cord rises abruptly a sort of woody promontory, in shape
almost conical; its sides covered with thick underwood, above
which is seen a bare and brown summit rising like an Alp in
miniature. The "defence of the nation" not being then in existence, Master Marsh met with no obstruction in reaching this
place of appointment long before the time prescribed.

So much, indeed, was his mind occupied by his adventure
and extraordinary cure that his original design had been abandoned, and Master Cobb remained unvisited. A rude hostel
in the neighborhood furnished entertainment for man and
horse; and here, a full hour before the rising of the moon, he
left Ralph and the other beasts, proceeding to his rendezvous
on foot and alone.

"You are punctual, Master Marsh," squeaked the shrill
voice of the Doctor, issuing from the thicket as the first silvery
gleam trembled on the aspens above. "'Tis well; now follow
me, and in silence."

The first part of the command Marsh hesitated not to obey;
the second was more difficult of observance.

"Who and what are you? Whither are you leading me?"
burst not unnaturally from his lips; but all question was at
once cut short by the peremptory tones of his guide.

"Hush! I say; your finger on your lip: there be hawks
abroad. Follow me, and that silently and quickly." The
little man turned as he spoke, and led the way through a
scarcely perceptible path, or track, which wound among the
underwood. The lapse of a few minutes brought them to the
door of a low building, so hidden by the surrounding trees that
few would have suspected its existence. It was a cottage of
rather extraordinary dimensions, but consisting of only one
floor. No smoke rose from its solitary chimney; no cheering
ray streamed from its single window, which was, however,
secured by a shutter of such thickness as to preclude the possibility of any stray beam issuing from within. The exact size
of the building it was, in that uncertain light, difficult to distinguish, a portion of it seeming buried in the wood behind.
The door gave way on the application of a key, and Marsh fol-

lowed his conductor resolutely, but cautiously, along a narrow passage, feebly lighted by a small taper that winked and twinkled at its farther extremity. The Doctor, as he approached, raised it from the ground, and, opening an adjoining door, ushered his guest into the room beyond.

It was a large and oddly furnished apartment, insufficiently lighted by an iron lamp that hung from the roof, and scarcely illumined the walls and angles, which seemed to be composed of some dark-colored wood. On one side, however, Master Marsh could discover an article bearing strong resemblance to a coffin; on the other was a large oval mirror in an ebony frame; and in the midst of the floor was described, in red chalk, a double circle, about six feet in diameter, its inner verge inscribed with sundry hieroglyphics, agreeably relieved at intervals with an alternation of skulls and cross-bones. In the very centre was deposited one skull of such surpassing size and thickness as would have filled the soul of a Spurzheim or De Ville with wonderment. A large book, a naked sword, an hour-glass, a chafing-dish, and a black cat, completed the list of movables,—with the exception of a couple of tapers which stood on each side of the mirror, and which the strange gentleman now proceeded to light from the one in his hand. As they flared up with what Marsh thought a most unnatural brilliancy, he perceived reflected in the glass behind a dial suspended over the coffin-like article already mentioned; the hand was fast verging towards the hour of nine. The eyes of the little Doctor seemed riveted on the horologe.

"Now strip thee, Master Marsh, and that quickly: untruss, I say! discard thy boots, doff doublet and hose, and place thyself incontinent in yonder bath."

The visitor cast his eyes again upon the formidable-looking article, and perceived that it was nearly filled with water. A cold bath, at such an hour and under such auspices, was anything but inviting: he hesitated, and turned his eyes alternately on the Doctor and the Black Cat.

"Trifle not the time, man, an you be wise," said the former. "Passion of my heart! let but you minute-hand reach the hour, and thou not immersed, thy life were not worth a pin's fee!"

The Black Cat gave vent to a single mew,—a most unnatural

8

sound for a mouser: it seemed as it were mewed through a
cow's horn.

"Quick, Master Marsh! uncase, or you perish!" repeated
his strange host, throwing as he spoke a handful of some
dingy-looking powders into the brasier. "Behold, the attack
is begun!" A thick cloud rose from the embers; a cold shivering shook the astonished Yeoman; sharp pricking pains penetrated his ankles and the palms of his hands; and as the
smoke cleared away, he distinctly saw and recognized in the
mirror the boudoir of Marston Hall.

The doors of the well-known ebony cabinet were closed; but
fixed against them, and standing out in strong relief from the
contrast afforded by the sable background, was a waxen image—of himself! It appeared to be secured, and sustained in
an upright posture, by large black pins driven through the feet
and palms, the latter of which were extended in a cruciform
position. To the right and left stood his wife and José; in the
middle, with his back towards him, was a figure which he had
no difficulty in recognizing as that of the Leech of Folkestone.
The latter had just succeeded in fastening the dexter hand of
the image, and was now in the act of drawing a broad and
keen-edged sabre from its sheath. The Black Cat mewed
again. "Haste, or you die!" said the Doctor. Marsh looked
at the dial; it wanted but four minutes of nine: he felt that
the crisis of his fate was come. Off went his heavy boots;
doublet to the right, galligaskins to the left; never was man
more swiftly disrobed. In two minutes, to use an Indian expression, he was "all face;" in another he was on his back and
up to his chin in a bath which smelt strongly as of brimstone
and garlic.

"Heed well the clock!" cried the Conjurer. "With the first
stroke of Nine plunge thy head beneath the water,—suffer not
a hair above the surface: plunge deeply, or thou art lost!"

The little man had seated himself in the centre of the circle
upon the large skull, elevating his legs at an angle of forty-five
degrees. In this position he spun round with a velocity to be
equalled only by that of a teetotum, the red roses on his insteps
seeming to describe a circle of fire. The best buckskins that
ever mounted at Melton had soon yielded to such rotatory fric-

tion; but he spun on; the cat mewed, bats and obscene birds
fluttered overhead; Erasmus was seen to raise his weapon; the
clock struck!—and Marsh, who had "ducked" at the instant,
popped up his head again, spitting and sputtering, half choked
with the infernal solution, which had insinuated itself into his
mouth and ears and nose. All disgust at his nauseous dip was,
however, at once removed when, casting his eyes on the glass,
he saw the consternation of the party whose persons it exhibited. Erasmus had evidently made his blow and failed; the
figure was unmutilated; the hilt remained in the hand of the
striker, while the shivered blade lay in shining fragments on
the floor.

The Conjurer ceased his spinning and brought himself to an
anchor; the Black Cat purred: its purring seemed strangely
mixed with the self-satisfied chuckle of a human being. Where
had Marsh heard something like it before?

He was rising from his unsavory couch when a motion from
the little man checked him. "Rest where you are, Thomas
Marsh: so far all goes well, but the danger is not yet over."
He looked again, and perceived that the shadowy triumvirate
were in deep and eager consultation; the fragments of the
shattered weapon appeared to undergo a close scrutiny. The
result was clearly unsatisfactory; the lips of the parties moved
rapidly, and much gesticulation might be observed, but no
sound fell upon the ear. The hand of the dial had nearly
reached the quarter: at once the parties separated; and Buckthorne stood again before the figure, his hand armed with a
long and sharp-pointed *misericorde*, a dagger little in use of
late, but such as, a century before, often performed the part of
a modern oyster-knife in tickling the osteology of a dismounted
cavalier through the shelly defences of his plate armor. Again
he raised his arm. "Duck!" roared the Doctor, spinning away
upon his cephalic pivot:—the Black Cat cocked his tail, and
seemed to mew the word "Duck!" Down went Master Marsh's
head; one of his hands had unluckily been resting on the edge
of the bath; he drew it hastily in, but not altogether scathe-
less: the stump of a rusty nail, projecting from the margin of
the bath, had caught and slightly grazed it. The pain was
more acute than is usually produced by such trivial accidents;

and Marsh, on once more raising his head, beheld the dagger of the Leech sticking in the little finger of the wax figure, which it had seemingly nailed to the cabinet door.

"By my truly, a scape of the narrowest!" quoth the Conjurer. "The next course, dive you not the readier, there is no more life in you than in a pickled herring. What! courage, Master Marsh; but be heedful: an they miss again, let them bide the issue!"

He drew his hand athwart his brow as he spoke, and dashed off the perspiration which the violence of his exercise had drawn from every pore. Black Tom sprang upon the edge of the bath and stared full in the face of the bather. His sea-green eyes were lambent with unholy fire, but their marvellous obliquity of vision was not to be mistaken;—the very countenance too! Could it be?—the features were feline, but their expression was that of the Jack-pudding! Was the mountebank a cat? or the cat a mountebank? It was all a mystery!—and Heaven knows how long Marsh might have continued staring at Grimalkin had not his attention been again called by Aldrovando to the magic mirror.

Great dissatisfaction, not to say dismay, seemed now to pervade the conspirators. Dame Isabel was closely inspecting the figure's wounded hand, while José was aiding the pharmacopolist to charge a huge petronel with powder and bullets. The load was a heavy one; but Erasmus seemed determined this time to make sure of his object. Somewhat of trepidation might be observed in his manner as he rammed down the balls, and his withered cheek appeared to have acquired an increase of paleness; but amazement rather than fear was the prevailing symptom, and his countenance betrayed no jot of irresolution. As the clock was about to chime half-past nine, he planted himself with a firm foot in front of the image, waved his unoccupied hand with a cautionary gesture to his companions, and, as they hastily retired on either side, brought the muzzle of his weapon within half a foot of his mark. As the shadowy form was about to draw the trigger, Marsh again plunged his head beneath the surface; and the sound of an explosion, as of fire-arms, mingled with the rush of water that poured into his ears. His immersion was but momentary, yet did he feel as though half suffocated: he sprang from the bath, and, as his eye fell on the mirror, he saw,—or thought he saw,—the Leech of Folkestone lying dead on the floor of his wife's boudoir, his head shattered to pieces, and his hand still grasping the stock of a bursten petronel.

He saw no more; his head swam, his senses reeled, the whole room was turning round, and, as he fell to the ground, the last impressions to which he was conscious were the chucklings of a hoarse laughter, and the mewings of a tom cat!

Master Marsh was found the next morning by his bewildered serving-man, stretched before the door of the humble hostel at which he sojourned. His clothes were somewhat torn and much bemired; and deeply did honest Ralph marvel that one so staid and grave as Master Marsh of Marston should thus have played the roisterer, missing, perchance, a profitable bargain for the drunken orgies of midnight wassail, or the endearments of some rustic light-o'-love. Tenfold was his astonishment increased when, after retracing in silence their journey of the preceding day, the Hall, on their arrival about noon, was found in a state of the uttermost confusion. No wife stood there to greet with the smile of bland affection her returning spouse; no page to hold his stirrup, or receive his gloves, his hat, and riding-rod. The doors were open, the rooms in most admired disorder; men and maidens peeping, hurrying hither and thither, and popping in and out, like rabbits in a warren. The lady of the mansion was nowhere to be found.

José, too, had disappeared; the latter had been last seen riding furiously towards Folkestone early in the preceding afternoon: to a question from Hodge Gardener he had hastily answered that he bore a missive of moment from his mistress. The lean apprentice of Erasmus Buckthorne declared that the page had summoned his master, in haste, about six of the clock, and that they had rode forth together, as he verily believed, on their way back to the Hall, where he had supposed Master Buckthorne's services to be suddenly required on some pressing emergency. Since that time he had seen nought of either of them; the gray cob, however, had returned late at night, masterless, with his girths loose and the saddle turned upside down.

Nor was Master Erasmus Buckthorne ever seen again. Strict

search was made through the neighborhood, but without success; and it was at length presumed that he must, for reasons which nobody could divine, have absconded, together with José and his faithless mistress. The latter had carried off with her the strong box, divers articles of valuable plate, and jewels of price. Her boudoir appeared to have been completely ransacked; the cabinet and drawers stood open and empty; the very carpet, a luxury then newly introduced into England, was gone. Marsh, however, could trace no vestige of the visionary scene which he affirmed to have been last night presented to his eyes.

Much did the neighbors marvel at his story :—some thought him mad; others that he was merely indulging in that privilege to which, as a traveller, he had a right indefeasible. Trusty Ralph said nothing, but shrugged his shoulders; and, falling into the rear, imitated the action of raising a wine-cup to his lips. An opinion, indeed, soon prevailed that Master Thomas Marsh had gotten, in common parlance, exceedingly drunk on the preceding evening, and had dreamt all that he so circumstantially related. This belief acquired additional credit when they whom curiosity induced to visit the woody knoll of Aldington Mount declared that they could find no building such as that described, nor any cottage near; save one, indeed, a low-roofed hovel, once a house of public entertainment, but now half in ruins. The "Old Cat and Fiddle"—so was the tenement called—had been long uninhabited; yet still exhibited the remains of a broken sign, on which the keen observer might decipher something like a rude portrait of the animal from which it derived its name. It was also supposed still to afford an occasional asylum to the smugglers of the coast, but no trace of any visit from sage or mountebank could be detected; nor was the wise Aldrovando, whom many remembered to have seen at the fair, ever found again on all that country-side.

Of the runaways nothing was ever certainly known. A boat, the property of an old fisherman who plied his trade on the outskirts of the town, had been seen to quit the bay that night; and there were those who declared that she had more hands on board than Carden and his son, her usual complement; but as the gale came on, and the frail bark was

eventually found keel upwards on the Goodwin Sands, it was
presumed that she had struck on that fatal quicksand in the
dark, and that all on board had perished.

Little Marian, whom her profligate mother had abandoned,
grew up to be a fine girl, and a handsome. She became, moreover, heiress to Marston Hall, and brought the estate into the
Ingoldsby family by her marriage with one of its scions.

Thus far Mrs. Botherby.

It is a little singular that, on pulling down the old Hall in
my grandfather's time, a human skeleton was discovered among
the rubbish ; under what particular part of the building I

could never with any accuracy ascertain ; but it was found
enveloped in a tattered cloth that seemed to have been once
a carpet, and which fell to pieces almost immediately on being
exposed to the air. The bones were perfect, but those of one
hand were wanting ; and the skull, perhaps from the laborer's
pickaxe, had received considerable injury ; the worm-eaten
stock of an old-fashioned pistol lay near, together with a rusty
piece of iron which a workman, more sagacious than his fellows,

pronounced a portion of the lock; but nothing was found which the utmost stretch of human ingenuity could twist into a barrel.

The portrait of the fair Marian hangs yet in the Gallery of Tappington; and near it is another, of a young man in the prime of life, which Mrs. Botherby affirms to be that of her father. It exhibits a mild and rather melancholy countenance, with a high forehead, and the peaked beard and moustaches of the seventeenth century. The signet-finger of the left hand is gone, and appears, on close inspection, to have been painted out by some later artist; possibly in compliment to the tradition, which, *teste Botherby,* records that of Mr. Marsh to have gangrened, and to have undergone amputation at the knuckle-joint. If really the resemblance of the gentleman alluded to, it must have been taken at some period antecedent to his marriage. There is neither date nor painter's name; but a little above the head, on the dexter side of the picture, is an escutcheon, bearing "Quarterly, Gules and Argent, in the first quarter a horse's head of the second;" beneath it are the words "*Ætatis suæ* 26." On the opposite side is the following mark, which Mr. Simpkinson declares to be that of a Merchant of the Staple, and pretends to discover, in the monogram comprised in it, all the characters which compose the name of THOMAS MARSH, of MARSTON.

RESPECT for the feelings of an honorable family,—nearly connected with the Ingoldsbys,—has induced me to veil the *real* "sponsorial and patronymic appellations" of my next hero under a *sobriquet* interfering neither with rhyme nor rhythm.[*] I shall merely add that every incident in the story bears on the face of it the stamp of veracity, and that many "persons of honor" in the county of Berks, who well recollected Sir George Rooks's expedition against Gibraltar, would, if they were now alive, gladly bear testimony to the truth of every syllable.

[*] Pack o' nonsense!—Everybody as belongs to him is dead and gone—and everybody knows that the poor young gentleman's real name wasn't *Sobriquet* at all, but Hampden Pye, Esq., and that one of his uncles—or cousins—used to make verses about the

Legend of Hamilton Tighe.

THE Captain is walking his quarter-deck,
  With a troubled brow and a bended neck;
One eye is down through the hatchway cast,
The other turns up to the truck on the mast;
Yet none of the crew may venture to hint
"Our Skipper hath gotten a sinister squint!"

The Captain again the letter hath read
Which the bumboat woman brought out to Spithead—
Still, since the good ship sailed away,
He reads that letter three times a day;
Yet the writing is broad and fair to see
As a Skipper may read, in his degree,
And the seal is as black, and as broad, and as flat,
As his own cockade in his own cocked hat:
He reads, and he says, as he walks to and fro,
"Curse the old woman—she bothers me so!"

He pauses now, for the topmen hail—
"On the larboard quarter a sail! a sail!"
That grim Old Captain he turns him quick,
And bawls through his trumpet for Hairy-faced Dick.

"The breeze is blowing—huzza! huzza!
The breeze is blowing—away! away!
The breeze is blowing—a race! a race!
The breeze is blowing—we near the chase!
Blood will flow, and bullets will fly,—
Oh where will be then young Hamilton Tighe?"

—"On the foeman's deck, where a man should be,
With his sword in his hand, and his foe at his knee.
Cockswain, or boatswain, or reefer may try,
But the first man on board will be Hamilton Tighe!"

king and the queen, and had a sack of money for doing it every year;—and that's his picture in the blue coat and little gold-laced cocked hat that hangs on the stairs over the door of the passage that leads to the blue room.—*Sobriquet!*—but there!—The Squire wrote it after dinner!—ELIZABETH BOTHERBY.

Hairy-faced Dick hath a swarthy hue,
Between a gingerbread-nut and a Jew,
And his pigtail is long, and bushy, and thick,
Like a pump-handle stuck on the end of a stick.
Hairy-faced Dick understands his trade ;
He stands by the breech of a long carronade,
The linstock glows in his bony hand,
Waiting that grim old Skipper's command.

" The bullets are flying—huzza ! huzza !
The bullets are flying—away ! away !"
The brawny boarders mount by the chains,
And are over their buckles in blood and in brains :
On the foeman's deck, where a man should be,
     Young Hamilton Tighe   Waves his cutlass high,
And *Capitaine Crapaud* bends low at his knee.

Hairy-faced Dick, linstock in hand,
Is waiting that grim-looking Skipper's command :—
     A wink comes sly   From that sinister eye—
Hairy-faced Dick at once lets fly,
And knocks off the head of Young Hamilton Tighe !

There's a lady sits lonely in bower and hall,
Her pages and handmaidens come at her call :
" Now, haste ye, my handmaidens, haste and see
How he sits there and glow'rs with his head on his knee !"
The maidens smile, and, her thought to destroy,
They bring her a little, pale, mealy-faced boy ;
And the mealy-faced boy says, " Mother, dear,
Now Hamilton's dead, I've a thousand a year !"

The lady has donned her mantle and hood,
She is bound for shrift at Saint Mary's Rood :—
" Oh ! the taper shall burn, and the bell shall toll,
And the mass shall be said for my stepson's soul,
And the tablet fair shall be hung on high,
Orate pro animâ Hamilton Tighe."

Her coach and four   Draws up to the door,
With her groom and her footman, and half a score more;
The lady steps into her coach alone,
They hear her sigh, and they hear her groan,
They close the door, and they turn the pin,
But there's One rides with her that never stept in!
All the way there, and all the way back,
The harness strains and the coach-springs crack,
The horses snort and plunge and kick,
Till the coachman thinks he is driving Old Nick;
And the grooms and the footmen wonder, and say
" What makes the old coach so heavy to-day?"
But the mealy-faced boy peeps in and sees
A man sitting there with his head on his knees!

'Tis ever the same,—in hall or in bower,
Wherever the place, whatever the hour,
That Lady mutters, and talks to the air,
And her eye is fixed on an empty chair;
But the mealy-faced boy still whispers with dread,
"She talks to a man with never a head!"

———

There's an old Yellow Admiral living at Bath,
As gray as a badger, as thin as a lath;
And his very queer eyes have such very queer leers,
They seem to be trying to peep at his ears;
That old Yellow Admiral goes to the Rooms,
And he plays long whist, but he frets and he fumes,
For all his Knaves stand upside down,
And the Jack of Clubs does nothing but frown;
And the Kings, and the Aces, and all the best trumps
Get into the hands of the other old frumps;
While, close to his partner, a man he sees
Counting the tricks with his head on his knees.

In Ratcliffe Highway there's an old marine store,
And a great black doll hangs out of the door;

There arc rusty locks, and dusty bags,
And musty phials, and fusty rags,
And a lusty old woman, called Thirsty Nan,
And her crusty old husband's a Hairy-faced man!

That Hairy-faced man is sallow and wan,
And his great thick pigtail is withered and gone;
And he cries, "Take away that lubberly chap
That sits there and grins with his head in his lap!"
And the neighbors say, as they see him look sick,
"What a rum old covey is Hairy-faced Dick!"

That Admiral, Lady, and Hairy-faced man
May say what they please, and may do what they can;
But one thing seems remarkably clear,—
They may die to-morrow, or live till next year,—
But wherever they live, or whenever they die,
They'll never get quit of young Hamilton Tighe!

———————

THE When,—the Where,—and the How,—of the succeeding
narrative speak for themselves. It may be proper, however, to
observe that the ruins here alluded to, and improperly termed
"the Abbey," are not those of Bolsover, described in a preceding page, but the remains of a Preceptory once belonging
to the Knights Templars, situate near Swynfield, Swinkefield,
or, as it is now generally spelt and pronounced, Swingfield,
Minnis, a rough tract of common land now undergoing the
process of enclosure, and adjoining the woods and arable lands
of Tappington, at the distance of some two miles from the
Hall, to the southeastern windows of which the time-worn
walls in question, as seen over the intervening coppices, present a picturesque and striking object.

The Witches' Frolic.

[Scene, the "Snuggery" at Tappington.—Grandpapa in a high-backed cane-bottomed elbow-chair of carved walnut-tree, dozing; his nose at an angle of forty-five degrees,—his thumbs slowly perform the rotatory motion described by lexicographers as "twiddling."—The "Hope of the family" astride on a walking-stick, with burnt-cork moustaches, and a pheasant's tail pinned in his cap, solaceth himself with martial music.—Roused by a strain of surpassing dissonance, Grandpapa *loquitur.*]

COME hither, come hither, my little boy Ned!
  Come hither unto my knee—
I cannot away with that horrible din,
That sixpenny drum, and that trumpet of tin.
Oh, better to wander frank and free
Through the Fair of good St. Bartlemy,
Than list to such awful minstrelsie.
Now lay, little Ned, those nuisances by,
And I'll rede ye a lay of Grammarye.

[Grandpapa riseth, yawneth like the crater of an extinct volcano, proceedeth slowly to the window, and apostrophizeth the Abbey in the distance.]

I love thy tower, Gray Ruin,
  I joy thy form to see,
   Though reft of all, Cell, cloister, and hall,
Nothing is left save a tottering wall
That, awfully grand and darkly dull,
Threatened to fall and demolish my skull,
As, ages ago, I wandered along
Careless thy grass-grown courts among,
In sky-blue jacket, and trousers laced,
The latter uncommonly short in the waist.
Thou art dearer to me, thou Ruin gray,
Than the Squire's veranda over the way;
   And fairer, I ween, The ivy-sheen
  That thy mouldering turret binds,
Than the Alderman's house about half a mile off,
  With the green Venetian blinds.
Full many a tale would my Grandam tell,
  In many a bygone day,

Of darksome deeds, which of old befell
   In thee, thou Ruin gray!
And I the readiest ear would lend,
   And stare like frightened pig!
While my Grandfather's hair would have stood up on end,
   Had he not worn a wig.

One tale I remember of mickle dread—
Now lithe and listen, my little boy Ned!

———

Thou mayest have read, my little boy Ned,
   Though thy mother thine idlesse blames,
In Doctor Goldsmith's history book,
   Of a gentleman called King James,
In quilted doublet, and great trunk breeches,
Who held in abhorrence Tobacco and Witches.

Well,—in King James's golden days,—
   For the days were golden then,—
They could not be less, for good Queen Bess
   Had died, aged threescore and ten,
     And her days, we know,   Were all of them so;
While the Court poets sung, and the Court gallants swore
That the days were as golden still as before.

Some people, 'tis true, a troublesome few,
   Who historical points would unsettle,
Have lately thrown out a sort of a doubt
   Of the genuine ring of the metal;
But who can believe to a monarch so wise
People would dare tell a parcel of lies!

—Well, then, in good King James's days,—
Golden or not does not matter a jot,—
You Ruin a sort of a roof had got;
For though, repairs lacking, its walls had been cracking
Since Harry the Eighth sent its people a-packing,

Though joists, and floors,   And windows, and doors,
Had all disappeared, yet pillars by scores
Remained, and still propped up a ceiling or two,
While the belfry was almost as good as new;
You are not to suppose matters looked just so
In the Ruin some two hundred years ago.

Just in the furthermost angle, where
There are still the remains of a winding stair,
One turret especially high in air
    Upreared its tall gaunt form;
As if defying the power of Fate, or
The hand of " Time the Innovator;"
    And though to the pitiless storm
Its weaker brethren all around
Bowing, in ruin had strewed the ground,
Alone it stood, while its fellows lay strewed,
Like a four-bottle man in a company "screwed,"—
Not firm on his legs, but by no means subdued.

One night,—'twas in Sixteen hundred and six,—
I like when I can, Ned, the date to fix,—
    The month was May,   Though I can't well say
At this distance of time the particular day—
But oh! that night, that horrible night!
—Folks ever afterwards said with affright
That they never had seen such a terrible sight.

The Sun had gone down fiery red;
And if, that evening, he laid his head
In Thetis's lap beneath the seas,
He must have scalded the goddess's knees.
He left behind him a lurid track
Of blood-red light upon clouds so black,
That Warren and Hunt, with the whole of their crew,
Could scarcely have given them a darker hue.

There came a shrill and a whistling sound,
Above, beneath, beside, and around,

Yet leaf ne'er moved on tree!
So that some people thought old Beelzebub must
Have been locked out of doors, and was blowing the dust
From the pipe of his street-door key.
And then a hollow moaning blast
Came, sounding more dismally still than the last,
And the lightning flashed, and the thunder growled,
And louder and louder the tempest howled,
And the rain came down in such sheets as would stagger a
Bard for a simile short of Niagara.

Rob Gilpin " was a citizen ;"
  But though of some " renown,"
Of no great " credit" in his own
  Or any other town.

He was a wild and roving lad,
  For ever in the alehouse boozing ;
Or romping,—which is quite as bad,—
  With female friends of his own choosing.

And Rob this very day had made,
  Not dreaming such a storm was brewing,
An assignation with Miss Slade,—
  Their trysting-place that same gray Ruin.

But Gertrude Slade became afraid,
  And to keep her appointment unwilling,
When she spied the rain on her window-pane
  In drops as big as a shilling ;
She put off her hat and her mantle again :
" He'll never expect me in all this rain !"

But little he recks of the fears of the sex,
  Or that maiden false to her tryst could be.
He had stood there a good half hour,
Ere yet had commenced that perilous shower,
  Alone by the trysting-tree !

Robin looks east, Robin looks west,
But he sees not her whom he loves the best;
Robin looks up, and Robin looks down,
But no one comes from the neighboring town.

The storm came at last;—loud roared the blast,
And the shades of evening fell thick and fast;
The tempest grew; and the straggling yew,
His leafy umbrella, was wet through and through.
Rob was half dead with cold and with fright,
When he spies in the Ruins a twinkling light—
A hop, two skips, and a jump, and straight
Rob stands within that postern gate.

And there were gossips sitting there,
  By one, by two, by three:

  Two were an old ill-favored pair:
But the third was young and passing fair,
With laughing eyes and with coal-black hair;
  A dainty quean was she!
Rob would have given his ears to sip
But a single salute from her cherry lip.

As they sat in that old and haunted room,
In each one's hand was a huge birch broom,
On each one's head was a steeple-crowned hat,
On each one's knee was a coal-black cat;
Each had a kirtle of Lincoln green—
It was, I trow, a fearsome scene.

"Now riddle me, riddle me right, Madge Gray,
What foot unhallowed wends this way?
Goody Price, Goody Price, now areed me right,
Who roams the old Ruins this drearisome night?"

Then up and spake that sonsie quean,
  And she spake both loud and clear:
"Oh, be it for weal, or be it for woe,
Enter friend, or enter foe,
  Rob Gilpin is welcome here!"—

9

"Now tread we a measure! a hall! a hall!
Now tread we a measure," quoth she—
　　　The heart of Robin　Beat quick and throbbing—
　"Roving Rob, tread a measure with me!"
"Ay, lassie!" quoth Rob, as her hand he gripes,
"Though Satan himself were blowing the pipes!"

Now around they go, and around, and around,
With hop-skip-and-jump, and frolicsome bound;
　　　Such sailing and gliding,　Such sinking and sliding,
　　　Such lofty curvetting,　And grand pirouetting,
Ned, you would swear that Monsieur Gilbert
And Miss Taglioni were capering there!

And oh! such awful music! ne'er
Fell sounds so uncanny on mortal ear.
There were the tones of a dying man's groans
Mixed with the rattling of dead men's bones:
Had you heard the shrieks, and the squeals, and the squeaks,
You'd not have forgotten the sound for weeks.

And around, and around, and around they go,
Heel to heel, and toe to toe,—
Prance and caper, curvet and wheel,
Toe to toe, and heel to heel.

"'Tis merry, 'tis merry, Cummers, I trow,
To dance thus beneath the nightshade bough!"—

"Goody Price, Goody Price, now riddle me right,
Where may we sup this frolicsome night?"

"Mine host of the Dragon hath mutton and veal;
The Squire hath partridge, and widgeon, and teal;
But old Sir Thopas hath daintier cheer,
A pasty made of the good red deer,
A huge grouse-pie, and a fine Florentine,
A fat roast goose, and a turkey and chine."—

"Madge Gray, Madge Gray,
Now tell me, I pray,
Where's the best wassail bowl to our roundelay?"

" There is ale in the cellars of Tappington Hall,
But the Squire* is a churl, and his drink is small ;
    Mine host of the Dragon   Hath many a flagon
Of double ale, lambs' wool, and *eau de vie*,
    But Sir Thopas, the Vicar,   Hath costlier liquor,—
A butt of the choicest *Malvoisie.*
    He doth not lack   Canary or sack ;
And a good pint stoup of Clary wine
Smacks merrily off with a turkey and chine !"

" Now away ! and away ! without delay,
Hey Cockalorum ! my Broomstick gay !
We must be back ere the dawn of the day :
Hey up the chimney ! away ! away !"—
    Old Goody Price   Mounts in a trice,
In showing her legs she is not over nice ;
    Old Goody Jones,   All skin and bones,
Follows " like winking."—Away go the crones,
Knees and nose in a line with the toes,
Sitting their brooms like so many Ducrows ;
    Latest and last   The damsel passed,
One glance of her coal-black eye she cast ;
She laughed with glee loud laughters three.
" Dost fear, Rob Gilpin, to ride with me ?"—
Oh, never might man unscathed espy
One single glance from that coal-black eye.
    —Away she flew !—   Without more ado
Rob seizes and mounts on a broomstick too,
" Hey up the chimney, lass !   Hey after you !"

It's a very fine thing, on a fine day in June,
To ride through the air in a Nassau Balloon ;
But you'll find very soon, if you aim at the Moon
In a carriage like that, you're a bit of a " Spoon,"

---

* Stephen Ingoldsby, surnamed "The Niggard," second cousin and successor to
"The Bad Sir Giles." (Visitation of Kent, 1666.) For an account of his murder by
burglars, and their subsequent execution, see Dodsley's "Remarkable Trials," etc.
Lond. 1776, vol. ii. p. 264, ex the present volume, Art. "Hand of Glory."

For the largest can't fly   Above twenty miles high,
And you're not half way then on your journey, nor nigh;
    While no man alive   Could ever contrive,
Mr. Green has declared, to get higher than five.
And the soundest Philosophers hold that, perhaps,
If you reached twenty miles your balloon would collapse,
    Or pass by such action   The sphere of attraction,
Getting into the track of some comet—Good lack!
'Tis a thousand to one that you'd never come back;
And the boldest of mortals a danger like that must fear,
Rashly protruding beyond our own atmosphere.
    No, no; when I try   A trip to the sky,
I shan't go in that thing of yours, Mr. Gye,
Though Messieurs Mouck Mason, and Spencer, and Beazly,
All join in saying it travels so easily.
    No; there's nothing so good   As a pony of wood—
Not like that which, of late, they stuck up on the gate
At the end of the Park, which caused so much debate,
And gave so much trouble to make it stand straight—
But a regular Broomstick—you'll find that the favorite—
Above all, when, like Robin, you haven't to pay for it.
    —Stay—really I dread—   I am losing the thread
Of my tale; and it's time you should be in your bed,
So lithe now, and listen, my little boy Ned!

———————

The Vicarage walls are lofty and thick,
And the copings are stone, and the sides are brick;
The casements are narrow, and bolted and barred,
And the stout oak door is heavy and hard;
Moreover, by way of additional guard,
A great big dog runs loose in the yard,
And a horse-shoe is nailed on the threshold sill,
To keep out aught that savors of ill,—
But, alack! the chimney-pot's open still!
—That great big dog begins to quail,
Between his hind legs he drops his tail.

Crouched on the ground, the terrified hound
Gives vent to a very odd sort of a sound;
It is not a bark, loud, open, and free,
As an honest old watch-dog's bark should be;
It is not a yelp, it is not a growl,
But a something between a whine and a howl;
And, hark!—a sound from the window high
Responds to the watch-dog's pitiful cry:
    It is not a moan,   It is not a groan:
It comes from a nose,—but is not what a nose
Produces in healthy and sound repose.
Yet Sir Thopas the Vicar is fast asleep,
And his respirations are heavy and deep!

He snores, 'tis true, but he snores no more
As he's aye been accustomed to snore before,
And as men of his kidney are wont to snore
(Sir Thopas's weight is sixteen stone four);—
He draws his breath like a man distressed
By pain or grief, or like one oppressed
By some ugly old Incubus perched on his breast.
    A something seems   To disturb his dreams,
And thrice on his ear, distinct and clear,
Falls a voice as of somebody whispering near
In still small accents, faint and few,
"Hey down the chimney-pot! Hey after you!"

Throughout the Vicarage, near and far,
There is no lack of bolt or of bar;
    There are plenty of locks   To closet and box,
Yet the pantry wicket is standing ajar!
And the little low door, through which you must go,
Down some half dozen steps, to the cellar below,
Is also unfastened, though no one may know,
By so much as a guess, how it comes to be so;
    For wicket and door,   The evening before,
Were both of them locked, and the key safely placed
On the bunch that hangs down from the Housekeeper's waist.

Oh! 'twas a jovial sight to view
In that snug little cellar that frolicsome crew!—
    Old Goody Price   Had got something nice,
A turkey-poult larded with bacon and spice;
    Old Goody Jones   Would touch nought that had bones,—
She might just as well mumble a parcel of stones.
Goody Jones, in sooth, had got never a tooth,
And a New-College pudding of marrow and plums
Is the dish of all others that suiteth her gums.

    Madge Gray was picking   The breast of a chicken;
Her coal-black eye, with its glance so sly,
Was fixed on Rob Gilpin himself, sitting by
With his heart full of love, and his mouth full of pie;
    Grouse-pie, with hare   In the middle, is fare
Which, duly concocted with science and care,
Doctor Kitchener says is beyond all compare;
    And a tenderer leveret   Robin had never ate;
So, in after times, oft he was wont to asseverate.

" Now pledge we the wine-cup!—a health!—a health!
Sweet are the pleasures obtained by stealth!
Fill up! fill up!—the brim of the cup
Is the part that aye holdeth the toothsomest sup!
Here's to thee, Goody Price!—Goody Jones, to thee!—
To thee, Roving Rob! and again to me!
Many a sip, never a slip,
Come to us four 'twixt the cup and the lip!"

    The cups pass quick,   The toasts fly thick,
Rob tries in vain out their meaning to pick,
But hears the words "Scratch," and "Old Bogey," and "Nick."
    More familiar grown,   Now he stands up alone,
Volunteering to give them a toast of his own.
    "A bumper of wine!   Fill thine!   Fill mine!
Here's a health to old Noah who planted the Vine!"
    Oh then what sneezing,   What coughing and wheezing,
Ensued in a way that was not over pleasing;
Goody Price, Goody Jones, and the pretty Madge Gray,
All seemed as their liquor had gone the wrong way.

But the best of the joke was, the moment he spoke
Those words which the party seemed almost to choke,
As by mentioning Noah some spell had been broke,
Every soul in the house at that instant awoke!
And, hearing the din from barrel and bin,
Drew at once the conclusion that thieves had got in.
Up jumped the Cook and caught hold of her spit;
Up jumped the Groom and took bridle and bit;
Up jumped the Gardener and shouldered his spade;
Up jumped the Scullion,—the Footman,—the Maid
(The two last, by the way, occasioned some scandal
By appearing together with only one candle,
Which gave for unpleasant surmises some handle);
Up jumped the Swineherd,—and up jumped the big boy,
A nondescript under him, acting as Pig-boy;
Butler, Housekeeper, Coachman—from bottom to top
Everybody jumped up without parley or stop,
With the weapon which first in their way chanced to
     drop,—
Whip, warming-pan, wig-block, mug, musket, and mop.
     Last of all doth appear,   With some symptoms of fear,
Sir Thopas in person to bring up the rear,
In a mixed kind of costume half *Pontificalibus*,
Half what scholars denominate Pure *Naturalibus*;
     Nay, the truth to express,   As you'll easily guess,
They have none of them time to attend much to dress;
     But He, or She,   As the case may be,
He or She seizes what He or She pleases,
Trunk-hosen or kirtles, and shirts or chemises,
And thus one and all, great and small, short and tall,
Muster at once in the Vicarage hall,
With upstanding locks, starting eyes, shortened breath,
Like the folks in the Gallery Scene in Macbeth,
When Macduff is announcing their Sovereign's death.
And hark!—what accents clear and strong
To the listening throng came floating along!
'Tis Robin encoring himself in a song—
     " Very good song! very well sung!
     Jolly companions every one!"

On, on to the cellar! away! away!
On, on to the cellar without more delay!
The whole *posse* rush onwards in battle array—
Conceive the dismay of the party so gay,
Old Goody Jones, Goody Price, and Madge Gray,
When the door bursting wide, they descried the allied
Troops, prepared for the onslaught, roll in like a tide,
And the spits, and the tongs, and the pokers beside!—
" Boot and saddle's the word! mount, Cummers, and ride!"—
Alarm was ne'er caused more strong and indigenous
By cats among rats, or a hawk in a pigeon-house;
　　Quick from the view　Away they all flew,
With a yell, and a screech, and a halliballoo,
" Hey up the chimney! Hey after you!"—
The Volscians themselves made an exit less speedy
From Corioli, " flutter'd like doves" by Macready.

　　They are gone,—save one,　Robin alone!
Robin, whose high state of civilization
Precludes all idea of aërostation;
　　And who now has no notion　Of more locomotion
Than suffices to kick, with much zeal and devotion,
Right and left at the party, who pounced on their victim,
And mauled him, and kicked him, and licked him, and pricked
　　him,
As they bore him away scarce aware what was done,
And believing it all but a part of the fun,
Hic—hiccoughing out the same strain he'd begun,
" Jol—jolly companions every one!"

*　　*　　*　　*　　*　　*　　*

　　Morning gray　Scarce burst into day
Ere at Tappington Hall there's the deuce to pay;
The tables and chairs are all placed in array
In the old oak-parlor, and in and out
Domestics and neighbors, a motley rout,
Are walking, and whispering, and standing about;
　　And the Squire is there　In his large arm-chair,
Leaning back with a grave magisterial air;

In the front of a seat a   Huge volume, called Fleta,
And Bracton, a tome of an old-fashioned look,
And Coke upon Lyttelton, then a new book;
    And he moistens his lips   With occasional sips
From a luscious sack-posset that smiles in a tankard
Close by on a side-table—not that he drank hard,
    But because at that day,   I hardly need say,
The Hong Merchants had not yet invented How Qua,
Nor as yet would you see Souchong or Bohea
At the tables of persons of any degree:
How our ancestors managed to do without tea
I must fairly confess is a mystery to me;
    Yet your Lydgates and Chaucers
    Had no cups and saucers;
Their breakfast, in fact, and the best they could get,
Was a sort of *déjeûner à la fourchette;*
    Instead of our slops   They had cutlets and chops,
And sack-possets, and ale in stoups, tankards, and pots;
And they wound up the meal with rumpsteaks and 'schalots.

Now the Squire lifts his hand   With an air of command,
And gives them a sign, which they all understand,
To bring in the culprit; and straightway the carter
And huntsman drag in that unfortunate martyr,
Still kicking, and crying " Come,—what are you arter?"
The charge is prepared, and the evidence clear,
" He was caught in the cellar a-drinking the beer!
And came there, there's very great reason to fear,
With companions,—to say but the least of them,—queer;
    Such as Witches, and creatures   With horrible features,
    And horrible grins,   And hooked noses and chins,
Who'd been playing the deuce with his Reverence's bins."
The face of his worship grows graver and graver,
As the parties detail Robin's shameful behavior;
Mister Buzzard, the clerk, while the tale is reciting,
Sits down to reduce the affair into writing,
    With all proper diction,   And due " legal fiction:"
Viz., " That he, the said prisoner, as clearly was shown,
Conspiring with folks to deponents unknown,

With divers—that is to say, two thousand—people,
In two thousand hats, each hat peaked like a steeple,
  With force and with arms, And with sorcery and charms,
  Upon two thousand brooms, Entered four thousand rooms,
To wit, two thousand pantries, and two thousand cellars,
Put in bodily fear twenty thousand in-dwellers,
And with sundry—that is to say, two thousand—forks,
Drew divers—that is to say, ten thousand—corks,
And, with malice prepense, down their two thousand throttles
Emptied various—that is to say, ten thousand—bottles ;
All in breach of the peace,—moved by Satan's malignity—
And in spite of King James, and his Crown, and his Dignity."

  At words so profound Rob gazes around,
But no glance sympathetic to cheer him is found.
  —No glance, did I say ! Yes, one !—Madge Gray !—
She is there in the midst of the crowd standing by,
And she gives him one glance from her coal-black eye,
One touch to his hand, and one word to his ear
(That's a line which I've stolen from Sir Walter, I fear),—
  While nobody near Seems to see her or hear ;
As his worship takes up, and surveys with a strict eye,
The broom now produced as the *corpus delicti*,
  Ere his fingers can clasp, It is snatched from his grasp,
The end poked in his chest with a force makes him gasp,
And despite the decorum so due to the *Quorum*,
His worship's upset, and so too is his jorum ;
And Madge is astride on the broomstick before 'em,—
" *Hocus Pocus !* Quick, *Presto !* and *Hey Cockalorum !*
Mount, mount for your life, Rob !—Sir Justice, adieu !—
—Hey up the chimney-pot ! hey after you !"
  Through the mystified group,
  With a halloo and a whoop,
 Madge on the pommel, and Robin *en croupe*,
The pair through the air ride as if in a chair,
While the party below stand mouth open and stare ;
" Clean bumbaized" and amazed, and fixed, all the room stick,
Oh ! what's gone with Robin,—and Madge,—and the broom-
  stick ?

Ay, "what's gone" indeed, Ned?—of what befell
Madge Gray and the broomstick, I never heard tell:
But Robin was found, that morn, on the ground,
In yon old gray Ruin again, safe and sound,
Except that at first he complained much of thirst,
And a shocking bad headache, of all ills the worst,
    And close by his knee A flask you might see,
But an empty one, smelling of *eau de vie.*

Rob from this hour is an altered man;
He runs home to his lodgings as fast as he can,
    Sticks to his trade, Marries Miss Slade,
Becomes a Teetotaller—that is, the same
As Teetotallers now, one in all but the name;
Grows fond of Small-beer, which is always a steady sign,
Never drinks spirits except as a medicine;
    Learns to despise Coal-black eyes,
Minds pretty girls no more than so many Guys;
Has a family, lives to be sixty, and dies!

    Now, my little boy Ned, Brush off to your bed,
Tie your nightcap on safe, or a napkin instead,
Or these terrible nights you'll catch cold in your head.
And remember my tale, and the moral it teaches,
Which you'll find much the same as what Solomon preaches:
Don't flirt with young ladies; don't practice soft speeches;
Avoid waltzes, quadrilles, pumps, silk hose, and knee-breeches;—
Frequent not gray Ruins,—shun riot and revelry,
Hocus Pocus, and Conjuring, and all sorts of devilry;—
Don't meddle with broomsticks,—they're Beelzebub's switches,
Of cellars keep clear,—they're the devil's own ditches;
And beware of balls, banquetings, brandy, and—witches;
Above all, don't run after black eyes!—if you do,—
Depend on't you'll find what I say will come true,—
Old Nick, some fine morning, will "hey after you!"

STRANGE as the events detailed in the succeeding narrative may appear, they are, I have not the slightest doubt, true to the letter. Whatever impression they make upon the reader, that produced by them on the narrator, I can aver, was neither light nor transient.

SINGULAR PASSAGE IN THE LIFE OF

The late Henry Harris, Doctor in Divinity,

AS RELATED BY THE REV. JASPER INGOLDSBY, M.A., HIS FRIEND AND EXECUTOR.

IN order that the extraordinary circumstance which I am about to relate may meet with the credit it deserves, I think it necessary to premise that my reverend friend, among whose papers I find it recorded, was, in his lifetime, ever esteemed as a man of good plain understanding, strict veracity, and unimpeached morals,—by no means of a nervous temperament, or one likely to attach undue weight to any occurrence out of the common course of events merely because his reflections might not, at the moment, afford him a ready solution of its difficulties.

On the truth of his narrative, as far as he was personally concerned, no one who knew him would hesitate to place the most implicit reliance. His history is briefly this :—He had married early in life, and was a widower at the age of thirty-nine, with an only daughter, who had then arrived at puberty, and was just married to a near connection of our own family. The sudden death of her husband, occasioned by a fall from his horse, only three days after her confinement, was abruptly communicated to Mrs. S—— by a thoughtless girl, who saw her master brought lifeless into the house, and, with all that inexplicable anxiety to be the first to tell bad news, so common among the lower orders, rushed at once into the sick-room with her intelligence. The shock was too severe; and though the young widow survived the fatal event several months, yet she gradually sank under the blow, and expired, leaving a boy, not a twelvemonth old, to the care of his maternal grandfather.

My poor friend was sadly shaken by this melancholy catastrophe; time, however, and a strong religious feeling, succeeded at length in moderating the poignancy of his grief—a consummation much advanced by his infant charge, who now succeeded, as it were by inheritance, to the place in his affections left vacant by his daughter's decease. Frederick S—— grew up to be a fine lad; his person and features were decidedly handsome; still there was, as I remember, an unpleasant expression in his countenance, and an air of reserve, attributed, by the few persons who called occasionally at the vicarage, to the retired life led by his grandfather, and the little opportunity he had, in consequence, of mixing in the society of his equals in age and intellect. Brought up entirely at home, his progress in the common branches of education was, without any great display of precocity, rather in advance of the generality of boys of his own standing; partly owing, perhaps, to the turn which even his amusements took from the first. His sole associate was the son of the village apothecary, a boy about two years older than himself, whose father, being really clever in his profession, and a good operative chemist, had constructed for himself a small laboratory, in which, as he was fond of children, the two boys spent a great portion of their leisure time, witnessing many of those little experiments so attractive to youth, and in time aspiring to imitate what they admired.

In such society, it is not surprising that Frederick S—— should imbibe a strong taste for the sciences which formed his principal amusement; or that when, in process of time, it became necessary to choose his walk in life, a profession so intimately connected with his favorite pursuit, as that of medicine, should be eagerly selected. No opposition was offered by my friend, who, knowing that the greater part of his own income would expire with his life, and that the remainder would prove an insufficient resource to his grandchild, was only anxious that he should follow such a path as would secure him that moderate and respectable competency which is, perhaps, more conducive to real happiness than a more elevated or wealthy station. Frederick was, accordingly, at the proper age, matriculated at

Oxford, with the view of studying the higher branches of medicine, a few months after his friend, John W——, had proceeded to Leyden, for the purpose of making himself acquainted with the practice of surgery in the hospitals and lecture-rooms attached to that university. The boyish intimacy of their younger days did not, as is frequently the case, yield to separation; on the contrary, a close correspondence was kept up between them. Dr. Harris was even prevailed upon to allow Frederick to take a trip to Holland to see his friend; and John returned the visit to Frederick at Oxford.

Satisfactory as, for some time, were the accounts of the general course of Frederick S——'s studies, by degrees rumors of a less pleasant nature reached the ears of some of his friends; to the vicarage, however, I have reason to believe they never penetrated. The good old Doctor was too well beloved in his parish for any one voluntarily to give him pain; and, after all, nothing beyond whispers and surmises had reached X——, when the worthy vicar was surprised on a sudden by a request from his grandchild that he might be permitted to take his name off the books of the university, and proceed to finish his education in conjunction with his friend W—— at Leyden. Such a proposal, made, too, at a time when the period for his graduating could not be far distant, both surprised and grieved the Doctor; he combated the design with more perseverance than he had ever been known to exert in opposition to any declared wish of his darling boy before, but, as usual, gave way when more strongly pressed, from sheer inability to persist in a refusal which seemed to give so much pain to Frederick, especially when the latter, with more energy than was quite becoming their relative situations, expressed his positive determination of not returning to Oxford, whatever might be the result of his grandfather's decision. My friend, his mind, perhaps, a little weakened by a short but severe nervous attack from which he had scarcely recovered, at length yielded a reluctant consent, and Frederick quitted England.

It was not till some months had elapsed after his departure that I had reason to suspect that the eager desire of availing himself of opportunities for study abroad, not afforded him at home, was not the sole, or even the principal, reason which had drawn Frederick so abruptly from his *Alma Mater.* A chance visit to the university, and a conversation with a senior fellow belonging to his late college, convinced me of this; still I found it impossible to extract from the latter the precise nature of his offence. That he had given way to most culpable indulgences I had before heard hinted; and when I recollected how he had been at once launched, from a state of what might be well called seclusion, into a world where so many enticements were lying in wait to allure—with liberty, example, everything to tempt him from the straight road—regret, I frankly own, was more the predominant feeling in my mind than either surprise or condemnation. But here was evidently something more than mere ordinary excess—some act of profligacy, perhaps of a deeper stain, which had induced his superiors, who, at first, had been loud in his praises, to desire him to withdraw himself quietly, but for ever; and such an intimation, I found, had, in fact, been conveyed to him from an authority which it was impossible to resist. Seeing that my informant was determined not to be explicit, I did not press for a disclosure, which, if made, would, in all probability, only have given me pain, and that the rather as my old friend the Doctor had recently obtained a valuable living from Lord M——, only a few miles distant from the market town in which I resided, where he now was, amusing himself in putting his grounds into order, ornamenting his house, and getting everything ready against his grandson's expected visit in the following autumn. October came, and with it came Frederick: he rode over more than once to see me, sometimes accompanied by the Doctor, between whom and myself the recent loss of my poor daughter Louisa had drawn the cords of sympathy still closer.

More than two years had flown on in this way, in which Frederick S—— had as many times made temporary visits to his native country. The time was fast approaching when he was expected to return and finally take up his residence in England, when the sudden illness of my wife's father obliged us to take a journey into Lancashire, my old friend, who had himself a curate, kindly offering to fix his quarters at my parsonage, and superintend the concerns of my parish till my return. Alas! when I saw him next he was on the bed of death!

My absence was necessarily prolonged much beyond what I had anticipated. A letter, with a foreign post-mark, had, as I afterwards found, been brought over from his own house to my venerable substitute in the interval, and, barely giving himself time to transfer the charge he had undertaken to a neighboring clergyman, he had hurried off at once to Leyden. His arrival there was, however, too late. Frederick *was dead!*—killed in a duel, occasioned, it was said, by no ordinary provocation on his part, although the flight of his antagonist had added to the mystery which enveloped its origin. The long journey, its melancholy termination, and the complete overthrow of all my poor friend's earthly hopes, were too much for him. He appeared too—as I was informed by the proprietor of the house in which I found him, when his summons at length had brought me to his bedside—to have received some sudden and unaccountable shock, which even the death of his grandson was inadequate to explain. There was, indeed, a wildness in his fast-glazing eye, which mingled strangely with the glance of satisfaction thrown upon me as he pressed my hand; he endeavored to raise himself, and would have spoken, but fell back in the effort, and closed his eyes for ever. I buried him there, by the side of the object of his more than parental affection—in a foreign land.

It is from the papers that I discovered in his travelling-case that I submit the following extracts, without, however, presuming to advance an opinion on the strange circumstances which they detail, or even as to the connection which some may fancy they discover between different parts of them.

The first was evidently written at my own house, and bears date August the 15th, 18—, about three weeks after my own departure for Preston.

It begins thus:—

"Tuesday, August 15.—Poor girl!—I forget who it is that says, 'The real ills of life are light in comparison with fancied evils;' and certainly the scene I have just witnessed goes some way towards establishing the truth of the hypothesis. Among the afflictions which flesh is heir to, a diseased imagination is far from being the lightest, even when considered separately, and without taking into the account those bodily pains and sufferings which—so close is the connection between mind and matter—are but too frequently attendant upon any disorder of the fancy. Seldom has my interest been more powerfully excited than by poor Mary Graham. Her age, her appearance, her pale, melancholy features, the very contour of her countenance, all conspire to remind me, but too forcibly, of one who, waking or sleeping, is never long absent from my thoughts. But enough of this.

"A fine morning had succeeded one of the most tempestuous nights I ever remember, and I was just sitting down to a substantial breakfast, which the care of my friend Ingoldsby's housekeeper, kind-hearted Mrs. Wilson, had prepared for me, when I was interrupted by a summons to the sick-bed of a young parishioner whom I had frequently seen in my walks, and had remarked for the regularity of her attendance at divine worship. Mary Graham is the elder of two daughters, residing with their mother, the widow of an attorney, who, dying suddenly in the prime of life, left his family but slenderly provided for. A strict though not parsimonious economy has, however, enabled them to live with an appearance of respectability and comfort; and from the personal attractions which both the girls possess, their mother is evidently not without hopes of seeing one, at least, of them advantageously settled in life. As far as poor Mary is concerned, I fear she is doomed to inevitable disappointment, as I am much mistaken if consumption has not laid its wasting finger upon her; while this last recurrence, of what I cannot but believe to be a formidable epileptic attack, threatens to shake out, with even added velocity, the little sand that may yet remain within the hour-glass of time. Her very delusion, too, is of such a nature as, by adding to bodily illness the agitation of superstitious terror, can scarcely fail to accelerate the catastrophe, which I think I see fast approaching.

"Before I was introduced into the sick-room, her sister, who had been watching my arrival from the window, took me into their little parlor, and, after the usual civilities, began to prepare me for the visit I was about to pay. Her countenance was marked at once with trouble and alarm, and in a low tone of voice, which some internal emotion, rather than the fear of disturbing the invalid in a distant room, had subdued almost to a

10

whisper, informed me that my presence was become necessary, not more as a clergyman than a magistrate; that the disorder with which her sister had, during the night, been so suddenly and unaccountably seized, was one of no common kind, but attended with circumstances which, coupled with the declarations of the sufferer, took it out of all ordinary calculations, and, to use her own expression, that 'malice was at the bottom of it.'

"Naturally supposing that these insinuations were intended to intimate the partaking of some deleterious substance on the part of the invalid, I inquired what reason she had for imagining, in the first place, that anything of a poisonous nature had been administered at all; and, secondly, what possible incitement any human being could have for the perpetration of so foul a deed towards so innocent and unoffending an individual. Her answer considerably relieved the apprehensions I had begun to entertain lest the poor girl should, from some unknown cause, have herself been attempting to rush uncalled into the presence of her Creator; at the same time, it surprised me not a little by its apparent want of rationality and common sense. She had no reason to believe, she said, that her sister had taken poison, or that any attempt upon her life had been made, or was, perhaps, contemplated, but that 'still malice was at work—the malice of villains or fiends, or of both combined; that no causes purely natural would suffice to account for the state in which her sister had been now twice placed, or for the dreadful sufferings she had undergone while in that state;' and that she was determined the whole affair should undergo a thorough investigation. Seeing that the poor girl was now herself laboring under a great degree of excitement, I did not think it necessary to enter at that moment into a discussion upon the absurdity of her opinion, but applied myself to the tranquillizing of her mind by assurances of a proper inquiry, and then drew her attention to the symptoms of the indisposition, and the way in which it had first made its appearance.

"The violence of the storm last night had, I found, induced the whole family to sit up far beyond their usual hour, till, wearied out at length, and, as their mother observed, 'tired of burning fire and candle to no purpose,' they repaired to their several chambers.

" The sisters occupied the same room ; Elizabeth was already
at her humble toilet, and had commenced the arrangement of
her hair for the night, when her attention was at once drawn
from her employment by a half-smothered shriek and exclamation from her sister, who, in her delicate state of health, had
found walking up two flights of stairs, perhaps a little more
quickly than usual, an exertion, to recover from which she had
seated herself in a large arm-chair.

" Turning hastily at the sound, she perceived Mary deadly
pale, grasping, as it were convulsively, each arm of the chair
which supported her, and bending forward in the attitude of
listening ; her lips were trembling and bloodless, cold drops of
perspiration stood upon her forehead, and in an instant after,
exclaiming in a piercing tone, ' Hark ! they are calling me
again ! it is—*it is the same voice ;*—Oh no, no !—Oh my God !
save me, Betsy—hold me—save me !' she fell forward upon the
floor.   Elizabeth flew to her assistance, raised her, and by her
cries brought both her mother, who had not yet got into bed, and
their only servant-girl, to her aid.   The latter was despatched
at once for medical help ; but, from the appearance of the sufferer, it was much to be feared that she would soon be beyond
the reach of art.   Her agonized parent and sister succeeded in
bearing her between them and placing her on a bed : a faint and
intermittent pulsation was for a while perceptible ; but in a few
moments a general shudder shook the whole body ; the pulse
ceased, the eyes became fixed and glassy, the jaw dropped, a
cold clamminess usurped the place of the genial warmth of life.
Before Mr. I—— arrived everything announced that dissolution
had taken place, and that the freed spirit had quitted its mortal
tenement.

" The appearance of the surgeon confirmed their worst apprehensions ; a vein was opened, but the blood refused to flow, and
Mr. I—— pronounced that the vital spark was indeed extinguished.

" The poor mother, whose attachment to her children was
perhaps the more powerful as they were the sole relatives or
connections she had in the world, was overwhelmed with a
grief amounting almost to frenzy.   It was with difficulty that
she was removed to her own room by the united strength of

her daughter and medical adviser. Nearly an hour had elapsed during the endeavor at calming her transports; they had succeeded, however, to a certain extent, and Mr. I—— had taken his leave, when Elizabeth, re-entering the bed-chamber in which her sister lay, in order to pay the last sad duties to her corpse, was horror-struck at seeing a crimson stream of blood running down the side of the counterpane to the floor. Her exclamation brought the girl again to her side, when it was perceived, to their astonishment, that the sanguine stream proceeded from the arm of the body, which was now manifesting signs of returning life. The half-frantic mother flew to the room, and it was with difficulty that they could prevent her, in her agitation, from so acting as to extinguish for ever the hope which had begun to rise in their bosoms. A long-drawn sigh, amounting almost to a groan, followed by several convulsive gaspings, was the prelude to the restoration of the animal functions in poor Mary: a shriek, almost preter-naturally loud considering her state of exhaustion, succeeded; but she did recover, and, with the help of restoratives, was well enough towards morning to express a strong desire that I should be sent for—a desire the more readily complied with inasmuch as the strange expressions and declarations she had made since her restoration to consciousness had filled her sister with the most horrible suspicions. The nature of these suspicions was such as would at any other time, perhaps, have raised a smile upon my lips; but the distress and even agony of the poor girl as she half hinted and half expressed them were such as entirely to preclude every sensation at all approaching to mirth. Without endeavoring, therefore, to combat ideas evidently too strongly impressed upon her mind at the moment to admit of present refutation, I merely used a few encouraging words, and requested her to precede me to the sick-chamber.

"The invalid was lying on the outside of the bed, partly dressed, and wearing a white dimity wrapping-gown, the color of which corresponded but too well with the deadly paleness of her complexion. Her cheek was wan and sunken, giving an extraordinary prominence to her eye, which gleamed with a lustrous brilliancy not unfrequently characteristic of the aber-

ration of intellect. I took her hand : it was chill and clammy,
the pulse feeble and intermittent, and the general debility of
her frame was such that I would fain have persuaded her to
defer any conversation which, in her present state, she might
not be equal to support. Her positive assurance that, until
she had disburdened herself of what she called her 'dreadful
secret,' she could know no rest either of mind or body, at
length induced me to comply with her wish, opposition to
which, in her then frame of mind, might perhaps be attended
with even worse effects than its indulgence. I bowed acquiescence, and in a low and faltering voice, with frequent interrup-
tions occasioned by her weakness, she gave me the following
singular account of the sensations which, she averred, had been
experienced by her during her trance :—

"'This, sir,' she began, 'is not the first time that the cruelty
of others has, for what purpose I am unable to conjecture, put
me to a degree of torture which I can compare to no suffering,
either of body or mind, which I have ever before experienced.
On a former occasion I was willing to believe it the mere effect
of a hideous dream, or what is vulgarly termed the nightmare;
but this repetition, and the circumstances under which I was
last *summoned*,—at a time, too, when I had not even composed
myself to rest,—fatally convince me of the reality of what I
have seen and suffered.

"'This is no time for concealment of any kind. It is now
more than a twelvemonth since I was in the habit of occasionally encountering in my walks a young man of prepossessing
appearance and gentlemanly deportment. He was always
alone, and generally reading; but I could not be long in doubt
that these rencounters, which became every week more frequent, were not the effect of accident, or that his attention,
when we did meet, was less directed to his book than to my
sister and myself. He even seemed to wish to address us, and
I have no doubt would have taken some other opportunity of
doing so had not one been afforded him by a strange dog
attacking us one Sunday morning in our way to church, which
he beat off, and made use of this little service to promote an
acquaintance. His name, he said, was Francis Somers, and
added that he was on a visit to a relation of the same name,

resident a few miles from X——. He gave us to understand
that he was himself studying surgery with the view to a medical appointment in one of the colonies. You are not to suppose, sir, that he had entered thus into his concerns at the first
interview; it was not till our acquaintance had ripened, and he
had visited our house more than once with my mother's sanction, that these particulars were elicited. He never disguised,
from the first, that an attachment to myself was his object orig-
inally in introducing himself to our notice. As his prospects
were comparatively flattering, my mother did not raise any
impediment to his attentions, and I own I received them with
pleasure.

"'Days and weeks elapsed; and although the distance at
which his relation resided prevented the possibility of an uninterrupted intercourse, yet neither was it so great as to preclude
his frequent visits. The interval of a day, or at most of two,
was all that intervened; and these temporary absences certainly did not decrease the pleasure of the meetings which they
terminated. At length a pensive expression began to exhibit
itself upon his countenance, and I could not but remark that at
every visit he became more abstracted and reserved. The eye
of affection is not slow to detect any symptom of uneasiness in
a quarter dear to it. I spoke to him, questioned him, on the
subject; his answer was evasive, and I said no more. My
mother too, however, had marked the same appearance of melancholy, and pressed him more strongly. He at length admitted that his spirits were depressed, and that their depression
was caused by the necessity of an early, though but a temporary, separation. His uncle, and only friend, he said, had
long insisted on his spending some months on the Continent,
with the view of completing his professional education, and
that the time was now fast approaching when it would be
necessary for him to commence his journey. A look made the
inquiry which my tongue refused to utter. "Yes, dearest
Mary," was his reply: "I have communicated our attachment
to him, partially at least; and though I dare not say that the
intimation was received as I could have wished, yet I have
perhaps, on the whole, no fair reason to be dissatisfied with his
reply.

" ' " The completion of my studies, and my settlement in the world, must, my uncle told me, be the first consideration ; when these material points were achieved, he should not interfere with any arrangement that might be found essential to my happiness ; at the same time he has positively refused to sanction any engagement at present, which may, he says, have a tendency to divert my attention from those pursuits on the due prosecution of which my future situation in life must depend. A compromise between love and duty was eventually wrung from me, though reluctantly ; I have pledged myself to proceed immediately to my destination abroad, with a full understanding that on my return, a twelvemonth hence, no obstacle shall be thrown in the way of what are, I trust, our mutual wishes.''

" ' I will not attempt to describe the feelings with which I received this communication, nor will it be necessary to say anything of what passed at the few interviews which took place before Francis quitted X———. The evening immediately previous to that of his departure he passed in this house, and, before we separated, renewed his protestations of an unchangeable affection, requiring a similar assurance from me in return. I did not hesitate to make it. " Be satisfied, my dear Francis," said I, "that no diminution in the regard I have avowed can ever take place, and though absent in body, my heart and soul will still be with you."—"Swear this," he cried with a suddenness and energy which surprised and rather startled me: "promise me that you will be with me *in spirit*, at least, when I am far away." I gave him my hand, but that was not sufficient. " One of these dark shining ringlets, my dear Mary," said he, "as a pledge that you will not forget your vow !" I suffered him to take the scissors from my work-box and to sever a lock of my hair, which he placed in his bosom. The next day he was pursuing his journey, and the waves were already bearing him from England.

" ' I had letters from him repeatedly during the first three months of his absence: they spoke of his health, his prospects, and of his love; but by degrees the intervals between each arrival became longer, and I fancied I perceived some falling off from that warmth of expression which had at first characterized his communications.

"'One night I had retired to rest rather later than usual, having sat by the bedside comparing his last brief note with some of his earlier letters, and was endeavoring to convince myself that my apprehensions of his fickleness were unfounded, when an undefinable sensation of restlessness and anxiety seized upon me. I cannot compare it to anything I had ever experienced before; my pulse fluttered, my heart beat with a quickness and violence which alarmed me, and a strange tremor shook my whole frame. I retired hastily to bed, in hopes of getting rid of so unpleasant a sensation, but in vain; a vague apprehension of I know not what occupied my mind, and vainly did I endeavor to shake it off. I can compare my feelings to nothing but those which we sometimes experience when about to undertake a long and unpleasant journey, leaving those we love behind us. More than once did I raise myself in my bed and listen, fancying that I heard myself called; and on each of these occasions the fluttering of my heart increased. Twice I was on the point of calling to my sister, who then slept in an adjoining room; but she had gone to bed indisposed, and an unwillingness to disturb either her or my mother checked me. The large clock in the room below at this moment began to strike the hour of twelve; I distinctly heard its vibrations, but ere its sounds had ceased a burning heat, as if a hot iron had been applied to my temple, was succeeded by a dizzinesss,— a swoon,—a total loss of consciousness as to where or in what situation I was.

"'A pain, violent, sharp, and piercing, as though my whole frame were lacerated by some keen-edged weapon, roused me from this stupor;—but where was I? Everything was strange around me; a shadowy dimness rendered every object indistinct and uncertain; methought, however, that I was seated in a large antique high-backed chair, several of which were near, their tall black carved frames and seats interwoven with a lattice-work of cane. The apartment in which I sat was one of moderate dimensions, and, from its sloping roof, seemed to be the upper story of the edifice, a fact confirmed by the moon shining without, in full effulgence, on a huge round tower, which its light rendered plainly visible through the open casement, and the summit of which appeared but little superior in elevation to the room I occupied. Rather to the right, and in the distance, the spire of some cathedral or lofty church was visible, while sundry gable ends and tops of houses told me I was in the midst of a populous but unknown city.

"'The apartment itself had something strange in its appearance; and, in the character of its furniture and appurtenances, bore little or no resemblance to any I had ever seen before. The fireplace was large and wide, with a pair of what are sometimes called andirons, betokening that wood was the principal if not the only fuel consumed within its recess; a fierce fire was now blazing in it, the light from which rendered visible the remotest parts of the chamber. Over a lofty old-fashioned mantlepiece, carved heavily in imitation of fruits and flowers, hung the half-length portrait of a gentleman in a dark-colored foreign habit, with a peaked beard and moustaches, one hand resting upon a table, the other supporting a sort of *baton*, or short military staff, the summit of which was surmounted by a silver falcon. Several antique chairs, similar in appearance to those already mentioned, surrounded a massive oaken table, the length of which much exceeded its width. At the lower end of this piece of furniture stood the chair I occupied; on the upper was placed a small chafing-dish filled with burning coals, and darting forth occasionally long flashes of various-colored fire, the brilliance of which made itself visible, even above the strong illumination emitted from the chimney. Two huge black japanned cabinets, with clawed feet, reflecting from their polished surfaces the effulgence of the flame, were placed one on each side the casement-window to which I have alluded, and with a few shelves loaded with books, many of which were also strewed in disorder on the floor, completed the list of the furniture in the apartment. Some strange-looking instruments, of unknown form and purpose, lay on the table near the chafing-dish, on the other side of which a miniature portrait of myself hung, reflected by a small oval mirror in a dark-colored frame, while a large open volume, traced with strange characters of the color of blood, lay in front; a goblet, containing a few drops of liquid of the same ensanguined hue, was by its side.

"'But of the objects which I have endeavored to describe,

none arrested my attention so forcibly as two others. These
were the figures of two young men, in the prime of life, only
separated from me by the table. They were dressed alike, each
in a long flowing gown, made of some sad-colored stuff, and
confined at the waist by a crimson girdle; one of them, the
shorter of the two, was occupied in feeding the embers of the
chafing-dish with a resinous powder, which produced and maintained a brilliant but flickering blaze, to the action of which
his companion was exposing a long lock of dark chestnut hair,
that shrank and shrivelled as it approached the flame. But,
O God!—that hair!—and the form of him who held it! that
face! those features!—not for one instant could I entertain a
doubt—it was He! Francis!—the lock he grasped was mine,
the very pledge of affection I had given him, and still, as it
partially encountered the fire, a burning heat seemed to scorch
the temple from which it had been taken, conveying a torturing
sensation that affected my very brain.

"'How shall I proceed?—but no, it is impossible,—not even
to you, sir, can I—dare I—recount the proceedings of that unhallowed night of horror and of shame. Were my life extended
to a term commensurate with that of the Patriarchs of old,
never could its detestable, its damning pollutions be effaced
from my remembrance; and oh! above all, never could I forget
the diabolical glee which sparkled in the eyes of my fiendish
tormentors, as they witnessed the worse than useless struggles
of their miserable victim. Oh! why was it not permitted me
to take refuge in unconsciousness, nay, in death itself, from the
abominations of which I was compelled to be, not only a witness, but a partaker? But it is enough, sir; I will not further
shock your nature by dwelling longer on the scene, the full
horrors of which words, if I even dared employ any, would be
inadequate to express; suffice it to say that after being subjected
to it, how long I knew not, but certainly for more than an hour,
a noise from below seemed to alarm my persecutors; a pause
ensued,—the lights were extinguished,—and, as the sound of a
footstep ascending a staircase became more distinct, my forehead
felt again the excruciating sensation of heat, while the embers,
kindling into a momentary flame, betrayed another portion of
the ringlet consuming in the blaze. Fresh agonies succeeded,

not less severe, and of a similar description to those which had
seized upon me at first; oblivion again followed, and on being
at length restored to consciousness, I found myself as you see
me now, faint and exhausted, weakened in every limb, and
every fibre quivering with agitation. My groans soon brought
my sister to my aid; it was long before I could summon resolu-
tion to confide, even to her, the dreadful secret, and when I had
done so, her strongest efforts were not wanting to persuade me
that I had been laboring under a severe attack of nightmare.
I ceased to argue, but I was not convinced: the whole scene
was then too present, too awfully real, to permit me to doubt
the character of the transaction; and if, when a few days had
elapsed, the hopelessness of imparting to others the conviction
I entertained myself produced in me an apparent acquiescence
with their opinion, I have never been the less satisfied that no
cause reducible to the known laws of nature occasioned my
sufferings on that hellish evening. Whether that firm belief
might have eventually yielded to time, whether I might at
length have been brought to consider all that had passed, and
the circumstances which I could never cease to remember, as a
mere phantasm, the offspring of a heated imagination, acting
upon an enfeebled body, I know not—last night, however, would
in any case have dispelled the flattering illusion—last night—
last night was the whole horrible scene acted over again. The
place—the actors—the whole infernal apparatus were the same;
—the same insults, the same torments, the same brutalities—all
were renewed, save that the period of my agony was not so prolonged. I became sensible to an incision in my arm, though
the hand that made it was not visible; at the same moment my
persecutors paused; they were manifestly disconcerted, and the
companion of him, whose name shall never more pass my lips,
muttered something to his abettor in evident agitation; the
formula of an oath of horrible import was dictated to me in
terms fearfully distinct. I refused it unhesitatingly; again and
again was it proposed, with menaces I tremble to think on—but
I refused; the same sound was heard—interruption was evidently apprehended,—the same ceremony was hastily repeated,
and I again found myself released, lying on my own bed, with
my mother and my sister weeping over me. O God! O God!

when and how is this to end ?—When will my spirit be left in peace ?—Where or with whom shall I find refuge ?'

" It is impossible to convey any adequate idea of the emotions with which this unhappy girl's narrative affected me. It must not be supposed that her story was delivered in the same continuous and uninterrupted strain in which I have transcribed its substance. On the contrary, it was not without frequent intervals, of longer or shorter duration, that her account was brought to a conclusion : indeed, many passages of her strange dream were not without the greatest difficulty and reluctance communicated at all. My task was no easy one ; never, in the course of a long life spent in the active duties of my Christian calling,—never had I been summoned to such a conference before.

" To the half-avowed and palliated confession of committed guilt I had often listened, and pointed out the only road to secure its forgiveness. I had succeeded in cheering the spirit of despondency, and sometimes even in calming the ravings of despair ; but here I had a different enemy to combat, an ineradicable prejudice to encounter, evidently backed by no common share of superstition, and confirmed by the mental weakness attendant upon severe bodily pain. To argue the sufferer out of an opinion so rooted was a hopeless attempt. I did, however, essay it ; I spoke to her of the strong and mysterious connection maintained between our waking images and those which haunt us in our dreams, and more especially during that morbid oppression commonly called nightmare. I was even enabled to adduce myself as a strong and living instance of the excess to which fancy sometimes carries her freaks on those occasions ; while, by an odd coincidence, the impression made upon my own mind, which I adduced as an example, bore no slight resemblance to her own. I stated to her that on my recovery from the fit of epilepsy which had attacked me about two years since, just before my grandson Frederick left Oxford, it was with the greatest difficulty I could persuade myself that I had not visited him, during the interval, in his rooms at Brazenose, and even conversed with himself and his friend W——, seated in his arm-chair, and gazing through the window full upon the statue of Cain, as it stands in the centre of the quad-

rangle. I told her of the pain I underwent both at the com-
mencement and termination of my attack; of the extreme
lassitude that succeeded; but my efforts were all in vain: she
listened to me, indeed, with an interest almost breathless, especially when I informed her of my having actually experienced
the very burning sensation in the brain alluded to, no doubt a
strong attendant symptom of this peculiar affection, and a proof
of the identity of the complaint; but I could plainly perceive
that I failed entirely in shaking the rooted opinion which possessed her, that her spirit had, by some nefarious and unhallowed means, been actually subtracted for a time from its
earthly tenement."

The next extract which I shall give from my old friend's
memoranda is dated August 24th, more than a week subsequent
to his first visit at Mrs. Graham's. He appears, from his
papers, to have visited the poor young woman more than once
during the interval, and to have afforded her those spiritual
consolations which no one was more capable of communicating.
His patient, for so in a religious sense she may well be termed,
had been sinking under the agitation she had experienced; and
the constant dread she was under of similar sufferings operated
so strongly on a frame already enervated that life at length
seemed to hang only by a thread. His papers go on to say—

"I have just seen poor Mary Graham,—I fear for the last
time. Nature is evidently quite worn out; she is aware that
she is dying, and looks forward to the termination of her existence here, not only with resignation but with joy. It is clear
that her dream, or what she persists in calling her 'subtraction,'
has much to do with this. For the last three days her behavior
has been altered; she has avoided conversing on the subject of
her delusion, and seems to wish that I should consider her as a
convert to my view of her case. This may, perhaps, be partly
owing to the flippancies of her medical attendant upon the subject, for Mr. I—— has, somehow or other, got an inkling that
she has been much agitated by a dream, and thinks to laugh
off the impression—in my opinion injudiciously; but though a

skillful and a kind-hearted, he is a young man, and of a disposition, perhaps, rather too mercurial for the chamber of a nervous invalid. Her manner has since been much more reserved to both of us: in my case, probably because she suspects me of betraying her secret."

"August 26th.—Mary Graham is yet alive, but sinking fast; her cordiality towards me has returned since her sister confessed yesterday that she had herself told Mr. I—— that his patient's mind 'had been affected by a terrible vision.' I am evidently restored to her confidence. She asked me this morning, with much earnestness, ' What I believed to be the state of departed spirits during the interval between dissolution and the final day of account? And whether I thought they would be safe, in another world, from the influence of wicked persons employing an agency more than human?' Poor child! One cannot mistake the prevailing bias of her mind. Poor child!"

"August 27th.—It is nearly over; she is sinking rapidly, but quietly and without pain. I have just administered to her the sacred elements, of which her mother partook. Elizabeth declined doing the same: she cannot, she says, yet bring herself to forgive the villain who has destroyed her sister. It is singular that she, a young woman of good plain sense in ordinary matters, should so easily adopt, and so pertinaciously retain, a superstition so puerile and ridiculous. This must be matter of a future conversation between us; at present, with the form of the dying girl before her eyes, it were vain to argue with her. The mother, I find, has written to young Somers, stating the dangerous situation of his affianced wife; indignant, as she justly is, at his long silence, it is fortunate that she has no knowledge of the suspicions entertained by her daughter. I have seen her letter; it is addressed to Mr. Francis Somers, in the Hogewoert, at

Leyden—a fellow-student, then, of Frederick's. I must remember to inquire if he is acquainted with this young man."

———

Mary Graham, it appears, died the same night. Before her
departure, she repeated to my friend the singular story she
had before told him, without any material variation from
the detail she had formerly given. To the last she persisted
in believing that her unworthy lover had practiced upon
her by forbidden arts. She once more described the apartment with great minuteness, and even the person of Francis's
alleged companion, who was, she said, about the middle height,
hard-featured, with a rather remarkable scar upon his left
cheek, extending in a transverse direction from below the
eye to the nose. Several pages of my reverend friend's man-
uscript are filled with reflections upon this extraordinary
confession, which, joined with its melancholy termination,
seems to have produced no common effect upon him. He
alludes to more than one subsequent discussion with the sur-
viving sister, and piques himself on having made some progress
in convincing her of the folly of her theory respecting the
origin and nature of the illness itself.

His memoranda on this and other subjects are continued
till about the middle of September, when a break ensues,
occasioned, no doubt, by the unwelcome news of his grandson's
dangerous state, which induces him to set out forthwith for
Holland. His arrival at Leyden was, as I have already said,
too late. Frederick S—— had expired after thirty hours'
intense suffering, from a wound received in a duel with a
brother student. The cause of quarrel was variously related;
but, according to his landlord's version, it had originated in
some silly dispute about a dream of his antagonist's, who had
been the challenger. Such, at least, was the account given
to him, as he said, by Frederick's friend and fellow-lodger,
W——, who had acted as second on the occasion, thus ac-
quitting himself of an obligation of the same kind due to the
deceased, whose services he had put in requisition about a year

before on a similar occasion, when he had himself been severely wounded in the face.

From the same authority I learned that my poor friend was much affected on finding that his arrival had been deferred too long. Every attention was shown him by the proprietor of the house, a respectable tradesman, and a chamber was prepared for his accommodation; the books and few effects of his deceased grandson were delivered over to him, duly inventoried, and, late as it was in the evening when he reached Leyden, he insisted on being conducted immediately to the apartments which Frederick had occupied, there to indulge the first ebullitions of his sorrow, before he retired to his own. Madame Müller accordingly led the way to an upper room, which, being situated at the top of the house, had been, from its privacy and distance from the street, selected by Frederick as his study. The Doctor entered, and taking the lamp from his conductress motioned to be left alone. His implied wish was of course complied with: and nearly two hours had elapsed before his kind-hearted hostess reascended, in the hope of prevailing upon him to return with her, and partake of that refreshment which he had in the first instance peremptorily declined. Her application for admission was unnoticed:—she repeated it more than once, without success; then, becoming somewhat alarmed at the continued silence, opened the door and perceived her new inmate stretched on the floor in a fainting fit. Restoratives were instantly administered, and prompt medical aid succeeded at length in restoring him to consciousness. But his mind had received a shock from which, during the few weeks he survived, it never entirely recovered. His thoughts wandered perpetually; and though, from the very slight acquaintance which his hosts had with the English language, the greater part of what fell from him remained unknown, yet enough was understood to induce them to believe that something more than the mere death of his grandson had contributed thus to paralyze his faculties.

When his situation was first discovered, a small miniature was found tightly grasped in his right hand. It had been the property of Frederick, and had more than once been seen by the Müllers in his possession. To this the patient made

continued reference, and would not suffer it one moment from
his sight: it was in his hand when he expired. At my request
it was produced to me. The portrait was that of a young
woman, in an English morning dress, whose pleasing and
regular features, with their mild and somewhat pensive expression, were not, I thought, altogether unknown to me.
Her age was apparently about twenty. A profusion of dark
chestnut hair was arranged in the Madonna style above a brow
of unsullied whiteness, a single ringlet depending on the left
side. A glossy lock of the same color, and evidently belonging
to the original, appeared beneath a small crystal, inlaid in
the back of the picture, which was plainly set in gold, and
bore in a cipher the letters M. G., with the date 18—. From
the inspection of this portrait I could at the time collect
nothing, nor from that of the Doctor himself, which, also,
I found the next morning in Frederick's desk, accompanied
by two separate portions of hair. One of them was a lock,
short and deeply tinged with gray, and had been taken, I
have little doubt, from the head of my old friend himself;
the other corresponded in color and appearance with that at
the back of the miniature. It was not till a few days had
elapsed, and I had seen the worthy Doctor's remains quietly
consigned to the narrow house, that, while arranging his
papers previous to my intended return upon the morrow,
I encountered the narrative I have already transcribed. The
name of the unfortunate young woman connected with it
forcibly arrested my attention. I recollected it immediately
as one belonging to a parishioner of my own, and at once
recognized the original of the female portrait as its owner.

I rose not from the perusal of his very singular statement
till I had gone through the whole of it. It was late, and
the rays of the single lamp by which I was reading did but
very faintly illumine the remoter parts of the room in which
I sat. The brilliancy of an unclouded November moon, then
some twelve nights old, and shining full into the apartment,
did much towards remedying the defect. My thoughts filled
with the melancholy details I had read, I rose and walked to
the window. The beautiful planet rose high in the firmament,
and gave to the snowy roofs of the houses, and pendent icicles,

11

all the sparkling radiance of clustering gems. The stillness
of the scene harmonized well with the state of my feelings.
I threw open the casement and looked abroad. Far below me
the waters of the principal canal shone like a broad mirror in
the moonlight. To the left rose the Burght, a huge round
tower of remarkable appearance, pierced with embrasures at
its summit; while a little to the right, and in the distance, the
spire and pinnacles of the Cathedral of Leyden rose in all
their majesty, presenting a *coup d'œil* of surpassing though
simple beauty. To a spectator of calm, unoccupied mind, the
scene would have been delightful. On me it acted with an
electric effect. I turned hastily to survey the apartment in
which I had been sitting. It was the one designated as the
study of the late Frederick S——. The sides of the room
were covered with dark wainscot; the spacious fireplace opposite to me, with its polished andirons, was surmounted by a
large old-fashioned mantlepiece, heavily carved in the Dutch
style with fruits and flowers; above it frowned a portrait, in a
Vandyke dress, with a peaked beard and moustaches; one hand
of the figure rested on a table, while the other bore a marshal's
staff, surmounted with a silver falcon; and either my imagination, already heated by the scene, deceived me, or a smile as
of malicious triumph curled the lip and glared in the cold
leaden eye that seemed fixed upon my own. The heavy
antique cane-backed chairs, the large oaken table, the book-
shelves, the scattered volumes,—all, all were there; while, to
complete the picture, to my right and left, as half breathless
I leaned my back against the casement, rose, on each side, a
tall, dark ebony cabinet, in whose polished sides the single
lamp upon the table shone reflected as in a mirror.

What am I to think?—Can it be that the story I have been
reading was written by my poor friend here, and under the influence of delirium?—Impossible! Besides, they all assure me
that from that fatal night of his arrival he never left his bed—
never put pen to paper. His very directions to have me summoned from England were verbally given, during one of those

few and brief intervals in which reason seemed partially to re-
sume her sway. Can it then be possible that——? W——?
where is he who alone may be able to throw light on this horrible mystery? No one knows. He absconded, it seems, immediately after the duel. No trace of him exists, nor, after
repeated and anxious inquiries, can I find that any student has
ever been known in the University of Leyden by the name of
Francis Somers.

> "There are more things in heaven and earth
> Than are dreamt of in your philosophy!"

FATHER JOHN INGOLDSBY, to whose papers I am largely
indebted for the saintly records which follow, was brought up
by his father, a cadet of the family, in the Romish faith, and
was educated at Douai for the church. Besides the manuscripts
now at Tappington, he was the author of two controversial
treatises on the connection between the Papal Hierarchy and
the Nine of Diamonds.

From his well-known loyalty, evinced by secret services to
the Royal cause during the Protectorate, he was excepted by
name out of the acts against the Papists, became superintend-
ent of the Queen Dowager's chapel at Somerset House, and
enjoyed a small pension until his death, which took place in the
third year of Queen Anne (1704), at the mature age of ninety-
six. He was an ecclesiastic of great learning and piety, but,
from the stiff and antiquated phraseology which he adopted, I
have thought it necessary to modernize it a little: this will
account for certain anachronisms that have unavoidably crept
in; the substance of his narratives has, however, throughout
been strictly adhered to.

His hair-shirt, almost as good as new, is still preserved at
Tappington,—but nobody ever wears it.

The Jackdaw of Rheims.

"Tunc miser Corvus adeo conscientiæ stimulis compunctus fuit, et execratio cum tantopere excarneficavit, ut exinde tabescere inciperet, maciem contraheret, omnem cibum aversaretur, nec ampliùs crocitaret: pennæ præterea ei defluebant, et alis pendulis omnes facetias intermisit, et tam macer apparuit ut omnes ejus miserescent." * *

"Tunc abbas sacerdotibus mandavit ut rursus furem absolverent; quo facto, Corvus, omnibus mirantibus, propediem convaluit, et pristinam sanitatem recuperavit."

De Illust. Ord. Cistere.

THE Jackdaw sat on the Cardinal's chair!
  Bishop, and Abbot, and Prior were there;
    Many a monk, and many a friar,
    Many a knight, and many a squire,
With a great many more of lesser degree—
In sooth a goodly company;
And they served the Lord Primate on bended knee.
    Never, I ween,   Was a prouder seen,
Read of in books, or dreamt of in dreams,
Than the Cardinal Lord Archbishop of Rheims!

    In and out   Through the motley rout,
That little Jackdaw kept hopping about;
    Here and there   Like a dog in a fair,
    Over comfits and cakes,   And dishes and plates,
Cowl and cope, and rochet and pall,
Mitre and crosier! he hopped upon all!
    With saucy air,   He perched on the chair
Where, in state, the great Lord Cardinal sat
In the great Lord Cardinal's great red hat;
    And he peered in the face   Of his Lordship's Grace,
With a satisfied look, as if he would say,
" We two are the greatest folks here to-day!"
    And the priests, with awe,   As such freaks they saw,
Said, " The devil must be in that little Jackdaw!"

The feast was over, the board was cleared,
The flawns and the custards had all disappeared,

And six little Singing-boys,—dear little souls!
In nice clean faces, and nice white stoles,
      Came, in order due,   Two by two,
Marching that grand refectory through!

A nice little boy held a golden ewer,
Embossed and filled with water, as pure
As any that flows between Rheims and Namur,
Which a nice little boy stood ready to catch
In a fine golden hand-basin made to match.
Two nice little boys, rather more grown,
Carried lavender-water and eau de Cologne;
And a nice little boy had a nice cake of soap,
Worthy of washing the hands of the Pope.
      One little boy more   A napkin bore,
Of the best white diaper, fringed with pink,
And a Cardinal's Hat marked in " permanent ink."

The great Lord Cardinal turns at the sight
Of these nice little boys dressed all in white:
      From his finger he draws   His costly turquoise;
And, not thinking at all about little Jackdaws,
      Deposits it straight   By the side of his plate,
While the nice little boys on his Eminence wait;
Till, when nobody's dreaming of any such thing,
That little Jackdaw hops off with the ring!

      There's a cry and a shout,   And a deuce of a rout,
And nobody seems to know what they're about,
But the monks have their pockets all turned inside out;
      The friars are kneeling,   And hunting, and feeling
The carpet, the floor, and the walls, and the ceiling.
      The Cardinal drew   Off each plum-colored shoe,
And left his red stockings exposed to the view;
      He peeps, and he feels   In the toes and the heels;
They turn up the dishes,—they turn up the plates,—
They take up the poker and poke out the grates,

—They turn up the rugs,   They examine the mugs:—
But no!—no such thing;—   They can't find THE RING!
And the Abbot declared that "when nobody twigged it,
Some rascal or other had popped in and prigged it!"

The Cardinal rose with a dignified look,
He called for his candle, his bell, and his book!
  In holy anger, and pious grief,
  He solemnly cursed that rascally thief!
  He cursed him at board, he cursed him in bed;
  From the sole of his foot to the crown of his head;
  He cursed him in sleeping, that every night
  He should dream of the devil, and wake in a fright;
  He cursed him in eating, he cursed him in drinking,
  He cursed him in coughing, in sneezing, in winking;
  He cursed him in sitting, in standing, in lying;
  He cursed him in walking, in riding, in flying,
  He cursed him in living, he cursed him in dying!—
Never was heard such a terrible curse!
  But what gave rise   To no little surprise,
Nobody seemed one penny the worse!

    The day was gone,   The night came on,
The Monks and the Friars they searched till dawn;
    When the Sacristan saw,   On crumpled claw,
Come limping a poor little lame Jackdaw;
    No longer gay,   As on yesterday;
His feathers all seemed to be turned the wrong way;—
His pinions drooped—he could hardly stand,—
His head was as bald as the palm of your hand;
    His eye so dim,   So wasted each limb,
That, heedless of grammar, they all cried, "THAT'S HIM!—
That's the scamp that has done this scandalous thing!
That's the thief that has got my Lord Cardinal's Ring!"
    The poor little Jackdaw,   When the monks he saw,
Feebly gave vent to the ghost of a caw;
And turned his bald head, as much as to say,
    "Pray, be so good as to walk this way!"

Slower and slower He limped on before,
Till they came to the back of the belfry door,
    Where the first thing they saw, 'Midst the sticks and
        the straw,
Was the RING in the nest of that little Jackdaw!

Then the great Lord Cardinal called for his book,
And off that terrible curse he took;
    The mute expression Served in lieu of confession,
And, being thus coupled with full restitution,
The Jackdaw got plenary absolution!
    —When those words were heard, That poor little bird
Was so changed in a moment, 'twas really absurd;
He grew sleek and fat; In addition to that,
A fresh crop of feathers came thick as a mat!

His tail waggled more Even than before;
But no longer it wagged with an impudent air,
No longer he perched on the Cardinal's chair.
    He hopped now about With a gait devout;
At Matins, at Vespers, he never was out;
And, so far from any more pilfering deeds,
He always seemed telling the Confessor's beads.
If any one lied,—or if any one swore,—
Or slumbered in prayer-time and happened to snore,
    That good Jackdaw Would give a great "Caw!"
As much as to say, "Don't do so any more!"
While many remarked, as his manners they saw,
That they "never had known such a pious Jackdaw!"
    He long lived the pride Of that country side,
And at last in the odor of sanctity died;
    When, as words were too faint His merits to paint,
The Conclave determined to make him a Saint;
And on newly-made Saints and Popes, as you know,
It's the custom, at Rome, new names to bestow,
So they canonized him by the name of Jim Crow!

A Lay of St. Dunstan.

"This holy childe Dunstan was borne in ye yere of our Lorde ix. hundred & xxv. that tyme reynynge in this londe Kinge Athelston.

"Whan it so was that Saynt Dunstan was wery of prayer than used he to werke in goldsmythes werke with his owne handes for to eschewe ydelnes."

Golden Legend.

ST. DUNSTAN stood in his ivied tower,
    Alembic, crucible, all were there;
When in came Nick to play him a trick,
    In guise of a damsel passing fair.
        Every one knows   How the story goes:
He took up the tongs and caught hold of his nose.
But I beg that you won't for a moment suppose
That I mean to go through, in detail, to you
A story at least as trite as it's true;
        Nor do I intend   An instant to spend
On the tale, how he treated his monarch and friend,
When bolting away to a chamber remote,
Inconceivably bored by his Witen-gemote,
        Edwy left them all joking,   And drinking, and
    smoking,
So tipsily grand, they'd stand nonsense from no King,
        But sent the Archbishop   Their Sovereign to fish up,
With a hint that perchance on his crown he might feel
    taps
Unless he came back straight and took off his heel-taps.
You must not be plagued with the same story twice,
And perhaps have seen this one, by W. DYCE,

At the Royal Academy, very well done,
And marked in the catalogue, Four, seven, one.

You might there view the Saint, who in sable arrayed is,
Coercing the Monarch away from the Ladies;
His right hand has hold of his Majesty's jerkin,
His left shows the door, and he seems to say, "Sir King,
Your most faithful Commons won't hear of your shirking;
Quit your tea, and return to your Barclai and Perkyn;
Or, by Jingo,* ere morning, no longer alive, a
Sad victim you'll lie to your love for Elgiva!"
    No further to treat   Of this ungallant feat,
What I mean to do now is succinctly to paint
One particular fact in the life of the Saint,
Which, somehow, for want of due care, I presume,
Has escaped the researches of Rapin and Hume,
In recounting a miracle, both of them men who a
Great deal fall short of Jacques, Bishop of Genoa,
An Historian who likes deeds like these to record—
See his *Aurea Legenda*, by 𝔚𝔩𝔶𝔫𝔨𝔶𝔫 𝔡𝔢 𝔚𝔩𝔬𝔯𝔡𝔢.

St. Dunstan stood again in his tower,
   Alembic, crucible, all complete;
He had been standing a good half hour,
And now he uttered the words of power,
   And called to his Broomstick to bring him a seat.

The words of power!—and what be they
To which e'en Broomsticks bow and obey?
Why,—'twere uncommonly hard to say,
As the prelate I named has recorded none of them,
   What they may be,   But I know they are three,
And ABRACADABRA, I take it, is one of them:

---

* St. Jingo, or Gengo (Gengulphus), sometimes styled "The Living Jingo," from the great tenaciousness of vitality exhibited by his severed members. See his Legend, as recorded hereafter in the present volume.

For I'm told that most Cabalists use that identical
Word, written thus, in what they call "a Pentacle."

However that be,   You'll doubtless agree
It signifies little to you or to me,
As not being dabblers in Grammarye;
Still, it must be confessed, for a Saint to repeat
Such language aloud is scarcely discreet;
For, as Solomon hints to folks given to chatter,
"A bird of the air may carry the matter;"
      And in sooth,   From my youth,   I remember a truth
Insisted on much in my earlier years,
To wit, "Little Pitchers have very long ears!"
Now, just such a "Pitcher" as those I allude to
Was outside the door, which his "ears" appeared glued to.

Peter, the Lay-brother, meagre and thin,
    Five feet one in his sandal shoon,
While the Saint thought him sleeping,
Was listening and peeping,
    And watching his master the whole afternoon.

This Peter the Saint had picked out from his fellows,
To look to his fire, and to blow with the bellows,
To put on the Wall's-Ends and Lambtons whenever he
Chose to indulge in a little *orfevrerie;*
    —Of course you have read   That St. Dunstan was bred
A Goldsmith, and never quite gave up the trade!
The Company—richest in London, 'tis said—
Acknowledge him still as their Patron and Head;
        Nor is it so long   Since a capital song
In his praise—now recorded their archives among—
Delighted the noble and dignified throng
Of their guests, who, the newspapers told the whole town,
With cheers "pledged the wine-cup to Dunstan's renown,"
When Lord Lyndhurst, The Duke, and Sir Robert were
        dining
At the Hall some time since with the Prime Warden Twining.—
—I am sadly digressing—a fault which sometimes
One can hardly avoid in these gossiping rhymes—
A slight deviation's forgiven! but then this is
Too long, I fear, for a decent parenthesis,
So I'll rein up my Pegasus sharp, and retreat, or
You'll think I've forgotten the Lay-brother Peter,
        Whom the Saint, as I said,   Kept to turn down his bed,
        Dress his palfreys and cobs,   And do other odd jobs,—
    As reducing to writing   Whatever he might, in
The course of the day or the night, be inditing,
And cleaning the plate of his mitre with whiting;
Performing, in short, all those duties and offices
Abbots exact from Lay-brothers and Novices.

        It occurs to me here   You'll perhaps think it queer
That St. Dunstan should have such a personage near,
        When he'd only to say   Those words,—be what they
            may,—
And his Broomstick at once his commands would obey.—
        That's true—but the fact is   'Twas rarely his practice
Such aid to resort to, or such means apply,
Unless he'd some "dignified knot" to untie,

Adopting, though sometimes, as now, he'd reverse it,
Old Horace's maxim *" nec Broomstick intersit."*—
—Peter, the Lay-brother, meagre and thin,
Heard all the Saint was saying within;
Peter, the Lay-brother, sallow and spare,
Peeped through the keyhole, and—what saw he there?—
Why,—A BROOMSTICK BRINGING A RUSH-BOTTOMED CHAIR!

What Shakspeare observes, in his play of King John,
        Is undoubtedly right,   That "ofttimes the sight
Of means to do ill deeds will make ill deeds done."
Here's Peter, the Lay-brother, pale-faced and meagre,
A good sort of man, only rather too eager
To listen to what other people are saying
When he ought to be minding his business or praying,
Gets into a scrape, and an awkward one, too,—
As you'll find if you've patience enough to go through
        The whole of the story   I'm laying before ye,—
Entirely from having " the means" in his view
Of doing a thing which he ought not to do!

        Still rings in his ear,   Distinct and clear,
Abracadabra! that word of fear!
And the two which I never yet happened to hear.
        Still doth he spy,   With fancy's eye,
The Broomstick at work, and the Saint standing by;
And he chuckles, and says to himself, with glee,
" Aha! that Broomstick shall work for *me!*"

        Hark!—that swell   O'er flood and o'er fell,
Mountain, and dingle, and moss-covered dell!
List!—'tis the sound of the Compline bell;
And St. Dunstan is quitting his ivied cell;
        Peter, I wot,   Is off like a shot,
Or a little dog scalded by something that's hot,
For he hears his master approaching the spot
Where he'd listened so long, though he knew he ought not:

Peter remembered his Master's frown—
He trembled—he'd not have been caught for a crown;
   Howe'er you may laugh, He'd rather, by half,
Have run up to the top of the tower and jumped down.

The Compline hour is past and gone,
Evening service is over and done;
   The Monks repair   To their frugal fare,
A snug little supper of something light
And digestible, ere they retire for the night,
For, in Saxon times, in respect to their cheer,
St. Austin's rule was by no means severe,
But allowed, from the Beverley Roll 'twould appear,
Bread and cheese, and spring onions, and sound table beer,
And even green peas, when they were not too dear;
Not like the Rule of La Trappe, whose chief merit is
Said to consist in its greater austerities;
And whose Monks, if I rightly remember their laws,
   Ne'er are suffered to speak,   Think only in Greek,
And subsist, as the Bears do, by sucking their paws.
   Astonished I am   The gay Baron Geramb
With his head sav'ring more of the Lion than Lamb
Could e'er be persuaded to join such a set—I
Extend the remark to Signor Ambrogetti.—
For a Monk of La Trappe is as thin as a rat,
While an Austin Friar was jolly and fat;
Though, of course, the fare to which I allude,
With as good table beer as ever was brewed,
Was all "caviare to the multitude,"
Extending alone to the clergy, together in
Hall assembled, and not to Lay-brethren.
St. Dunstan himself sits there at his post,
   On what they say is   Called a Dais,
O'erlooking the whole of his clerical host,
And eating poached eggs with spinach and toast;

Five Lay-brothers stand behind his chair,
But where is the sixth?—Where's Peter?—Ay, WHERE?

'Tis an evening in June,   And a little half moon,
A brighter no fond lover ever set eyes on
        Gleaming and beaming,   And dancing the stream in,
Has made her appearance above the horizon;
Just such a half moon as you see, in a play,
On the turban of Mustapha Mulcy Bey,
Or the fair Turk who weds with the "Noble Lord Bateman;"
—*Vide* plate in George Cruikshanks' memoirs of that great
        man.
She shines on a turret remote and lone,.
A turret with ivy and moss overgrown,
And lichens that thrive on the cold dank stone;
Such a tower as a poet of no mean *calibre*
I once knew and loved, poor, dear Reginald Heber,
Assigns to oblivion*—a den for a She-Bear;
        Within it are found,   Strewed above and around,
On the hearth, on the table, the shelves, and the ground,
All sorts of instruments, all sorts of tools,
To name which, and their uses, would puzzle the Schools,
And make very wise people look very like fools;
        Pincers and hooks,   And black-letter books,
All sorts of pokers and all sorts of tongs,
And all sorts of hammers, and all that belongs
To Goldsmiths' work, chemistry, alchemy,—all,
        In short, that a Sage,   In that erudite age,
Could require, was at hand, or at least within call.
In the midst of the room lies a Broomstick!—and there
A Lay-brother sits in a rush-bottomed chair!

Abracadabra, that fearful word,
And the two which, I said, I have never yet heard,
        Are uttered.—'Tis done!   Peter, full of his fun,
Cries, "Broomstick! you lubberly son of a gun!

---

* And cold oblivion, 'midst the ruin laid,
Folds her dank wing beneath the ivy shade.
                                        Palestine.

Bring ale!—bring a flagon—a hogshead—a tun!
'Tis the same thing to you; I have nothing to do;
And, 'fore George, I'll sit here, and I'll drink till all's blue!"

No doubt you've remarked how uncommonly quick
A Newfoundland puppy runs after a stick,
Brings it back to his master, and gives it him—Well,
   So potent the spell,
The Broomstick perceived it was vain to rebel,
So ran off like that puppy;—some cellar was near,
For in less than ten seconds 'twas back with the beer!
Peter seizes the flagon; but ere he can suck
Its contents, or enjoy what he thinks his good luck,
The Broomstick comes in with a tub in a truck;
  Continues to run   At the rate it begun,
And, *au pied de lettre*, next brings in a tun;
A fresh one succeeds, then a third, then another,
Discomfiting much the astounded Lay-brother;
Who, had he possessed fifty pitchers or stoups,
They all had been too few; for, arranging in groups
The barrels, the Broomstick next *started the hoops:*
  The ale deluged the floor,   But still, through the door,
Said Broomstick kept bolting, and bringing in more.
  E'en Macbeth to Macduff
  Would have cried "Hold! enough!"
If half as well drenched with such "perilous stuff,"
And Peter, who did not expect such a rough visit,
Cried lustily, "Stop!—That will do, Broomstick!—*Sufficit!*"

  But ah, well-a-day! The Devil, they say,
'Tis easier at all times to raise than to lay.
  Again and again   Peter roared out in vain
His Abracadabra, and t'other words twain:—
  As well might one try   A pack in full cry
To check, and call off from their headlong career,
By bawling out "Yoicks!" with one's hand at one's ear.
The longer he roared and the louder and quicker,
The faster the Broomstick was bringing in liquor.

The poor Lay-brother knew   Not on earth what to do—
He caught hold of the Broomstick and snapt it in two.—
    Worse and worse!—like a dart,   Each part made a
      start,
And he found he'd been adding more fuel to fire,
For *both* now came loaded with Meux's entire;
Combe's, Delafield's, Hanbury's, Truman's—no stopping—
Goding's, Charrington's, Whitbread's, continued to drop in,
With Hodson's pale ale, from the Sun Brewhouse, Wapping.
The firms differed then, but I can't put a tax on
My memory to say what their names were in Saxon.
    To be sure the best beer   Of all did not appear;
For I've said 'twas in June, and so late in the year
The "Trinity Audit Ale" is not come-at-able,
—As I've found to my great grief when dining at that table.

Now extremely alarmed, Peter screamed without ceasing,
For a flood of brown stout he was up to his knees in,
Which, thanks to the Broomstick, continued increasing;
    He feared he'd be drowned,   And he yelled till the
      sound
Of his voice, winged by terror, at last reached the ear
Of St. Dunstan himself, who had finished *his* beer,
And had put off his mitre, dalmatic, and shoes,
And was just stepping into his bed for a snooze.

His Holiness paused when he heard such a clatter;
He could not conceive what on earth was the matter.
Slipping on a few things, for the sake of decorum,
He issued forthwith from his *Sanctum sanctorum*,
And calling a few of the Lay-brothers near him,
Who were not yet in bed, and who happened to hear him,
    At once led the way,   Without further delay,
To the tower where he'd been in the course of the day.

Poor Peter!—alas! though St. Dunstan was quick,
There were two there before him—Grim Death and Old Nick!—

When they opened the door out the malt-liquor flowed,
Just as when the great Vat burst in Tott'n'am Court Road;
The Lay-brothers nearest were up to their necks
In an instant, and swimming in strong double X;
While Peter, who, spite of himself, now had drunk hard,
After floating awhile, like a toast in a tankard,
    To the bottom had sunk,   And was spied by a monk,
Stone-dead, like poor Clarence, half drowned and half drunk.

In vain did St. Dunstan exclaim, "*Vade retro
Strongbeerum!—discede a Lay-fratre Petro!*"
    Queer Latin, you'll say,   That prefix of "*Lay*,"
And *Strongbeerum!*—I own they'd have called me a block-
    head if
At school I had ventured to use such a Vocative;
'Tis a barbarous word, and to me it's a query
If you'll find it in Patrick, Morell, or Moreri;
But the fact is, the Saint was uncommonly flurried,
And apt to be loose in his Latin when hurried;
The brown-stout, however, obeys to the letter,
Quite as well as if talked to, in Latin much better,
    By a grave Cambridge Johnian,   Or graver Oxonian,
Whose language, we all know, is quite Ciceronian.
It retires from the corpse, which is left high and dry;
But in vain do they snuff and hot towels apply,
And other means used by the faculty try,
    When once a man's dead   There's no more to be
    said;
Peter's " Beer with an *e* " was his " Bier with an *i!*"

MORAL.

By way of a moral permit me to pop in
The following maxims :—Beware of eaves-dropping!—
Don't make use of language that isn't well scanned!—
Don't meddle with matters you don't understand!—
Above all, what I'd wish to impress on both sexes
Is,—Keep clear of Broomsticks, Old Nick, and three XXX's.
  12

L'Envoye.

In Goldsmiths' Hall there's a handsome glass case,
And in it a stone figure, found on the place.
When, thinking the old Hall no longer a pleasant one,
They pulled it all down, and erected the present one.
If you look, you'll perceive that this stone figure twists
A thing like a broomstick in one of its fists.
It's so injured by time, you can't make out a feature;
But it is not St. Dunstan,—so doubtless it's Peter.

GENGULPHUS, or, as he is usually styled in this country,
"Jingo," was perhaps more in the mouths of the "general"
than any other Saint, on occasions of adjuration (see note, page
169). Mr. Simpkinson from Bath has kindly transmitted me
a portion of a primitive ballad, which has escaped the researches
of Ritson and Ellis, but is yet replete with beauties of no common order. I am happy to say that, since these Legends first
appeared, I have recovered the whole of it. *Vide infra.*

"A Franklyn's dogge lepèd ober a style,
And hys name was littel Byngo.
B with a Y—Y with an N—
N with a G—G with an O,
They callèd hym littel Byngo!

Thys Franklyn, Syrs, he brewèd goode ayle,
And he callèd it Rare goode Styngo!
S, T, Y, N, G, O!
He callèd it Rare goode Styngo!

Nowe is notte thys a prettie song?
I thinke it is, bye Jyngo!
I wythe a Y—N, G, O—
I sweare yt is, bye Jyngo!"

𝕬 𝕷𝖆𝖞 𝖔𝖋 𝕾𝖙. 𝕲𝖊𝖓𝖌𝖚𝖑𝖕𝖍𝖚𝖘.

"Non multo post, Gengulphus, in domo suâ dormiens, occisus est à quodam clerico
qui cum uxore suâ adulterare solebat. Cujus corpus dum, in fereto, in sepulturam
portaretur, multi infirmi de tactu sanati sunt."

"Cum hoc illius uxori referretur ab ancillâ sua, scilicet dominum suum, quam mar-
tyrem sanctum, miracula facere, irridens illa, et subsurrans, ait, 'Ita Gengulphus
miracula facitat ut pulvinarium meum cantat,'" etc., etc.—*Wolfii Memorab.*

G ENGULPHUS comes from the Holy Land,
     With his scrip, and his bottle, and sandal shoon;
Full many a day hath he been away,
     Yet his lady deems him returned full soon.

Full many a day hath he been away,
     Yet scarce had he crossed ayont the sea,
Ere a spruce young spark of a Learned Clerk
     Had called on his Lady, and stopped to tea.

This spruce young guest, so trimly drest,
     Stayed with that Lady, her revels to crown;
They laughed, and they ate and they drank of the best,
     And they turned the old castle quite upside down.

They would walk in the park, that spruce young Clerk,
     With that frolicsome Lady so frank and free,
Trying balls and plays, and all manner of ways,
     To get rid of what French people called *Ennui*.

———

Now the festive board with viands is stored,
     Savory dishes be there, I ween,
Rich puddings and big, a barbecued pig,
     And ox-tail soup in a China tureen.

There's a flagon of ale as large as a pail—
     When, cockle on hat, and staff in hand,
While on nought they are thinking save eating and drinking,
     Gengulphus walks in from the Holy Land!

" You must be pretty deep to catch weasels asleep,"
  Says the proverb: that is, "take the Fair unawares;"
A maid o'er the banisters chancing to peep,
  Whispers, " Ma'am, here's Gengulphus a-coming up stairs."

Pig, pudding, and soup, the electrified group,
  With the flagon, pop under the sofa in haste,
And contrive to deposit the Clerk in the closet,
  As the dish least of all to Gengulphus's taste.

Then oh! what rapture, what joy was exprest,
  When "poor dear Gengulphus" at last appeared!
She kissed and she pressed "the dear man" to her breast,
  In spite of his great, long, frizzly beard.

Such hugging and squeezing! 'twas almost unpleasing,
  A smile on her lip, and a tear in her eye;*
She was so very glad that she seemed half mad,
  And did not know whether to laugh or to cry.

Then she calls up the maid, and the table-cloth's laid,
  And she sends for a pint of the best Brown Stout;
On the fire, too, she pops some nice mutton-chops,
  And she mixes a stiff glass of "Cold Without."

Then again she began at the "poor dear" man ;
  She pressed him to drink, and she pressed him to eat,
And she brought a foot-pan, with hot water and bran,
  To comfort his "poor dear" travel-worn feet.

" Nor night nor day since he'd been away,
  Had she had any rest," she " vowed and declared ;"
She "never could eat one morsel of meat,
  For thinking how 'poor dear' Gengulphus fared."

She " really did think she had not slept a wink
  Since he left her, although he'd been absent so long;"
He here shook his head,—right little he said,
  But he thought she was "coming it rather too strong."

_____

* Ενι δακρυσι γελασασα.—HOM.

Now his palate she tickles with the chops and the pickles
    Till, so great the effect of that stiff gin grog,
His weakened body, subdued by the toddy,
    Falls out of the chair, and he lies like a log.

Then out comes the Clerk from his secret lair;
    He lifts up the legs, and she lifts up the head,
And, between them, this most reprehensible pair
    Undress poor Gengulphus and put him to bed.

Then the bolster they place athwart his face,
    And his nightcap into his mouth they cram;
And she pinches his nose underneath the clothes,
    Till the "poor dear soul" goes off like a lamb.

And now they tried the deed to hide;
    For a little bird whispered, "Perchance you may swing;
Here's a corpse in the case with a sad swelled face,
    And a Medical Crowner's a queer sort of thing!"

So the Clerk and wife, they each took a knife,
    And the nippers that nipped the loaf-sugar for tea;
With the edges and points they severed the joints
    At the clavicle, elbow, hip, ankle, and knee.

Thus limb from limb they dismembered him
    So entirely, that e'en when they came to his wrists,
With those great sugar-nippers they nipped off his "flippers,"
    As the Clerk, very flippantly, termed his fists.

When they'd cut off his head, entertaining a dread
    Lest folks should remember Gengulphus's face,
They determined to throw it where no one could know it,
    Down the well,—and the limbs in some different place.

But first the long beard from the chin they sheared,
    And managed to stuff that sanctified hair,
With a good deal of pushing, all into the cushion
    That filled up the seat of a large arm-chair.

They contrived to pack up the trunk in a sack,
  Which they hid in an osier-bed outside the town,
The Clerk bearing arms, legs, and all on his back,
  As that vile Mr. Greenacre served Mrs. Brown.

But to see now how strangely things sometimes turn out,
  And that in a manner the least expected!
Who could surmise a man ever could rise
  Who'd been thus carbonadoed, cut up, and dissected?

No doubt 'twould surprise the pupils at Guy's;
  I am no unbeliever—no man can say that o' me—
But St. Thomas himself would scarce trust his own eyes
  If he saw such a thing in his School of Anatomy.

You may deal as you please with Hindoos and Chinese,
  Or a Mussulman making his heathen *salaam,* or
A Jew or a Turk, but it's other guess work
  When a man has to do with a Pilgrim or Palmer.

By chance the Prince Bishop, a Royal Divine,
  Sends his cards round the neighborhood next day, and urges his
Wish to receive a snug party to dine
  Of the resident clergy, the gentry, and burgesses.

At a quarter past five they are all alive
  At the palace, for coaches are fast rolling in;
And to every guest his card had expressed
  "Half-past" as the hour for a "greasy chin."

Some thirty are seated, and handsomely treated
  With the choicest Rhine wines in his Highness's stock,
When a Count of the Empire, who felt himself heated,
  Requested some water to mix with his Hock.

The Butler, who saw it, sent a maid out to draw it,
  But scarce had she given the windlass a twirl,
Ere Gengulphus's head, from the well's bottom, said
  In mild accents, "Do help us out, that's a good girl!"

Only fancy her dread when she saw a great head
  In her bucket;—with fright she was ready to drop:—
Conceive, if you can, how she roared and she ran,
  With the head rolling after her, bawling out "Stop!"

She ran and she roared, till she came to the board
  Where the Prince Bishop sat with his party around,
When Gengulphus's poll, which continued to roll
  At her heels, on the table bounced up with a bound.

Never touching the cates, or the dishes or plates,
  The decanters or glasses, the sweetmeats or fruits,
The head smiles, and begs them to bring him his legs,
  As a well-spoken gentleman asks for his boots.

Kicking open the casement, to each one's amazement,
  Straight a right leg steps in, all impediment scorns,
And near the head stopping, a left follows hopping
  Behind,—for the left leg was troubled with corns.

Next, before the beholders, two great brawny shoulders,
  And arms on their bent elbows, dance through the throng,
While two hands assist, though nipped off at the wrist,
  The said shoulders in bearing a body along.

They march up to the head, not one syllable said,
  For the thirty guests all stare in wonder and doubt,
As the limbs in their sight arrange and unite,
  Till Gengulphus, though dead, looks as sound as a trout.

I will venture to say, from that hour to this day,
  Ne'er did such an assembly behold such a scene;
Or a table divide fifteen guests of a side
  With a dead body placed in the centre between.

Yes, they stared—well they might at so novel a sight:
  No one uttered a whisper, a sneeze, or a hem,
But sat all bolt upright, and pale with affright;
  And they gazed at the dead man, the dead man at them.

The Prince Bishop's Jester, on punning intent,
　As he viewed the whole thirty, in jocular terms
Said, " They put him in mind of a Council of *Trente*
　Engaged in reviewing the Diet of Worms."

But what should they do?—Oh! nobody knew
　What was best to be done, either stranger or resident ;
The Chancellor's self read his Puffendorf through
　In vain, for his books could not furnish a precedent.

The Prince Bishop muttered a curse, and a prayer,
　Which his double capacity hit to a nicety ;
His Princely, or Lay, half induced him to swear,
　His Episcopal moiety said "*Benedicite!*"

The Coroner sat on the body that night,
　And the jury agreed,—not a doubt could they harbor,—
" That the chin of the corpse—the sole thing brought to light—
　Had been recently shaved by a very bad barber."

They sent out Von Taünsend, Von Bürnie, Von Roe,
　Von Maine, and Von Rowantz—through châlets and châteaux,
Towns, villages, hamlets, they told them to go,
　And they stuck up placards on the walls of the Stadthaus.

"MURDER!!

" WHEREAS, a dead gentleman, surname unknown,
　Has been recently found at his Highness's banquet,
Rather shabbily drest in an Amice, or gown,
　In appearance resembling a second-hand blanket ;

" And WHEREAS, there's great reason indeed to suspect
　That some ill-disposed person, or persons, with malice
Aforethought, have killed, and begun to dissect
　The said Gentleman, not very far from the palace ;

" THIS IS TO GIVE NOTICE!—Whoever shall seize,
　And such person, or persons, to justice surrender,
Shall receive—such REWARD—as his Highness shall please,
　On conviction of him, the aforesaid offender.

"And, in order the matter more clearly to trace
  To the bottom, his Highness, the Prince Bishop, further,
Of his clemency, offers free PARDON and Grace
  To all such as have *not* been concerned in the murther.

" Done this day, at our palace,—July twenty-five,—
  By command,
              (Signed)
                      Johann Von Rüssell.
      N. B.
Deceased rather in years—had a squint when alive;
  And smells slightly of gin—linen mark'd with a G."

The Newspapers, too, made no little ado,
  Though a different version each managed to dish up;
Some said, " The Prince Bishop had run a man through,"
  Others said, " An assassin had killed the Prince Bishop."

The "Ghent Herald" fell foul of the " Bruxelles Gazette,"
  The " Bruxelles Gazette," with much sneering ironical,
Scorned to remain in the "Ghent Herald's" debt,
  And the "Amsterdam Times" quizzed the "Nuremberg
      Chronicle."

In one thing, indeed, all the journals agreed,
  Spite of " politics," " bias," or " party collision ;"
Viz.: to " give," when they'd "further accounts" of the deed,
  " Full particulars" soon, in " a later Edition."

But now, while on all sides they rode and they ran,
  Trying all sorts of means to discover the caitiffs,
Losing patience, the holy Gengulphus began
  To think it high time to " astonish the natives."

First, a Rittmeister's Frau, who was weak in both eyes,
  And supposed the most short-sighted woman in Holland,
Found greater relief, to her joy and surprise,
  From one glimpse of his "squint" than from glasses by Dollond.

By the slightest approach to the tip of his nose,
  Megrims, headache, and vapors were put to the rout;

And one single touch of his precious great toes
  Was a certain specific for chilblains and gout.

Rheumatics,—sciatica,—tic-douloureux!
  Apply to his shin-bones—not one of them lingers;—
All bilious complaints in an instant withdrew
  If the patient was tickled with one of his fingers.

Much virtue was found to reside in his thumbs;
  When applied to the chest they cured scantness of breathing,
Sea-sickness, and colic; or, rubbed on the gums,
  Were "A blessing to Mothers," for infants in teething.

Whoever saluted the nape of his neck,
  Where the mark remained visible still of the knife,
Notwithstanding east winds perspiration might check,
  Was safe from sore throat for the rest of his life.

Thus, while each acute and each chronic complaint
  Giving way, proved an influence clearly divine,
They perceived the dead gentleman must be a Saint,
  So they locked him up, body and bones, in a shrine.

Through country and town his new Saintship's renown
  As a first-rate physician kept daily increasing,
Till, as Alderman Curtis told Alderman Brown,
  It seemed as if "wonders had never *done ceasing.*"

The Three Kings of Cologne began, it was known,
  A sad falling off in their off'rings to find,
His feats were so many—still the greatest of any,
  In every sense of the word, was—behind;

For the German Police were beginning to cease
  From exertions which each day more fruitless appeared,
When Gengulphus himself, his fame still to increase,
  Unravelled the whole by the help of—his beard!

If you look back you'll see the aforesaid *barbe gris,*
  When divorced from the chin of its murdered proprietor,
Had been stuffed in the seat of a kind of settee,
  Or double-armed chair, to keep the thing quieter.

It may seem rather strange that it did not arrange
  Itself in its place when the limbs joined together;
P'rhaps it could not get out, for the cushion was stout,
  And constructed of good, strong, maroon-colored leather.

Or, what is more likely, Gengulphus might choose,—
  For Saints, e'en when dead, still retain their volition,—
It should rest there, to aid some particular views
  Produced by his very peculiar position.

Be that as it may, on the very first day
  That the widow Gengulphus sat down on that settee,
What occurred almost frightened her senses away,
  Beside scaring her handmaidens, Gertrude and Betty.

They were telling their mistress the wonderful deeds
  Of the new Saint, to whom all the Town said their orisons:
And especially how, as regards invalids,
  His miraculous cures far outrivalled Von Morison's.

"The cripples," said they, "fling their crutches away,
  And people born blind now can easily see us!"—
But she (we presume a disciple of Hume)
  Shook her head, and said angrily, "*Credat Judæus!*

"Those rascally liars, the Monks and the Friars,
  To bring grist to their mill these devices have hit on.—
He works miracles! pooh!—I'd believe it of you
  Just as soon, you great Geese,—or the Chair that I sit on!"

The Chair!—At that word,—it seems really absurd,
  But the truth must be told,—what contortions and grins
Distorted her face!—she sprang up from her place
  Just as though she'd been sitting on needles and pins!

For, as if the Saint's beard the rash challenge had heard
  Which she uttered, of what was beneath her forgetful,
Each particular hair stood on end in the chair,
  Like a porcupine's quills when the animal's fretful.

That stout maroon leather they pierced altogether,
    Like tenter-hooks holding when clenched from within;
And the maids cried, "Good gracious! how very tenacious!"
    —They as well might endeavor to pull off her skin!

She shrieked with the pain, but all efforts were vain;
    In vain did they strain every sinew and muscle,—
The cushion stuck fast!—From that hour to her last,
    She could never get rid of that comfortless "Bustle"!

And e'en as Macbeth, when devising the death
    Of his King, heard "the very stones prate of his whereabouts,"
So this shocking bad wife heard a voice all her life
    Crying "Murder!" resound from the cushion—or thereabouts.

With regard to the Clerk, we are left in the dark
    As to what his fate was; but I cannot imagine he
Got off scot-free, though unnoticed it be
    Both by Ribadaneira and Jacques de Voragine;

For cut-throats, we're sure, can be never secure,
    And "History's Muse" still to prove it her pen holds,
As you'll see if you look in a rather scarce book,
    "*God's Revenge against Murder,*" by one Mr. Reynolds.

MORAL.

Now, you grave married Pilgrims, who wander away,
    Like Ulysses of old* (*vide* Homer and Naso),
Don't lengthen your stay to three years and a day,
    And when you *are* coming home, just write and say so!

And you, learned Clerks, who're *not* given to roam,
    Stick close to your books, nor lose sight of decorum;
Don't visit a house when the master's from home!
    Shun drinking,—and study the "*Vitæ Sanctorum.*"

Above all, you gay ladies, who fancy neglect
    In your spouses, allow not your patience to fail;
But remember Gengulphus's wife! and reflect
    On the moral enforced by my terrible tale!

---

* Qui mores Hominum multorum vidit et urbes.

MR. BARNEY MAGUIRE has laid claim to the next Saint as a countrywoman ; and " Why wouldn't he," when all the world knows the O'Dells were a fine ould ancient family, sated in Tipperary

> " Ere the Lord Mayor stole his collar of gowld,
> And sowld it away to a trader"?*

He is manifestly wrong ; but, as he very rationally observes, " No matter for that,—she's a Saint any way !"

The Lay of St. Odille.

ODILLE was a maid of a dignified race :
   Her father, Count Otto, was lord of Alsace ;
     Such an air, such a grace, Such a form, such a face,
All agreed, 'twere a fruitless endeavor to trace
In the Court, or within fifty miles of the place.
Many ladies in Strasburg were beautiful, still
They were beat all to sticks by the lovely Odille.

But Odille was devout, and, before she was nine,
Had " experienced a call " she considered divine,
To put on the veil at St. Ermengarde's shrine.—
Lords, Dukes, and Electors, and Counts Palatine,
Came to seek her in marriage from both sides the Rhine ;
     But vain their design, They are all left to pine,
Their oglings and smiles are all useless ; in fine,
Not one of these gentlefolks, try as they will,
Can draw " Ask my papa " from the cruel Odille.

At length one of her suitors, a certain Count Herman,
A highly respectable man as a German,
Who smoked like a chimney, and drank like a Merman,
Paid his court to her father, conceiving his firman

---

* The " Inglorious Memory " of this ould ancient transaction is still, we understand, kept up in Dublin by an annual proclamation at one of the city gates. The jewel which has replaced the abstracted ornament is said to have been presented by King William, and worn by Daniel O'Connell, Esq.

Would soon make her bend,   And induce her to lend
An ear to a love-tale in lieu of a sermon.
He gained the old Count, who said, " Come, Mynheer, fill !—
Here's luck to yourself and my daughter Odille !"

The Lady Odille was quite nervous with fear
When a little bird whispered that toast in her ear ;
She murmured, " Oh dear ! my Papa has got queer,
I am sadly afraid, with that nasty strong beer !
He's so very austere, and severe, that it's clear,
If he gets in his 'tantrums,' I can't remain here ;
But St. Ermengarde's convent is luckily near :
    It were folly to stay   *Pour prendre congé,*
I shall put on my bonnet and e'en run away !"
—She unlocked the back door and descended the hill,
On whose crest stood the towers of the sire of Odille.

—When he found she'd levanted, the Count of Alsace
At first turned remarkably red in the face ;
He anathematized, with much unction and grace,
Every soul who came near, and consigned the whole race
Of runaway girls to a very warm place ;
    With a frightful grimace   He gave orders for chase ;
His vassals set off at a deuce of a pace,
And of all whom they met, high or low, Jack or Jill,
Asked, " Pray have you seen anything of Lady Odille ?"

Now I think I've been told,—for I'm no sporting man,—
That the " knowing ones" call this by far the best plan,
" Take the lead and then keep it !"—that is, if you can.—
Odille thought so too, so she set off and ran,
    Put her best leg before,   Starting at score,
As I said some lines since, from that little back door,
And, not being missed until half after four,
Had what hunters call " law" for a good hour and more ;
    Doing her best,   Without stopping to rest,
Like " Young Lochinvar who came out of the West."
" 'Tis done !—I am gone !—over briar, brook, and rill,
They'll be sharp lads who catch me !" said young Miss Odille.

But you've all read in Æsop, or Phædrus, or Gay,
How a tortoise and hare ran together one day;
    How the hare, making play, "Progressed right slick away,"
As "them tarnation chaps" the Americans say;
While the tortoise, whose figure is rather *outré*
For racing, crawled straight on, without let or stay,
Having no post-horse duty or turnpikes to pay,
    Till, ere noon's ruddy ray   Changed to eve's sober gray,
Though her form and obesity caused some delay,
Perseverance and patience brought up her lee-way,
And she chased her fleet-footed "praycursor" until
She o'ertook her at last;—so it fared with Odille!

For although, as I said, she ran gayly at first,
And showed no inclination to pause, if she durst,
She at length felt opprest with the heat, and with thirst
Its usual attendant; nor was that the worst,—
Her shoes went down at heel; at last one of them burst.
    Now a gentleman smiles   At a trot of ten miles;
But not so the Fair; then consider the stiles,
And as then ladies seldom wore things with a frill
Round the ankle, these stiles sadly bothered Odille.

Still, despite all the obstacles placed in her track,
She kept steadily on, though the terrible crack
In her shoe made of course her progression more slack,
Till she reached the Swartz Forest (in English the Black);
    I cannot divine   How the boundary line
Was passed which is somewhere there formed by the Rhine—
    Perhaps she'd the knack   To float o'er on her back—
Or, perhaps, cross'd the old bridge of boats at Brisach
(Which Vauban, some years after, secured from attack
By a bastion of stone which the Germans call "Wacke");
All I know is, she took not so much as a snack,
Till, hungry and worn, feeling wretchedly ill,
On a mountain's brow sank down the weary Odille.

I said on its "brow," but I should have said "crown,"
For 'twas quite on the summit, bleak, barren, and brown,

And so high that 'twas frightful indeed to look down
Upon Friburg, a place of some little renown,
That lay at its foot; but imagine the frown
That contracted her brow, when full many a clown
She perceived coming up from that horrid post-town.
    They had followed her trail,
    And now thought without fail,
As little boys say, to "lay salt on her tail;"
While the Count, who knew no other law but his will,
Swore that Herman that evening should marry Odille.

Alas, for Odille! poor dear! what could she do?
Her father's retainers now had her in view,
As she found from their raising a joyous halloo;
While the Count, riding on at the head of his crew,
In their snuff-colored doublets and breeches of blue,
Was huzzaing and urging them on to pursue—
    What, indeed, *could* she do?   She very well know
If they caught her how much she should have to go through;
But then—she'd so shocking a hole in her shoe!
And to go further on was impossible;—true
She might jump o'er the precipice;—still there are few,
In her place, who could manage their courage to screw
Up to bidding the world such a sudden adieu:—
Alack! how she envied the birds as they flew;
No Nassau balloon, with its wicker canoe,
Came to bear her from him she loathed worse than a Jew;
So she fell on her knees in a terrible stew,
    Crying, "Holy St. Ermengarde!
    Oh, from these vermin guard
Her whose last hope rests entirely on you;—
Don't let papa catch me, dear Saint!—rather kill
At once, *sur-le-champ*, your devoted Odille!"

It's delightful to see those who strive to oppress
Get balked when they think themselves sure of success.
The Saint came to the rescue!—I fairly confess
I don't see, as a Saint, how she well could do less

Than to get such a votary out of her mess.
Odille had scarce closed her pathetic address
When the rock, gaping wide as the Thames at Sheerness,
Closed again, and secured her within its recess

    In a natural grotto,   Which puzzled Count Otto,
Who could not conceive where the deuce she had got to.
'Twas her voice!—but 'twas *Vox et præterea Nil!*
Nor could any one guess what was gone with Odille!

Then burst from the mountain a splendor that quite
Eclipsed, in its brilliance, the finest Bude light,
And there stood St. Ermengarde, drest all in white,
A palm-branch in her left hand, her beads in her right;
While, with faces fresh gilt, and with wings burnished bright,
A great many little boys' heads took their flight
Above and around to a very great height,
And seemed pretty lively considering their plight,
    Since every one saw,   With amazement and awe,
They could never sit down, for they hadn't *de quoi.*—
    All at the sight,   From the knave to the knight,
Felt a very unpleasant sensation, called fright;
    While the Saint, looking down   With a terrible frown,
Said, "My Lords, you are done most remarkably brown!—
I am really ashamed of you both;—my nerves thrill
At your scandalous conduct to poor dear Odille!

"Come, make yourselves scarce!—it is useless to stay,
You will gain nothing here by a longer delay.
'Quick! Presto! Begone!' as the conjurers say;
For as to the lady, I've stowed her away
In this hill, in a stratum of London blue clay;
And I shan't, I assure you, restore her to-day
Till you faithfully promise no more to say 'Nay,'
But declare, 'if she will be a nun, why she may.'
For this you've my word, and I never yet broke it!—
So put that in your pipe, my Lord Otto, and smoke it!—
One hint to your vassals,—a month at 'the Mill'
Shall be nuts to what they'll get who worry Odille!"

13

The Saint disappeared as she ended, and so
Did the little boys' heads, which, above and below,
As I told you a very few stanzas ago,
Had been flying about her, and jumping Jim Crow;
Though, without any body, or leg, foot, or toe,
How they managed such antics, I really don't know;
Be that as it may, they all " melted like snow
Off a dyke," as the Scotch say in sweet Edinbro',
   And there stood the Count, With his men, on the mount,
Just like " twenty-four jackasses all on a row."
What was best to be done—'twas a sad bitter pill—
But gulp it he must, or else lose his Odille.

The lord of Alsace therefore altered his plan,
And said to himself, like a sensible man,
" I can't do as I would,—I must do as I can;
It will not do to lie under any Saint's ban,
For your hide, when you do, they all manage to tan;
So Count Herman must pick up some Betsy or Nan,
Instead of my girl,—some Sue, Polly, or Fan;—
If he can't get the corn he must do with the bran,
And make shift with the pot if he can't have the pan."
   With such proverbs as these He went down on his knees,
And said, " Blessed St. Ermengarde, just as you please—
They shall build a new convent,—I'll pay the whole bill
(Taking discount),—its Abbess shall be my Odille."

There are some of my readers, I'll venture to say,
Who have never seen Friburg, though some of them may,
And others, 'tis likely, may go there some day.
Now, if ever you happen to travel that way,
I do beg and pray,—'twill your pains well repay,—
That you'll take what the Cockney folks call a " po-shay"
(Though in Germany these things are more like a dray),
You may reach this same hill with a single relay,—
   And do look how the rock, Through the whole of its block,
Is split open, as though by some violent shock
From an earthquake, or lightning, or horrid hard knock

From the club-bearing fist of some jolly old cock
Of a Germanized giant, Thor, Woden, or Lok;
  And see how it rears   Its two monstrous great cars,
For when once you're between them such each side appears;
And list to the sound of the water one hears
Drip, drip, from the fissures, like raindrops or tears,—
Odille's, I believe,—which have flowed all these years;
—I think they account for them so;—but the rill
I am sure is connected some way with Odille.

MORAL.

Now then for a moral, which always arrives
At the end, like the honey-bees take to their hives,
And the more one observes it the better one thrives,—
We have all heard it said in the course of our lives,
"Needs must when a certain old gentleman drives;"
'Tis the same with a lady,—if once she contrives
To get hold of the ribbons, how vainly one strives
To escape from her lash or to shake off her gyves!
Then let's act like Count Otto, and while one survives,
Succumb to *our* She-Saints—videlicet wives!
  (*Aside.*)
That is, if one has not "a good bunch of fives."—
(I can't think how that last line escaped from my quill,
For I'm sure it has nothing to do with Odille.)
  Now, young ladies, to you:—   Don't put on the shrew!—
And don't be surprised if your father looks blue
When you're pert, and won't act as he wants you to do!
Be sure that you never elope;—there are few,—
Believe me, you'll find what I say to be true,—
Who run restive, but find as they bake they must brew,
And come off at last with "a hole in their shoe;"
Since not even Clapham, that sanctified ville,
Can produce enough saints to save *every* Odille.

Nycolas, epitryn of ye epte* of Pancrats, was borne of ryche and holpe kynne, And his fader was named Epiphanus, and his moder Iohane.

HE was born on a cold frosty morning, on the 6th of December (upon which day his feast is still observed), but in what *anno Domini* is not so clear; his baptismal register, together with that of his friend and colleague, St. Thomas at Hill, having been "lost in the great fire of London."

St. Nicholas was a great patron of Mariners, and,—saving your presence,—of Thieves also, which honorable fraternity have long rejoiced in the appellation of his "Clerks." Cervantes's story of Sancho's detecting a sum of money in a swindler's walking-stick is merely a Spanish version of a "Lay of St. Nicholas" extant "in choice Italian" a century before honest Miguel was born.

A Lay of St. Nicholas.

"Statim sacerdoti apparuit diabolus in specie puellæ pulchritudinis miræ, et ecce Divus, fide catholicâ, et cruce, et aquâ benedicta armatus venit, et aspersit aquam in nomine Sanctæ et Individuæ Trinitatis, quam, quasi ardentem, diabolus, nequaquam sustinere valens, mugitibus fugit."—ROGER HOVEDEN.

"LORD Abbot! Lord Abbot! I'd fain confess;
    I am a-weary, and worn with woe;
Many a grief doth my heart oppress,
    And haunt me whithersoever I go!"

On bended knee spake the beautiful Maid:
    "Now lithe and listen, Lord Abbot, to me!"—
"Now naye, Fair Daughter," the Lord Abbot said,
    "Now naye, in sooth it may hardly be.

"There is Mess Michael, and holy Mess John,
    Sage Penitauncers I ween be they!
And hard by doth dwell, in St. Catherine's cell,
    Ambrose, the Anchoret old and gray!"

* Parish.

—" Oh, I will have none of Ambrose or John,
  Though sage Penitauncers I trow they be;
Shrive me may none save the Abbot alone,
  Now listen, Lord Abbot, I speak to thee.

" Nor think foul scorn, though mitre adorn
  Thy brow, to listen to shrift of mine!
I am a Maiden royally born,
  And I come of old Plantagenet's line.

" Though hither I stray in lowly array,
  I am a damsel of high degree;
And the Compte of Eu, and the Lord of Ponthieu,
  They serve my father on bended knee!

" Counts a many, and Dukes a few,
  A suitoring came to my father's Hall;
But the Duke of Lorraine, with his large domain,
  He pleased my father beyond them all.

" Dukes a many, and Counts a few,
  I would have wedded right cheerfullie;
But the Duke of Lorraine was uncommonly plain,
  And I vow'd that he ne'er should my bridegroom be!

" So hither I fly, in lowly guise,
  From their gilded domes and their princely halls;
Fain would I dwell in some holy cell,
  Or within some Convent's peaceful walls!"

—Then out and spake that proud Lord Abbot,
  " Now rest thee, Fair Daughter, withouten fear,
Nor Count nor Duke but shall meet the rebuke
  Of Holy Church an he seek thee here:

" Holy Church denieth all search
  'Midst her sanctified ewes and her saintly rams,
And the wolves doth mock who would scathe her flock,
  Or, especially, worry her little pet lambs.

"Then lay, Fair Daughter, thy fears aside,
  For here this day shalt thou dine with me!"—
"Now naye, now naye," the fair maiden cried;
  "In sooth, Lord Abbot, that scarce may be!

"Friends would whisper, and foes would frown,
  Sith thou art a Churchman of high degree,
And ill mote it match with thy fair renown
  That a wandering damsel dine with thee!

"There is Simon the Deacon hath pulse in store,
  With beans and lettuces fair to see;
His lenten fare now let me share,
  I pray thee, Lord Abbot, in charitie!"

—"Though Simon the Deacon hath pulse in store,
  To our patron Saint foul shame it were
Should wayworn guest, with toil oppressed,
  Meet in his Abbey such churlish fare.

"There is Peter the Prior, and Francis the Friar,
  And Roger the Monk shall our convives be;
Small scandal I ween shall then be seen;
  They are a goodly companie!"

The Abbot hath donned his mitre and ring,
  His rich dalmatic, and maniple fine;
And the choristers sing, as the lay-brothers bring
  To the board a magnificent turkey and chine.

The turkey and chine, they are done to a nicety;
  Liver, and gizzard, and all are there;
Ne'er mote Lord Abbot pronounce *Benedicite*
  Over more luscious or delicate fare.

But no pious stave, no *Pater* or *Ave*,
  Pronounced, as he gazed on that maiden's face;
She asked him for stuffing, she asked him for gravy,
  She asked him for gizzard;—but not for Grace!

Yet gayly the Lord Abbot smiled, and pressed,
    And the blood-red wine in the wine-cup filled ;
And he helped his guest to a bit of the breast,
    And he sent the drumsticks down to be grilled.

There was no lack of old Sherris sack,
    Of Hippocras fine, or of Malmsey bright ;
And aye, as he drained off his cup with a smack,
    He grew less pious and more polite.

She pledged him once, and she pledged him twice,
    And she drank as Lady ought not to drink ;
And he pressed her hand 'neath the table thrice,
    And he winked as Abbot ought not to wink.

And Peter the Prior, and Francis the Friar,
    Sat each with a napkin under his chin ;
But Roger the Monk got excessively drunk,
    So they put him to bed, and they tucked him in !

The lay-brothers gazed on each other, amazed ;
    And Simon the Deacon, with grief and surprise,
As he peeped through the keyhole, could scarce fancy real
    The scene he beheld, or believe his own eyes.

In his ear was ringing the Lord Abbot singing,—
    He could not distinguish the words very plain,
But 'twas all about " Cole," and " jolly old Soul,"
    And " Fiddlers," and " Punch," and things quite as profane.

Even Porter Paul, at the sound of such revelling,
    With fervor himself began to bless ;
For he thought he must somehow have let the Devil in,—
    And perhaps was not very much out in his guess.

The Accusing Byers* " flew up to Heaven's Chancery,"
    Blushing like scarlet with shame and concern ;
The Archangel took down his tale, and in answer he
    Wept—(See the works of the late Mr. Sterne).

* The Prince of Peripatetic Informers, and terror of Stage Coachmen, when such things were. Alack! alack! the Railroads have ruined his "vested interest."

Indeed, it is said, a less taking both were in
   When, after a lapse of a great many years,
They booked Uncle Toby five shillings for swearing,
   And blotted the fine out again with their tears!

But St. Nicholas' agony who may paint?
   His senses at first were well-nigh gone;
The beatified saint was ready to faint
   When he saw in his Abbey such sad goings on!

For never, I ween, had such doings been seen
   There before, from the time that most excellent Prince,
Earl Baldwin of Flanders, and other Commanders,
   Had built and endowed it some centuries since.

—But hark!—'tis a sound from the outermost gate!
   A startling sound from a powerful blow.—
Who knocks so late?—it is half after eight
   By the clock,—and the clock's five minutes too slow.

Never, perhaps, had such loud double raps
   Been heard in St. Nicholas' Abbey before;
All agreed "it was shocking to keep people knocking,"
   But none seemed inclined to "answer the door."

Now a louder bang through the cloisters rang,
   And the gate on its hinges wide open flew;
And all were aware of a Palmer there,
   With his cockle hat, staff, and his sandal shoe.

Many a furrow and many a frown
   By toil and time on his brow were traced;
And his long loose gown was of ginger brown,
   And his rosary dangled below his waist.

Now seldom, I ween, is such costume seen,
   Except at a stage-play or masquerade;
But who doth not know it was rather the go
   With Pilgrims and Saints in the second Crusade?

With noiseless stride did that Palmer glide
  Across that oaken floor;
And he made them all jump, he gave such a thump
  Against the Refectory door!

Wide open it flew, and plain to the view
  The Lord Abbot they all mote see;
In his hand was a cup, and he lifted it up,
  "Here's the Pope's good health with three!!"

Rang in their ears three deafening cheers,
  "Huzza! huzza! huzza!"
And one of the party said, "Go it, my hearty!"—
  When out spake that Pilgrim gray—

"A boon, Lord Abbot! a boon! a boon!
  Worn is my foot, and empty my scrip;
And nothing to speak of since yesterday noon
  Of food, Lord Abbot, hath passed my lip.

"And I am come from a far countree,
  And have visited many a holy shrine;
And long have I trod the sacred sod
  Where the Saints do rest in Palestine!"—

"An thou art come from a far countree,
  And if thou in Paynim lands hast been,
Now rede me aright the most wonderful sight,
  Thou Palmer gray, that thine eyes have seen.

"Arede me aright the most wonderful sight,
  Gray Palmer, that ever thine eyes did see,
And a manchette of bread, and a good warm bed,
  And a cup o' the best, shall thy guerdon be!"

"Oh! I have been east, and I have been west,
  And I have seen many a wonderful sight;
But never to me did it happen to see
  A wonder like that which I see this night!

"To see a Lord Abbot, in rochet and stole,
　　With Prior and Friar,—a strange mar-velle!—
O'er a jolly full bowl sitting cheek by jowl,
　　And hob-nobbing away with a Devil from Hell!"

He felt in his gown of ginger brown,
　　And he pulled out a flask from beneath;
It was rather tough work to get out the cork,
　　But he drew it at last with his teeth.

O'er a pint and a quarter of holy water,
　　He made a sacred sign;
And he dashed the whole on the *soi-disant* daughter
　　Of old Plantagenet's line!

Oh! then did she reek, and squeak, and shriek,
　　With a wild unearthly scream;
And fizzled, and hissed, and produced such a mist,
　　They were all half choked by the steam.

Her dove-like eyes turned to coals of fire,
　　Her beautiful nose to a horrible snout,
Her hands to paws, with nasty great claws,
　　And her bosom went in, and her tail came out.

On her chin there appeared a long Nanny-goat's beard,
　　And her tusks and her teeth no man mote tell;
And her horns and her hoofs gave infallible proofs
　　'Twas a frightful fiend from the nethermost hell!

The Palmer threw down his ginger gown,
　　His hat and his cockle, and, plain to sight,
Stood St. Nicholas' self, and his shaven crown
　　Had a glow-worm halo of heavenly light.

The fiend made a grasp the Abbot to clasp;
　　But St. Nicholas lifted his holy toe,
And, just in the nick, let fly such a kick
　　On his elderly Namesake, he made him let go.

And out of the window he flew like a shot,
　For the foot flew up with a terrible thwack,
And caught the foul demon about the spot
　Where his tail joins on to the small of his back.

And he bounded away like a foot-ball at play,
　Till into the bottomless pit he fell slap,
Knocking Mammon the meagre o'er pursy Belphegor,
　And Lucifer into Beëlzebub's lap.

Oh! happy the slip from his Succubine grip
　That saved the Lord Abbot—though, breathless with fright,
In escaping he tumbled, and fractured his hip,
　And his left leg was shorter thenceforth than his right!

———

On the banks of the Rhine, as he's stopping to dine,
　From a certain Inn-window the traveller is shown
Most picturesque ruins, the scene of these doings,
　Some miles up the river, southeast of Cologne.

And, while "*sour-kraut*" she sells you, the landlady tells you
　That there, in those walls, now all roofless and bare,
One Simon, a Deacon, from a lean grew a sleek one,
　On filling a *ci-devant* Abbot's state chair.

How a *ci-devant* Abbot, all clothed in drab, but
　Of texture the coarsest, hair shirt, and no shoes
(His mitre and ring, and all that sort of thing,
　Laid aside), in yon Cave lived a pious recluse;

How he rose with the sun, limping "dot and go one"
　To yon rill of the mountain, in all sorts of weather,
Where a Prior and a Friar, who lived somewhat higher
　Up the rock, used to come and eat cresses together;

How a thirsty old codger, the neighbors called Roger,
　With them drank cold water in lieu of old wine!

What its quality wanted he made up in quantity,
    Swigging as though he would empty the Rhine!

And how, as their bodily strength failed, the mental man
    Gained tenfold vigor and force in all four;
And how, to the day of their death, the "Old Gentleman"
    Never attempted to kidnap them more.

And how, when at length, in the odor of sanctity,
    All of them died without grief or complaint,
The Monks of St. Nicholas said 'twas ridiculous
    Not to suppose every one was a Saint.

And how, in the Abbey, no one was so shabby
    As not to say yearly four masses a head,
On the eve of that supper, and kick on the crupper
    Which Satan received, for the souls of the dead!

How folks long held in reverence their reliques and memories,
    How the *ci-devant* Abbot's obtained greater still,
When some cripples, on touching his fractured *os femoris*,
    Threw down their crutches and danced a quadrille!

And how Abbot Simon (who turned out a prime one)
    These words, which grew into a proverb full soon,
O'er the late Abbot's grotto stuck up as a motto,
    "𝔚𝔥𝔬 𝔰𝔲𝔭𝔭𝔢𝔰 𝔴𝔦𝔱𝔥 𝔱𝔥𝔢 𝔇𝔢𝔟𝔦𝔩𝔩𝔢 𝔰𝔥𝔬𝔩𝔡𝔢 𝔥𝔞𝔟𝔢 𝔞 𝔩𝔬𝔫𝔤
    𝔰𝔭𝔬𝔬𝔫𝔢!"

ROHESIA, daughter of Ambrose, and sister to Sir Everard
Ingoldsby, was born about the beginning of the sixteenth century, and was married in 1526, at St. Giles's, Cripplegate, in
the city of London. The following narrative contains all else
that is known of

The Lady Rohesia.

THE Lady Rohesia lay on her death-bed!

So said the doctor, and doctors are generally allowed to be judges in these matters; besides, Doctor Butts was the Court Physician: he carried a crutch-handled staff, with its cross of the blackest ebony—*raison de plus.*

"Is there no hope, Doctor?" said Beatrice Grey.

"Is there no hope?" said Everard Ingoldsby.

"Is there no hope?" said Sir Guy de Montgomeri. He was the Lady Rohesia's husband;—he spoke the last.

The Doctor shook his head. He looked at the disconsolate widower *in posse*, then at the hour-glass; its waning sand seemed sadly to shadow forth the sinking pulse of his patient. Dr. Butts was a very learned man. "*Ars longa, vita brevis!*" said Dr. Butts.

"I am very sorry to hear it," quoth Sir Guy de Montgomeri. Sir Guy was a brave knight, and a tall; but he was no scholar.

"Alas! my poor sister!" sighed Ingoldsby.

"Alas! my poor mistress!" sobbed Beatrice.

Sir Guy neither sighed nor sobbed; his grief was too deep-seated for outward manifestation.

"And how long, Doctor——" The afflicted husband could not finish the sentence.

Dr. Butts withdrew his hand from the wrist of the dying lady. He pointed to the horologe; scarcely a quarter of its sand remained in the upper moiety. Again he shook his head. The eye of the patient waxed dimmer, the rattling in the throat increased.

"What's become of Father Francis?" whimpered Beatrice.

"The last consolations of the church——" suggested Everard.

A darker shade came over the brow of Sir Guy.

"Where *is* the Confessor?" continued his grieving brother-in-law.

"In the pantry," cried Marion Hacket pertly, as she tripped down stairs in search of that venerable ecclesiastic;—"in the pantry, I warrant me." The bower-woman was not wont to be in the wrong: in the pantry was the holy man discovered—at his devotions.

"*Pax vobiscum!*" said Father Francis, as he entered the chamber of death.

"*Vita brevis!*" retorted Dr. Butts. He was not a man to be browbeat out of his Latin,—and by a paltry Friar Minim, too. Had it been a bishop, indeed, or even a mitred abbot;—but a miserable Franciscan!

"*Benedicite!*" said the Friar.

"*Ars longa!*" returned the Leech.

Dr. Butts adjusted the tassels of his falling band, drew his short sad-colored cloak closer around him, and, grasping his cross-handled walking-staff, stalked majestically out of the apartment. Father Francis had the field to himself.

The worthy chaplain hastened to administer the last rites of the church. To all appearance he had little time to lose. As he concluded, the dismal toll of the passing-bell sounded from the belfry tower; little Hubert, the bandy-legged sacristan, was pulling with all his might. It was a capital contrivance, that same passing-bell; which of the Urbans or Innocents invented it is a query; but, whoever he was, he deserved well of his country and of Christendom.

Ah! our ancestors were not such fools, after all, as we, their degenerate children, conceit them to have been. The passing-bell—a most solemn warning to imps of every description—is not to be regarded with impunity; the most impudent *Succubus* of them all dare as well dip his claws in holy water as come within the verge of its sound. Old Nick himself, if he sets any value at all upon his tail, had best convey himself clean out of hearing, and leave the way open to Paradise. Little Hubert continued pulling with all his might—and St. Peter began to look out for a customer.

The knell seemed to have some effect even upon the Lady Rohesia: she raised her head slightly; inarticulate sounds issued from her lips,—inarticulate, that is, to the profane ears of the laity. Those of Father Francis, indeed, were sharper; nothing, as he averred, could be more distinct than the words, "A thousand marks to the priory of St. Mary Rouncival."

Now the Lady Rohesia Ingoldsby had brought her husband

broad lands and large possessions; much of her ample dowry, too, was at her own disposal,—and nuncupative wills had not yet been abolished by act of Parliament.

"Pious soul!" ejaculated Father Francis. "A thousand marks, she said——"

"If she did I'll be shot!" said Sir Guy de Montgomeri.

"—A thousand marks!" continued the Confessor, fixing his cold gray eye upon the knight, as he went on heedless of the interruption;—"a thousand marks! and as many *Aves* and *Paters* shall be duly said—as soon as the money is paid down."

Sir Guy shrank from the monk's gaze; he turned to the window, and muttered to himself something that sounded like "Don't you wish you may get it?"

The bell continued to toll. Father Francis had quitted the room, taking with him the remains of the holy oil he had been using for Extreme Unction. Everard Ingoldsby waited on him down stairs.

"A thousand thanks!" said the latter.

"A thousand marks!" said the friar.

"A thousand devils!" growled Sir Guy de Montgomeri from the top of the landing-place.

But his accents fell unheeded: his brother-in-law and the friar were gone; he was left alone with his departing lady and Beatrice Grey.

Sir Guy de Montgomeri stood pensively at the foot of the bed; his arms were crossed upon his bosom, his chin was sunk upon his breast; his eyes were filled with tears; the dim rays of the fading watchlight gave a darker shade to the furrows on his brow, and a brighter tint to the little bald patch on the top of his head,—for Sir Guy was a middle-aged gentleman, tall and portly withal, with a slight bend in his shoulders, but that not much; his complexion was somewhat florid, especially about the nose; but his lady was *in extremis*, and at this particular moment he was paler than usual.

"Bim! bome!" went the bell. The knight groaned audibly, Beatrice Grey wiped her eye with her little square apron

of lace de Malines; there was a moment's pause—a moment of intense affliction; she let it fall,—all but one corner,
which remained between her finger and thumb. She looked at
Sir Guy; drew the thumb and forefinger of her other hand
slowly along its border, till they reached the opposite extremity.
She sobbed aloud. "So kind a lady!" said Beatrice Grey.—
"So excellent a wife!" responded Sir Guy.—"So good!" said
the damsel.—"So dear!" said the knight.—"So pious!" said
she.—"So humble!" said he.—"So good to the poor!"—"So
capital a manager!"—"So punctual at matins!"—"Dinner
dished to moment!"—"So devout!" said Beatrice.—"So fond
of me!" said Sir Guy.—"And of Father Francis!"—"What
the devil do you mean by that?" said Sir Guy de Montgomeri.

The knight and the maiden had rung their antiphonic changes
on the fine qualities of the departing lady, like the *Strophe* and
Antistrophe of a Greek play. The cardinal virtues once disposed of, her minor excellences came under review. She would
drown a witch, drink lambs' wool at Christmas, beg Dominie
Dumps's boys a holiday, and dine upon sprats on Good Friday!
A low moan from the subject of these eulogies seemed to intimate that the enumeration of her good deeds was not altogether lost on her,—that the parting spirit felt and rejoiced in
the testimony.

"She was too good for earth!" continued Sir Guy.

"Ye-ye-yes!" sobbed Beatrice.

"I did not deserve her!" said the knight.

"No-o-o-o!" cried the damsel.

"Not but that I made her an excellent husband, and a kind;
but she is going, and—and—where, or when, or how—shall I
get such another?"

"Not in broad England—not in the whole wide world!"
responded Beatrice Grey; "that is, not *just* such another!"
Her voice still faltered, but her accents on the whole were more
articulate; she dropped the corner of her apron, and had recourse to her handkerchief; in fact, her eyes were getting red,
—and so was the tip of her nose.

Sir Guy was silent; he gazed for a few moments steadfastly
on the face of his lady. The single word, "Another!" fell from

his lips like a distant echo ;—it is not often that the viewless nymph repeats more than is necessary.

"Bim! bome!" went the bell. Bandy-legged Hubert had been tolling for half an hour; he began to grow tired, and St. Peter fidgety.

"Beatrice Grey!" said Sir Guy de Montgomeri, "what's to be done? What's to become of Montgomeri Hall?—and the buttery,—and the servants? And what—what's to become of *me*, Beatrice Grey?"—There was pathos in his tones, and a solemn pause succeeded. "I'll turn monk myself!" said Sir Guy.

"Monk?" said Beatrice.

"I'll be a Carthusian!" repeated the knight, but in a tone less assured: he relapsed into a reverie.—Shave his head!—he did not so much mind that,—he was getting rather bald already; —but, beans for dinner,—and those without butter—and then a horse-hair shirt!

The knight seemed undecided: his eye roamed gloomily around the apartment; it paused upon different objects, but as if it saw them not; its sense was shut, and there was no speculation in its glance: it rested at last upon the fair face of the sympathizing damsel at his side, beautiful in her grief.

Her tears had ceased; but her eyes were cast down, mournfully fixed upon her delicate little foot, which was beating the devil's tattoo.

There is no talking to a female when she does not look at you. Sir Guy turned round,—he seated himself on the edge of the bed; and, placing his hand beneath the chin of the lady, turned up her face in an angle of fifteen degrees.

"I don't think I shall take the vows, Beatrice; but what's to become of me? Poor, miserable, old—that is, poor, miserable, middle-aged man that I am!—No one to comfort, no one to care for me!"—Beatrice's tears flowed afresh, but she opened not her lips.—"'Pon my life!" continued he, "I don't believe there is a creature now would care a button if I were hanged to-morrow!"

"Oh! don't say so, Sir Guy!" sighed Beatrice; "you know there's—there's Master Everard, and—and Father Francis——"

" Pish!" cried Sir Guy testily.

"And—there's your favorite old bitch."

14

" I am not thinking of old bitches!" quoth Sir Guy de Mont-gomeri.

Another pause ensued; the knight had released her chin, and taken her hand; it was a pretty little hand, with long taper fingers and filbert-formed nails, and the softness of the palm said little for its owner's industry.

"Sit down, my dear Beatrice," said the knight thoughtfully; "you must be fatigued with your long watching. Take a seat, my child."—Sir Guy did not relinquish her hand; but he sidled along the counterpane, and made room for his companion between himself and the bed-post.

Now this is a very awkward position for two people to be placed in, especially when the right hand of the one holds the right hand of the other:—in such an attitude, what the deuce can the gentleman do with his left? Sir Guy closed his till it became an absolute fist, and his knuckles rested on the bed a little in the rear of his companion.

"Another!" repeated Sir Guy, musing; "if, indeed, I could find such another!" He was talking to his thought, but Beatrice Grey answered him.

"There's Madam Fitzfoozle."

"A frump!" said Sir Guy.

"Or the Lady Bumbarton."

"With her hump!" muttered he.

"There's the Dowager——"

"Stop—stop!" said the knight, "stop one moment!"—He paused; he was all on the tremble; something seemed rising in his throat, but he gave a great gulp and swallowed it. "Bea-trice," said he, "what think you of"—his voice sank into a most seductive softness,—"what think you of—Beatrice Grey?"

The murder was out: the knight felt infinitely relieved: the knuckles of his left hand unclosed spontaneously; and the arm he had felt such a difficulty in disposing of found itself,— nobody knows how,—all at once, encircling the jimp waist of the pretty Beatrice. The young lady's reply was expressed in three syllables. They were, "Oh, Sir Guy!" The words might be somewhat indefinite, but there was no mistaking the look. Their eyes met; Sir Guy's left arm contracted itself spasmod-ically; when the eyes meet,—at least, as theirs met,—the lips are very apt to follow the example. The knight had taken one long loving kiss—nectar and ambrosia! He thought on Doctor Butts and his *repetatur haustus,*—a prescription Father Francis had taken infinite pains to translate for him: he was about to repeat it, but the dose was interrupted *in transitu.* Doubtless the adage,

> "There's many a slip
> 'Twixt the cup and the lip,"

hath reference to medicine. Sir Guy's lip was again all but in conjunction with that of his bride elect.

It has been hinted already that there was a little round polished patch on the summit of the knight's *pericranium,* from which his locks had gradually receded; a sort of *oasis,*—or rather a *Mont Blanc* in miniature, rising above the highest point of vegetation. It was on this little spot, undefended alike by Art and Nature, that at this interesting moment a blow descended, such as we must borrow a term from the Sister Island adequately to describe,—it was a "Whack!"

Sir Guy started upon his feet; Beatrice Grey started upon hers: but a single glance to the rear reversed her position,—she fell upon her knees and screamed.

The knight, too, wheeled about, and beheld a sight which might have turned a bolder man to stone.—It was She!—the all-but-defunct Rohesia—there she sat, bolt upright!—her eyes no longer glazed with the film of impending dissolution, but scintillating like flint and steel; while in her hand she grasped the bed-staff,—a weapon of mickle might, as her husband's bloody coxcomb could now well testify. Words were yet wanting, for the quinsy, which her rage had broken, still impeded her utterance; but the strength and rapidity of her guttural intonations augured well for her future eloquence.

Sir Guy de Montgomeri stood for a while like a man distraught; this resurrection—for such it seemed—had quite overpowered him. "A husband ofttimes makes the best physician," says the proverb; he was a living personification of its truth. Still it was whispered he had been content with Dr. Butts; but his lady was restored to bless him for many years.—Heavens, what a life he led!

The Lady Rohesia mended apace; her quinsy was cured; the

bell was stopped, and little Hubert, the sacristan, kicked out of the chapelry. St. Peter opened his wicket and looked out; —there was nobody there; so he flung to the gate in a passion, and went back to his lodge, grumbling at being hoaxed by a runaway ring.

Years rolled on. The improvement of Lady Rohesia's temper did not keep pace with that of her health; and one fine morning Sir Guy de Montgomeri was seen to enter the *porte-cochère* of Durham House, at that time the town residence of Sir Walter Raleigh. Nothing more was ever heard of him; but a boat full of adventurers was known to have dropped down with the tide that evening to Deptford Hope, where lay the good ship the Darling, commanded by Captain Keymis, who sailed next morning on the Virginia voyage.

A brass plate, some eighteen inches long, may yet be seen in Denton chancel, let into a broad slab of Bethersden marble; it represents a lady kneeling, in her wimple and hood; her hands are clasped in prayer, and beneath is an inscription in the characters of the age—

> "Praie for ye sowle of ye Ladn Rohse,
> And for alle Christen sowles!"

The date is illegible; but it appears that she survived King Henry the Eighth, and that the dissolution of monasteries had lost St. Mary Rouncival her thousand marks. As for Beatrice Gray, it is well known that she was alive in 1559, and then had virginity enough left to be a maid of honor to "good Queen Bess."

It was during the "Honey (or, as it is sometimes termed, the 'Treacle') Moon" that Mr. and Mrs. Seaforth passed through London. A "good-natured friend," who dropped in to dinner, forced them in the evening to the theatre for the purpose of getting rid of him. I give Charles's account of the Tragedy, just as it was written, without altering even the last couplet—for there would be no making "Egerton" rhyme with "Story."

The Tragedy.

"Quæque ipse miserrima vidi."—VIRGIL.

CATHERINE of Cleves was a Lady of rank :
   She had lands and fine houses, and cash in the Bank ;
    She had jewels and rings,   And a thousand smart things ;
    Was lovely and young,   With a *rather* sharp tongue,
And she wedded a noble of high degree
With the star of the order of *St. Esprit ;*
    But the Duke de Guise   Was, by many degrees,
Her senior, and not very easy to please ;
He'd a sneer on his lip, and a scowl with his eye,
And a frown on his brow,—and he looked like a Guy,—
    So she took to intriguing   With Monsieur St. Megrin,
A young man of fashion, and figure, and worth,
But with no great pretensions to fortune or birth ;
    He would sing, fence, and dance,   With the best man in
      France,
And took his rappee with genteel *nonchalance ;*
He smiled, and he flattered, and flirted with ease,
And was very superior to Monseigneur de Guise.
Now Monsieur St. Megrin was curious to know
If the Lady approved of his passion or no ;
    So, without more ado,   He put on his *surtout,*
And went to a man with a beard like a Jew,
    One Signor Ruggieri,   A Cunning-man near, he
Could conjure, tell fortunes, and calculate tides,
Perform tricks on the cards, and Heaven knows what besides.
Bring back a strayed cow, silver ladle, or spoon,
And was thought to be thick with the Man in the Moon.
    The Sage took his stand   With his wand in his hand,
Drew a circle, then gave the dread word of command,
Saying solemnly—" *Presto !—Hey, quick !—Cock-a-lorum ! !* "
When the Duchess immediately popped up before 'em.
Just then a Conjunction of Venus and Mars,
Or something peculiar above in the stars,
Attracted the notice of Signor Ruggieri,
Who " bolted," and left him alone with his deary.—

Monsieur St. Megrin went down on his knees,
And the Duchess shed tears large as marrow-fat peas,
  When,—fancy the shock,— A loud double knock
Made the Lady cry "Get up, you fool!—there's De Guise!"
   'Twas his Grace, sure enough; So Monsieur, looking
    bluff,
Strutted by, with his hat on, and fingering his ruff,
While, unseen by either, away flew the Dame
Through the opposite keyhole, the same way she came;
  But, alack! and alas! A mishap came to pass,
In her hurry she, somehow or other, let fall
A new silk *Bandana* she'd worn as a shawl;
  She had used it for drying Her bright eyes while crying,
And blowing her nose, as her Beau talked of dying!

Now the Duke, who had seen it so lately adorn her,
And knew the great C with the Crown in the corner,
The instant he spied it, smoked something amiss,
And said, with some energy, "D—— it! what's this?"
  He went home in a fume, And bounced into her room,
Crying, "So, Ma'am, I find I've some cause to be jealous!
Look here!—here's a proof you run after the fellows!
—Now take up that pen,—if it's bad choose a better,—
And write, as I dictate, this moment a letter
  To Monsieur—you know who!" The Lady looked blue,
But replied with much firmness, "Hang me if I do!"
  De Guise grasped her wrist With his great bony fist,
And pinched it, and gave it so painful a twist,
That his hard iron gauntlet the flesh went an inch in,—
She did not mind death, but she could not stand pinching;
  So she sat down and wrote This polite little note:—

  "Dear Mister St. Megrin, The Chiefs of the League in
  Our house mean to dine This evening at nine;
   I shall, soon after ten, Slip away from the men,
And you'll find me up stairs in the drawing-room then;
Come up the back way, or those impudent thieves
Of Servants will see you. Yours,
        "CATHERINE OF CLEVES."

She directed and scaled it, all pale as a ghost,
And De Guise put it into the Twopenny Post.

St. Megrin had almost jumped out of his skin
For joy that day when the post came in ;
 He read the note through, Then began it anew,
And thought it almost too good news to be true.—
 He clapped on his hat, And a hood over that,
With a cloak to disguise him, and make him look fat ;
So great his impatience from half after Four
He was waiting till Ten at De Guise's back door.
When he heard the great clock of St. Genevieve chime
He ran up the back staircase six steps at a time.
 He had scarce made his bow, He hardly knew how,
 When alas! and alack! There was no getting back,
For the drawing-room door was banged to with a whack ;—
 In vain he applied To the handle and tried,
Somebody or other had locked it outside!
And the Duchess in agony mourned her mishap,
" We are caught like a couple of rats in a trap."

 Now the Duchess's Page, About twelve years of age,
For so little a boy was remarkably sage ;
And just in the nick, to their joy and amazement,
Popped the Gas-lighter's ladder close under the casement.
 But all would not do,— Though St. Megrin got through
The window,—below stood De Guise and his crew,
And though never man was more brave than St. Megrin,
Yet fighting a score is extremely fatiguing ;
 He thrust *carte* and *tierce* Uncommonly fierce,
But not Beëlzebub's self could their cuirasses pierce ;
 While his doublet and hose, Being holiday clothes,
Were soon cut through and through from his knees to his nose ;
Still an old crooked sixpence the Conjurer gave him
From pistol and sword was sufficient to save him ;
 But when beat on his knees, That confounded De Guise
Came behind with the " fogle " that caused all this breeze,
Whipped it tight round his neck, and when backward he'd
  jerked him,
The rest of the rascals jumped on him and Burked him.

The poor little Page, too, himself got no quarter, but
    Was served the same way,   And was found the next day
With his heels in the air, and his head in the water-butt.
    Catherine of Cleves   Roared "Murder!" and "Thieves!"
    From the window above   While they murdered her love;
Till, finding the rogues had accomplished his slaughter,
She drank Prussic acid without any water,
And died like a Duke-and-a-Duchess's daughter!

MORAL.

Take warning, ye fair, from this tale of the Bard's,
And don't go where fortunes are told on the cards,
But steer clear of Conjurers,—never put query
To "Wise Mrs. Williams," or folks like Ruggieri.
When alone in your room shut the door close, and lock it!
Above all,—KEEP YOUR HANDKERCHIEF SAFE IN YOUR
    POCKET!
Lest you too should stumble, and Lord Leveson Gower, he
Be called on,—sad poet!—to tell your sad story!

———

IT was in the summer of 1838 that a party from Tappington reached the metropolis with a view of witnessing the coronation of their youthful Queen, whom God long preserve!—This purpose they were fortunate enough to accomplish by the purchase of a peer's tickets from a stationer in the Strand, who was enabled so to dispose of some, greatly to the indignation of the hereditary Earl Marshal. How Mr. Barney managed to insinuate himself into the Abbey remains a mystery; his characteristic modesty and address doubtless assisted him, for there he unquestionably was. The result of his observations was thus communicated to his associates in the Servants' Hall, upon his return, to the infinite delectation of Mademoiselle Pauline, over a *Cruiskeen* of his own concocting.

Mr. Barney Maguire's Account of the Coronation.

AIR.—" *The Groves of Blarney.*"

OCH! the Coronation! what celebration
   For emulation can with it compare?
When to Westminster the Royal Spinster,
   And the Duke of Leinster, all in order did repair!
'Twas there you'd see the New Polishemen
   Making a skrimmage at half after four,
And the Lords and Ladies, and the Miss O'Gradys,
   All standing round before the Abbey door.

Their pillows scorning, that self-same morning
   Themselves adorning, all by the candle-light,
With roses and lilies, and daffy-down-dillies,
   And gould and jewels, and rich di'monds bright.
And then approaches five hundred coaches,
   With General Dullbeak.—Och! 'twas mighty fine
To see how asy bould Corporal Casey,
   With his sword drawn, prancing made them kape the line.

Then the Guns' alarums, and the King of Arums,
   All in his Garters and his Clarence shoes,
Opening the massy doors to the bould Ambassydors,
   The Prince of Potboys, and great haythen Jews;
'Twould have made you crazy to see Esterhazy
   All jools from his jasey to his di'mond boots,
With Alderman Harmer, and that swate charmer,
   The female heiress, Miss Anja-ly Coutts.

And Wellington, walking with his swoord drawn, talking
   To Hill and Hardinge, haroes of great fame:
And Sir De Lacy, and the Duke Dalmasy
   (They called him Sowlt afore he changed his name),
Themselves presading Lord Melbourne, lading
   The Queen, the darling, to her royal chair,

And that fine ould fellow, the Duke of Pell-Mello,
   The Queen of Portingal's Chargy-de-fair.

Then the Noble Prussians, likewise the Russians,
   In fine laced jackets with their goulden cuffs,
And the Bavarians, and the proud Hungarians,
   And Everythingarians all in furs and muffs.
Then Misthur Spaker, with Misthur Pays the Quaker,
   All in the Gallery you might persave;
But Lord Brougham was missing, and gone a-fishing,
   Ounly crass Lord Essex would not give him lave.

There was Baron Alten himself exalting,
   And Prince Von Schwartzenberg, and many more,
Och! I'd be bothered and entirely smothered
   To tell the half of 'em was to the fore;
With the swate Peeresses, in their crowns and dresses,
   And Aldermanesses, and the Boord of Works;
But Mehemet Ali said, quite gintaly,
   "I'd be proud to see the likes among the Turks!"

Then the Queen, Heaven bless her! och! they did dress her
   In her purple garments and her goulden Crown;
Like Venus or Hebe, or the Queen of Sheby,
   With eight young ladies houlding up her gown.
Sure 'twas grand to see her, also for to he-ar
   The big drums bating, and the trumpets blow,
And Sir George Smart! Oh! he played a Consarto,
   With his four-and-twenty fiddlers all on a row!

Then the Lord Archbishop held a goulden dish up,
   For to resave her bounty and great wealth,
Saying, "Plase your Glory, great Queen Vic-tory!
   Ye'll give the Clargy lave to dhrink your health!"
Then his Riverence, retrating, discoorsed the mating;
   "Boys! Here's your Queen! deny it if you can!
And if any bould traitour, or infarior craythur,
   Sneezes at that, I'd like to see the man!"

Then the Nobles kneeling to the Powers appealing,
  "Heaven send your Majesty a glorious reign!"
And Sir Claudius Hunter he did confront her,
  All in his scarlet gown and goulden chain.
The great Lord May'r, too, sat in his chair, too,
  But mighty sarious, looking fit to cry,
For the Earl of Surrey, all in his hurry,
  Throwing the thirteens, hit him in his eye.

Then there was preaching, and good store of speeching,
  With Dukes and Marquises on bended knee;
And they did splash her with raal Macasshur,
  And the Queen said, "Ah! then thank ye all for me!"—
Then the trumpets braying, and the organ playing,
  And sweet trombones, with their silver tones;
But Lord Rolle was rolling;—'twas mighty consoling
  To think his Lordship did not break his bones!

Then the crames and custard, and the beef and mustard,
  All on the tombstones like a poultherer's shop;
With lobsters and white-bait, and other swate-meats,
  And wine and nagus, and Imperial Pop!
There was cakes and apples in all the Chapels,
  With fine polonies, and rich mellow pears,—
Och! the Count Von Strogonoff, sure he got prog enough,
  The sly ould Divil, undernathe the stairs.

Then the cannons thundered, and the people wondered,
  Crying, "God save Victoria, our Royal Queen!"—
—Och! if myself should live to be a hundred,
  Sure it's the proudest day that I'll have seen.
And now, I've ended, what I pretended,
  This narration splendid in swate poe-thry,
Ye dear bewitcher, just hand the pitcher,
  Faith, it's myself that's getting mighty dhry.

As a *pendant* to the foregoing, I shall venture to insert Mr.
Simpkinson's lucubrations on a subject to him, as a *Savant* of
the first class, scarcely less interesting.   The aerial voyage to
which it alludes took place about a year and a half previously
to the august event already recorded, and the excitement mani-
fested in the learned Antiquary's effusion may give some faint
idea of that which prevailed generally among the Sons of
Science at that memorable epoch.

The "Monstre" Balloon.

OH! the balloon, the great balloon,
    It left Vauxhall one Monday at noon,
And every one said we should hear of it soon,
With news from Aleppo or Scanderoon.
But very soon after folks changed their tune:
"The netting had burst—the silk—the shalloon;—
It had met with a trade-wind—a deuced monsoon—
It was blown out to sea—it was blown to the moon—
They ought to have put off their journey till June;
Sure none but a donkey, a goose, or baboon
Would go up in November in any balloon!"

Then they talked about Green—"Oh! where's Mister Green?
And where's Mr. Holland who hired the machine?
And where is Monck Mason, the man that has been
Up so often before—twelve times or thirteen—
And who writes such nice letters describing the scene?
And where's the cold fowl, and the ham, and poteen?
The pressed beef, with the fat cut off—nothing but lean,
And the portable soup in the patent tureen?
Have they got to Grand Cairo or reached Aberdeen?
Or Jerusalem—Hamburg—or Ballyporeen?
No! they have not been seen!   Oh! they haven't been seen!"

Stay! here's Mister Gye—Mr. Frederick Gye—
"At Paris," says he, " I've been up very high,
A couple of hundred of toises, or nigh,
A cockstride the Tuileries' pantiles, to spy
With Dollond's best telescope stuck at my eye,
And my umbrella under my arm like Paul Pry,
But I could see nothing at all but the sky;
So I thought with myself 'twas of no use to try
Any longer; and, feeling remarkably dry
From sitting all day stuck up there, like a Guy,
I came down again, and—you see—here am I!"

But here's Mr. Hughes!—What says young Mr. Hughes?—
" Why, I'm sorry to say we've not got any news
Since the letter they threw down in one of their shoes,
Which gave the mayor's nose such a deuce of a bruise,
As he popped up his eye-glass to look at their cruise
Over Dover; and which the folks flocked to peruse
At Squiers's bazaar, the same evening, in crews—
Politicians, news-mongers, town-council, and blues,
Turks, Heretics, Infidels, Jumpers, and Jews,
Scorning Bachelor's papers, and Warren's reviews:
But the wind was then blowing towards Helvoetsluys,
And my father and I are in terrible stews,
For so large a balloon is a sad thing to lose!"—

Here's news come at last!—Here's news come at last!—
A vessel's come in, which has sailed very fast;
And a gentleman serving before the mast,—
Mister Nokes,—has declared that " the party has past
Safe across to the Hague, where their grapnel they cast,
As a fat burgomaster was staring aghast
To see such a monster come borne on the blast,
And it caught in his waistband, and there it stuck fast!"—
Oh fie! Mister Nokes,—for shame, Mr. Nokes!
To be poking your fun at us plain-dealing folks—
Sir, this isn't a time to be cracking your jokes,
And such jesting your malice but scurvily cloaks;

Such a trumpery tale every one of us smokes,
And we know very well your whole story's a hoax!—

"Oh! what shall we do?—Oh! where will it end?—
Can nobody go?—Can nobody send
To Calais—or Bergen-op-zoom—or Ostend?
Can't you go there yourself?—Can't you write to a friend,
For news upon which we may safely depend?"—

Huzza! huzza! one and eight-pence to pay
For a letter from Hamborough, just come to say
They descended at Weilburg, about break of day;
And they've lent them the palace there during their stay,
And the town is becoming uncommonly gay,
And they're feasting the party, and soaking their clay
With Johannisberg, Rudesheim, Moselle, and Tokay!
And the Landgraves, and Margraves, and Counts beg and pray
That they won't think, as yet, about going away;
Notwithstanding, they don't mean to make much delay,
But pack up the balloon in a wagon or dray,
And pop themselves into a German "*po-shay*,"
And get on to Paris by Lisle and Tournay;
Where they boldly declare, any wager they'll lay
If the gas people there do not ask them to pay
Such a sum as must force them at once to say "Nay,"
They'll inflate the balloon in the Champs-Elysées,
And be back again here the beginning of May.—

Dear me! what a treat for a juvenile *fête!*
What thousands will flock their arrival to greet!
There'll be hardly a soul to be seen in the street,
For at Vauxhall the whole population will meet,
And you'll scarcely get standing-room, much less a seat,
For this all preceding attraction must beat;
Since they'll unfold what we want to be told,—
How they coughed, how they sneezed, how they shivered with
    cold,
How they tippled the "cordial" as racy and old
As Hodges, or Deady, or Smith ever sold,

And how they all then felt remarkably bold ;
How they thought the boiled beef worth its own weight in gold,
And how Mr. Green was beginning to scold
Because Mr. Mason would try to lay hold
Of the moon, and had very near overboard rolled !

And there they'll be seen, they'll be all to be seen,—
The great-coats, the coffee-pots, mugs, and tureen !
With the tight-rope, and fireworks, and dancing between,
If the weather should only prove fair and serene ;
And there, on a beautiful transparent screen,
In the middle you'll see a large picture of Green,
Mr. Holland on one side, who hired the machine,
Mr. Mason on t'other, describing the scene ;
And Fame, on one leg, in the air, like a queen,
With three wreaths and a trumpet, will over them lean ;
While Envy, in serpents and black bombazin,
Looks on from below with an air of chagrin !
Then they'll play up a tune in the Royal Saloon,
And the people will dance by the light of the moon,
And keep up the ball till the next day at noon ;
And the peer and the peasant, the lord and the loon,
The haughty grandee and the low picaroon,
The six-foot life-guardsman and little gossoon,
Will all join in three cheers for the " Monstre" Balloon !

It is much to be regretted that I have not as yet been able to discover more than a single specimen of my friend "Suckle-thumbkin's" Muse. The event it alludes to, probably the *euthanasia* of the late Mr. Greenacre, will scarcely have yet faded from the recollection of an admiring public. Although, with the usual diffidence of a man of fashion, Augustus has "sunk" the fact of his own presence on that interesting occasion, I have every reason to believe that, in describing the party at the *auberge* hereafter mentioned, he might have said, with a brother Exquisite, "*Quorum pars magna fui.*"

HON. MR. SUCKLETHUMBKIN'S STORY.

The Execution.

A SPORTING ANECDOTE.

MY Lord Tomnoddy got up one day;
    It was half after two, He had nothing to do,
So his Lordship rang for his cabriolet.

    Tiger Tim   Was clean of limb,
His boots were polished, his jacket was trim;
With a very smart tie in his smart cravat,
And a smart cockade on the top of his hat;
Tallest of boys, or shortest of men,
He stood in his stockings just four foot ten;
And he asked, as he held the door on the swing,
"Pray, did your Lordship please to ring?"

My Lord Tomnoddy he raised his head,
And thus to Tiger Tim he said:
    "Malibran's dead, Duvernay's fled,
Taglioni has not yet arrived in her stead;
Tiger Tim, come tell me true,
What may a Nobleman find to do?"—
Tim looked up, and Tim looked down,
He paused, and he put on a thoughtful frown,
And he held up his hat, and he peeped in the crown;
He bit his lip, and he scratched his head,
He let go the handle, and thus he said,
As the door, released, behind him banged:
"An't please you, my Lord, there's a man to be hanged."

My Lord Tomnoddy jumped up at the news,
    "Run to M'Fuze, And Lieutenant Tregooze,
And run to Sir Carnaby Jenks, of the Blues.

Rope-dancers a score   I've seen before—
Madam Sacchi, Antonio, and Master Black-more;
　　But to see a man swing   At the end of a string,
With his neck in a noose, will be quite a new thing!"

My Lord Tomnoddy stept into his cab—
Dark rifle green, with a lining of drab;
　　Through street and through square
　　His high-trotting mare,
Like one of Ducrow's, goes pawing the air.
Adown Piccadilly and Waterloo Place
Went the high-trotting mare at a very quick pace;
　　She produced some alarm,   But did no great harm,
Save frightening a nurse with a child on her arm,
　　Spattering with clay   Two urchins at play,
Knocking down—very much to the sweeper's dismay—
An old woman who wouldn't get out of the way,
　　And upsetting a stall   Near Exeter Hall,
Which made all the pious Church-Mission folks squall.
　　But eastward afar   Through Temple Bar,
My Lord Tomnoddy directs his car;
　　Never heeding their squalls,
　　Or their calls, or their bawls,
He passes by Waithman's Emporium for shawls,
And, merely just catching a glimpse of St. Paul's,
　　Turns down the Old Bailey,
　　Where in front of the gaol, he
Pulls up at the door of the gin-shop, and gayly
Cries, "What must I fork out to-night, my trump,
For the whole first floor of the Magpie and Stump?"

———

The clock strikes Twelve—it is dark midnight—
Yet the Magpie and Stump is one blaze of light.
　　The parties are met;   The tables are set;
There is "punch," "cold *without*," "hot *with*," heavy wet,
Ale-glasses and jugs,   And rummers and mugs,
　　And sand on the floor, without carpets or rugs,
　15

Cold fowl and cigars,   Pickled onions in jars,
Welsh rabbits and kidneys—rare work for the jaws—
And very large lobsters, with very large claws ;
      And there is M'Fuze,   And Lieutenant Tregooze ;
And there is Sir Carnaby Jenks, of the Blues,
All come to see a man " die in his shoes !"

      The clock strikes One !   Supper is done,
And Sir Carnaby Jenks is full of his fun,
Singing " Jolly companions every one !"
      My Lord Tomnoddy   Is drinking gin-toddy,
And laughing at ev'ry thing, and ev'ry body.—

      The clock strikes Two ! and the clock strikes Three !
—" Who so merry, so merry as we ?"
      Save Captain M'Fuze,   Who is taking a snooze,
While Sir Carnaby Jenks is busy at work
Blacking his nose with a piece of burnt cork.

      The clock strikes Four !—   Round the debtors' door
Are gathered a couple of thousand or more ;
      As many await   At the press-yard gate,
Till slowly its folding doors open, and straight
The mob divides, and between their ranks
A wagon comes loaded with posts and planks.

      The clock strikes Five !   The Sheriffs arrive,
And the crowd is so great that the street seems alive ;
      But Sir Carnaby Jenks   Blinks, and winks.
A candle burns down in the socket, and stinks.
      Lieutenant Tregooze   Is dreaming of Jews,
And acceptances all the bill-brokers refuse ;
      My Lord Tomnoddy   Has drunk all his toddy,
And just as the dawn is beginning to peep,
The whole of the party are fast asleep.

Sweetly, oh ! sweetly, the morning breaks,
      With roseate streaks,
Like the first faint blush on a maiden's cheeks ;

Seemed as that mild and clear blue sky
Smiled upon all things far and high,
On all—save the wretch condemn'd to die!
Alack! that ever so fair a Sun,
As that which its course has now begun,
Should rise on such scene of misery!—
Should gild with rays so light and free
That dismal, dark-frowning Gallows-tree!

And hark!—a sound comes, big with fate;
The clock from St. Sepulchre's tower strikes—Eight!—
List to that low funereal bell:
It is tolling, alas! a living man's knell!—
And see!—from forth that opening door
They come—HE steps that threshold o'er
Who never shall tread upon threshold more!
—God! 'tis a fearsome thing to see
That pale wan man's mute agony,—
The glare of that wild, despairing eye,
Now bent on the crowd, now turned to the sky,
As though 'twere scanning, in doubt and in fear,
The path of the Spirit's unknown career;
Those pinioned arms, those hands that ne'er
Shall be lifted again,—not even in prayer;
That heaving chest!—Enough—'tis done!
The bolt has fallen!—The spirit is gone—
For weal or for woe is known but to One!—
—Oh! 'twas a fearsome sight!—Ah me,
A deed to shudder at,—not to see.

Again that clock! 'tis time, 'tis time!
The hour is past: with its earliest chime
The cord is severed, the lifeless clay
By "dungeon villains" is borne away:
Nine!—'twas the last concluding stroke!
And then—my Lord Tomnoddy awoke!
And Tregooze and Sir Carnaby Jenks arose,
And Captain M'Fuze, with the black on his nose:

And they stared at each other, as much as to say,
    "Hollo! Hollo!   Here's a rum Go!
Why, Captain!—my Lord!—Here's the devil to pay!
The fellow's been cut down and taken away!
    What's to be done?   We've miss'd all the fun!—
Why, they'll laugh at and quiz us all over the town,
We are all of us done so uncommonly brown!"

What *was* to be done?—'twas perfectly plain
That they could not well hang the man over again:
What *was* to be done?—The man was dead!
Nought *could* be done—nought could be said;
So—my Lord Tomnoddy went home to bed!

THE following communication will speak for itself:—

"On their own actions modest men are dumb!"

Some Account of a New Play,

IN A FAMILIAR EPISTLE TO MY BROTHER-IN-LAW, LIEUT. SEA-
FORTH, H.P., LATE OF THE HON. E.I.C.'S SECOND REGT.
OF BOMBAY FENCIBLES.

"The play's the thing!"—*Hamlet.*

TAVISTOCK HOTEL, *Nov.* 1839.
DEAR CHARLES,
            In reply to your letter, and Fanny's,
Lord Brougham, it appears, isn't dead,—though Queen
        Anne is;
'Twas a " plot" and a " farce"—you hate farces, you say—
Take another " plot," then, viz., the plot of the Play.

The Countess of Arundel, high in degree,
As a lady possessed of an earldom in fee,
Was imprudent enough, at fifteen years of age,—
A period of life when we're not over sage,—
To form a *liaison*—in fact, to engage
Her hand to a Hop-o'-my-thumb of a Page.
  This put her Papa— She had no Mamma—
As may well be supposed, in a deuce of a rage.

Mr. Benjamin Franklin was wont to repeat,
In his budget of proverbs, "Stol'n kisses are sweet!"
  But they have their alloy:— Fate assumed, to annoy
Miss Arundel's peace, and embitter her joy,
The equivocal shape of a fine little Boy.

When, through "the young stranger," her secret took wind,
The old Lord was neither "to haud nor to bind;"
  He bounced up and down, And so fearful a frown
Contracted his brow, you'd have thought he'd been blind.
  The young lady, they say, Having fainted away,
Was confined to her room for the whole of that day;
While her beau—no rare thing in the old feudal system—
Disappeared the next morning, and nobody missed him.

The fact is, his Lordship,—who hadn't, it seems,
Formed the slightest idea, not ev'n in his dreams,
That the pair had been wedded according to law,—
Conceived that his daughter had made a *faux pas*;
  So he bribed at a high rate A sort of a Pirate
To knock out the poor dear young Gentleman's brains,
And gave him a handsome *douceur* for his pains.
The Page thus disposed of, his Lordship now turns
His attention at once to the Lady's concerns;
  And, alarmed for the future, Looks out for a suitor
One not fond of raking, nor giv'n to "the pewter,"
But adapted to act both the husband and tutor;—
Finds a highly respectable middle-aged widower,
Marries her off, and thanks Heaven that he's rid of her.

Relieved from his cares,　The old Peer now prepares
To arrange in good earnest his worldly affairs;
Has his will made anew by a Special Attorney,
Sickens,—takes to his bed,—and sets out on his journey.
　　Which way he travelled　Has not been unravelled;
To speculate much on the point were too curious,
If the climate he reached were serene or sulphureous.
To be sure, in his balance-sheet all must declare
One item—the Page—was an awkward affair;
But, *per contra*, he'd lately endowed a new Chantry
For Priests, with ten marks, and the run of the pantry.
　　Be that as it may,　It's sufficient to say
That his tomb in the chancel stands there to this day,
Built of Bethersden marble—a dark bluish-gray.
The figure, a fine one of pure alabaster,
Some cleanly churchwarden has covered with plaster;
　　While some Vandal or Jew,　With a taste for *virtu*,
Has knocked off his toes, to place, I suppose,
In some Pickwick Museum, with part of his nose;
　　From his belt and his sword　And his *misericorde*
The enamel's been chipped out, and never restored;
His *ci-gît* in old French is inscribed all around,
And his head's in his helm, and his heel's on his hound;
The palms of his hands, as if going to pray,
Are joined and upraised o'er his bosom—　But stay!
I forgot that his tomb's not described in the Play!

＊　　＊　　＊　　＊　　＊　　＊　　＊

Lady Arundel, now in her own right a Peeress,
Perplexes her noddle with no such nice queries,
But produces in time, to her husband's great joy,
Another remarkably "fine little boy."
　　As novel connections　Oft change the affections,
And turn all one's love into different directions,
Now to young "Johnny Newcome" she seems to confine
　　hers,
Neglecting the poor little dear out at dry-nurse;
　　Nay, far worse than that,　She considers "the brat"
As a bore,—fears her husband may smell out a rat.

For her legal adviser   She takes an old Miser,
A sort of " poor cousin."   She might have been wiser ;
    For this arrant deceiver,   By name Maurice Beevor,
A shocking old scamp, should her own issue fail,
By the law of the land stands the next in entail ;
So, as soon as she asked him to hit on some plan
To provide for her eldest, away the rogue ran
To that self-same unprincipled sea-faring man ;
In his ear whispered low   *   *   *—" Bully Gaussen " said
    " Done !—
I Burked the papa, now I'll Bishop the son !"
    'Twas agreed ; and, with speed   To accomplish the deed,
He adopted a scheme he was sure would succeed.

    By long cock-and-bull stories,   Of Candish and Norcys,
Of Drake, and bold Raleigh (then fresh in his glories,
Acquired 'mongst the Indians, and Rapparee Torics),
    He so worked on the lad,   That he left, which was bad,
The only true friend in the world that he had,
Father Onslow, a priest, though to quit him most loth,
Who in childhood had furnished his pap and his broth,
At no small risk of scandal, indeed, to his cloth.

    The kidnapping crimp   Took the foolish young imp
On board of his cutter so trim and so jimp,
Then, seizing him just as you'd handle a shrimp,
Twirled him thrice in the air with a whirligig motion,
And soused him at once neck and heels in the ocean ;
    This was off Plymouth Sound,
    And he must have been drowned,
For 'twas nonsense to think he could swim to dry ground,
    If " A very great Warman,   Called Billy the Norman,"
Had not just at that moment sailed by, outward bound.
    A shark of great size,   With his great glassy eyes,
Sheered off as he came, and relinquished the prize :
So he picked up the lad,* swabbed and dry-rubbed and mopped
    him,
And, having no children, resolved to adopt him.

        * An incident very like one in Jack Sheppard—
            A work some have lauded, and others have peppered—

Full many a year   Did he hand, reef, and steer,
And by no means considered himself as small beer,
When old Norman at length died and left him his frigate,
With lots of pistoles in his coffer to rig it.
     A sailor ne'er moans;   So, consigning the bones
Of his friend to the locker of one Mr. Jones,
     For England he steers.—   On the voyage it appears
That he rescued a maid from the Dey of Algiers;
And at length reached the Sussex coast, where, in a
      bay,
Not a great way from Brighton, most cosily lay
His vessel at anchor, the very same day
That the Poet begins—thus commencing his Play:

Act I.

Giles Gaussen accosts old Sir Maurice de Beevor,
And puts the poor Knight in a deuce of a fever,
By saying the boy, whom he took out to please him,
Is come back a Captain on purpose to tease him.—
Sir Maurice, who gladly would see Mr. Gaussen
Breaking stones on the highway, or sweeping a crossing,
Dissembles—observes, It's of no use to fret,—
And hints he may find some more work for him yet;
Then calls at the castle, and tells Lady A.
That the boy they had ten years ago sent away
Is returned a grown man, and, to come to the point,
Will put her son Percy's nose clean out of joint;
But adds, that herself she no longer need vex,
If she'll buy him (Sir Maurice) a farm near the Ex.
" Oh! take it," she cries; " but secure every document."—
" A bargain," says Maurice,—" including the stock, you
      meant?"—

> Where a Dutch pirate kidnaps and tosses Thames Darrel
> Just so in the sea, and he's saved by a barrel,—
> On the coast, if I recollect rightly, it's flung whole,
> And the hero, half drowned, scrambles out of the bung-hole.

[It ain't no sich thing!—the hero ain't bung'd in no barrel at all.—He's picked up by
a captain, just as Norman was arterwards.—Print. Dev.]

The Captain, meanwhile,   With a lover-like smile,
And a fine cambric handkerchief, wipes off the tears
From Miss Violet's eyelash, and hushes her fears.
(That's the Lady he saved from the Dey of Algiers.)
Now arises a delicate point, and this is it—
The young Lady herself is but down on a visit.
        She's perplexed; and, in fact,   Does not know how to
            act.
It's her very first visit—and then to begin
By asking a stranger, a gentleman, in—
One with moustaches too—and a tuft on his chin—
        She "really don't know—   He had much better go,"—
Here the Countess steps in from behind, and says " No!—
Fair sir, you are welcome. Do, pray, stop and dine—
You'll take our pot-luck—and we've decentish wine."
He bows, looks at Miss,—and he does not decline.

Act II.

After dinner the Captain recounts, with much glee,
All he's heard, seen, and done since he first went to sea,
        All his perils and scrapes,   And his hair-breadth escapes,
Talks of boa-constrictors, and lions, and apes,
And fierce "Bengal Tigers," like that which, you know,
If you've ever seen any respectable "Show,"
" Carried off the unfortunate Mr. Munro."
Then, diverging awhile, he adverts to the mystery
Which hangs, like a cloud, o'er his own private history—
How he ran off to sea—how they set him afloat
(Not a word, though, of barrel or bung-hole—*See Note*),
        How he happened to meet   With the Algerine fleet,
And forced them, by sheer dint of arms, to retreat,
Thus saving his Violet—(One of his feet
Here just touched her toe, and she moved on her seat),—
        How his vessel was battered—   In short he so chat-
            tered,
Now lively, now serious, so ogled and flattered,
That the ladies much marvelled a person should be able
To " make himself," both said, " so very agreeable."

Captain Norman's adventures were scarcely half done
When Percy Lord Ashdale, her Ladyship's son,
   In a terrible fume, Bounces into the room,
And talks to his guest as you'd talk to your groom,
Claps his hand on his rapier, And swears he'll be through
    him—
The Captain does nothing at all but "pooh! pooh!" him—
   Unable to smother His hate of his brother,
He rails at his cousin, and blows up his mother.—
"Fie! fie!" says the first.—Says the latter, "In sooth,
This is sharper by far than a keen serpent's tooth!"
(A remark, by the way, which King Lear had made years ago,
When he asked for his Knights, and his Daughters said,
    "Here's a go!")—
   This made Ashdale ashamed; But he must not be blamed
Too much for his warmth, for like many young fellows he
Was apt to lose temper when tortured by jealousy.
   Still speaking quite gruff, He goes off in a huff;
Lady A., who is now what some call "up to snuff,"
   Straight determines to patch Up a clandestine match
Between the Sea-Captain she dreads like Old Scratch,
And Miss,—whom she does not think any great catch
For Ashdale;—besides, he won't kick up such shindies
Were she once fairly married and off to the Indies.

Act III.

Miss Violet takes from the Countess her tone:
She agrees to meet Norman "by moonlight alone,"
   And slip off to his bark, "The night being dark,"
Though "the moon," the Sea-Captain says, rises in Heaven
"One hour before midnight," *i. e.* at eleven.
   From which speech I infer,— Though perhaps I may
    err,—
That, though weatherwise, doubtless, 'midst surges and surf, he
When "capering on shore" was by no means a Murphy.

He starts off, however, at sunset to reach
An old chapel in ruins, that stands on the beach,

Where the Priest is to bring, as he's promised by letter, a
Paper to prove his name, " birthright," *et cetera*.

Being rather too late,   Gaussen, lying in wait,
Gives poor Father Onslow a knock on the pate,
But bolts, seeing Norman, before he has wrested
From the hand of the Priest, as Sir Maurice requested,
The marriage certificate duly attested.—
Norman kneels by the clergyman fainting and gory,
And begs he won't die till he's told him his story ;

The Father complies,   Reopens his eyes,
And tells him all how and about it—and dies !

ACT IV.

Norman, now called Le Mesnil, instructed of all,
Goes back, though it's getting quite late for a call,
Hangs his hat and his cloak on a peg in the hall,
And tells the proud Countess it's useless to smother
The fact any longer—he knows she's his Mother !

His Pa's wedded Spouse.—   She questions his *νους*,
And threatens to have him turned out of the house.—

He still perseveres,   Till, in spite of her fears,
She admits he's the son she had cast off for years,
And he gives her the papers " all blistered with tears,"
When Ashdale, who chances his nose in to poke,

Takes his hat and his cloak,   Just as if in a joke,
Determined to put in his wheel a new spoke,
And slips off thus disguised, when he sees by the dial it
's time for the rendezvous fixed with Miss Violet.—
—Captain Norman, who, after all, feels rather sore
At his mother's reserve, vows to see her no more,
Rings the bell for the servant to open the door,
And leaves his Mamma in a fit on the floor.

ACT V.

Now comes the catastrophe !—Ashdale, who's wrapt in
The cloak, with the hat and the plume of the Captain,
Leads Violet down through the grounds to the chapel
Where Gaussen's concealed—he springs forward to grapple

The man he's erroneously led to suppose
Captain Norman himself by the cut of his clothes.

In the midst of their strife,   And just as the knife
Of the Pirate is raised to deprive him of life,
The Captain comes forward, drawn there by the squeals
Of the Lady, and, knocking Giles head over heels,

Fractures his " nob,"   Saves the hangman a job,
And executes justice most strictly, the rather,
'Twas the spot where that rascal had murdered his father.

Then in comes the mother,   Who, finding one brother
Had the instant before saved the life of the other,

Explains the whole case.   Ashdale puts a good face
On the matter; and, since he's obliged to give place,
Yields his coronet up with a pretty good grace;
Norman vows he won't have it—the kinsmen embrace,—
And the Captain, the first in this generous race,

To remove every handle   For gossip and scandal,
Sets the whole of the papers alight with the candle;
An arrangement takes place—on the very same night, all
Is settled and done, and the points the most vital
Are, N. takes the personals ;—A., in requital,
Keeps the whole real property, Mansion, and Title.—
V. falls to the share of the Captain, and tries a
Sea voyage, as a Bride, in the " Royal Eliza."—
Both are pleased with the part they acquire as joint heirs,
And old Maurice Beevor is bundled down stairs !

MORAL.

The public, perhaps, with the drama might quarrel
If deprived of all epilogue, prologue, and moral ;
This may serve for all three then :—

                     " Young Ladies of property,
Let Lady A.'s history serve as a stopper t'ye ;
Don't wed with low people beneath your degree,
And if you've a baby, don't send it to sea !

" Young Noblemen, shun everything like a brawl ;
And be sure when you dine out, or go to a ball,

Don't take the best hat that you find in the hall,
And leave one in its stead that's worth nothing at all!

"Old Knights, don't give bribes!—above all, never urge a man
To steal people's things, or to stick an old Clergyman!

" And you, ye Sea Captains! who've nothing to do
But to run round the world, fight, and drink till all's blue,
And tell us tough yarns, and then swear they are true,
Reflect, notwithstanding your seafaring life,
That you can't get on well long, without you've a wife;
So get one at once, treat her kindly and gently,
Write a nautical novel,—and send it to Bentley !"

It has been already hinted that Mr. Peters had been a
"traveller" in his day. The only story which his lady would
ever allow "her P." to finish—he began as many as would furnish an additional volume to the "Thousand and One Nights"
—is the last I shall offer. The subject, I fear me, is not over
new, but will remind my friends

"Of something better they have seen before."

MR. PETERS'S STORY.

The Bagman's Dog.

Stant littore Puppies !—VIRGIL.

IT was a litter, a litter of five,
    Four are drowned, and one left alive,
He was thought worthy alone to survive,
And the Bagman resolved upon bringing him up,
To eat of his bread and drink of his cup,
He was such a dear little cock-tailed pup!

The Bagman taught him many a trick ;
He would carry, and fetch, and run after a stick,
 Could well understand   The word of command,
 And appear to doze   With a crust on his nose
Till the Bagman permissively waved his hand :
Then to throw up and catch it he never would fail,
As he sat up on end, on his little cock-tail.
Never was puppy so *bien instruit,*
Or possessed of such natural talent as he ;
 And as he grew older,   Every beholder
Agreed he grew handsomer, sleeker, and bolder.—

Time, however his wheels we may clog,
Wends steadily still with onward jog,
And the cock-tailed puppy's a curly-tailed dog !
 When, just at the time   He was reaching his prime,
And all thought he'd be turning out something sublime,
 One unlucky day,   How, no one could say,
Whether soft *liaison* induced him to stray,
Or some kidnapping vagabond coaxed him away,
 He was lost to the view,   Like the morning dew ;—
He had been, and was not—that's all that they knew.
And the Bagman stormed, and the Bagman swore
As never a Bagman had sworn before ;
But storming or swearing but little avails
To recover lost dogs with great curly tails.—

In a large paved court, close by Billiter Square,
Stands a mansion, old, but in thorough repair,
The only thing strange, from the general air
Of its size and appearance, is how it got there ;
In front is a short semicircular stair
 Of stone steps,—some half score,—
 Then you reach the ground floor,
With a shell-patterned architrave over the door.

It is spacious, and seems to be built on the plan
Of a Gentleman's house in the reign of Queen Anne ;

Which is odd, for although,   As we very well know,
Under Tudors and Stuarts the City could show
Many Noblemen's seats above Bridge and below,
Yet that fashion soon after induced them to go
From St. Michael Cornhill, and St. Mary-le-Bow,
To St. James, and St. George, and St. Anne in Soho.—
Be this as it may, at the date I assign
To my tale,—that's about Seventeen Sixty-nine,—
This mansion, now rather upon the decline,
Had less dignified owners,—belonging, in fine,
To Turner, Dry, Weipersyde, Rogers, and Pyne—
A respectable House in the Manchester line.

There were a score   Of Bagmen, and more,
Who had travell'd full oft for the firm before;
But just at this period they wanted to send
Some person on whom they could safely depend,—
A trustworthy body, half agent, half friend,—
On some mercantile matter as far as Ostend;
And the person they pitched on was Anthony Blogg,
A grave, steady man, not addicted to grog,—
The Bagman, in short, who had lost this great dog.

"The Sea! the Sea! the open Sea!—
That is the place where we all wish to be,
Rolling about on it merrily!"
   So all sing and say   By night and by day,
In the *boudoir*, the street, at the concert, and play,
In a sort of coxcombical roundelay;—
You may roam through the City, transversely or straight,
From Whitechapel turnpike to Cumberland gate,
And every young Lady who thrums a guitar,
Ev'ry moustachio'd Shopman who smokes a cigar,
   With affected devotion,   Promulgates his notion,
Of being a "Rover" and "child of the Ocean"—
Whate'er their age, sex, or condition may be,
They all of them long for the " Wide, Wide Sea!"

But however they dote,   Only set them afloat
In any craft bigger at all than a boat,
 Take them down to the Nore,   And you'll see that, before
The " Wessel " they " Woyage " in has made half her way
Between Shell-Ness Point and the pier at Herne Bay,
Let the wind meet the tide in the slightest degree,
They'll be all of them heartily sick of " the Sea !"

I've stood in Margate, on a bridge of size
 Inferior far to that described by Byron,
Where " palaces and pris'ns on each hand rise,"—
 —That too's a stone one, this is made of iron—
 And little donkey-boys your steps environ,
Each proffering for your choice his tiny hack,
 Vaunting its excellence ; and should you hire one,
For sixpence, will he urge, with frequent thwack,
The much-enduring beast to Buenos Ayres—and back.

And there, on many a raw and gusty day,
 I've stood, and turned my gaze upon the pier,
And seen the crews, that did embark so gay
 That self-same morn, now disembark so queer ;
 Then to myself I've sighed and said, " Oh dear !
Who would believe yon sickly-looking man's a
 London Jack Tar,—a Cheapside Buccaneer !"
But hold, my Muse !—for this terrific stanza
Is all too stiffly grand for our extravaganza.

" So now we'll go up, up, up,
 And now we'll go down, down, down,
And now we'll go backwards and forwards,
 And now we'll go roun', roun', roun'."—
—I hope you've sufficient discernment to see,
Gentle Reader, that here the discarding the *d*
Is a fault which you must not attribute to me ;

Thus my nurse cut it off when, "with counterfeit glee,"
She sung, as she danced me about on her knee,
In the year of our Lord eighteen hundred and three:—
All I mean to say is that the Muse is now free
From the self-imposed trammels put on by her betters,
And no longer like Filch, 'midst the felons and debtors
At Drury Lane, dances her hornpipe in fetters.

  Resuming her track, At once she goes back
To our hero, the Bagman.—Alas! and Alack!
  Poor Anthony Blogg Is as sick as a dog,
Spite of sundry unwonted potations of grog,
By the time the Dutch packet is fairly at sea,
With the sands called the Goodwins a league on her lee.

And now, my good friends, I've a fine opportunity
To obfuscate you all by sea terms with impunity,
  And talking of "calking," And "quarter-deck walking,"
  "Fore and aft," And "abaft,"
"Hookers," "barkeys," and "craft"
(At which Mr. Poole has so wickedly laught),
Of binnacles,—bilboes,—the boom called the spanker,
The best bower cable,—the jib,—and sheet anchor;
Of lower-deck guns, and broadsides and chases,
Of taffrails and topsails, and splicing main-braces,
And "Shiver my timbers!" and other odd phrases
Employed by old pilots with hard-featured faces;—
Of the expletives seafaring Gentlemen use,
The allusions they make to the eyes of their crews;—
  How the Sailors, too, swear, How they cherish their hair,
And what very long pigtails a great many wear.—
But, Reader, I scorn it—the fact is, I fear,
To be candid, I can't make these matters so clear
As Marryat, or Cooper, or Captain Chamier,
Or Sir E. Lytton Bulwer, who brought up the rear
Of the "Nauticals," just at the end of the year
Eighteen thirty-nine—(how Time flies!—Oh, dear!)—
With a well-written preface, to make it appear
That his play, the "Sea-Captain," 's by no means small beer.
16

There!—" brought up the rear"—you see there's a mistake
Which none of the authors I've mentioned would make:
I ought to have said, that he "sail'd in their wake."—
So I'll merely observe, as the water grew rougher
The more my poor hero continued to suffer,
Till the Sailors themselves cried, in pity, " Poor Buffer!"

  Still rougher it grew, And still harder it blew,
And the thunder kicked up such a hallibaloo,
That even the Skipper began to look blue;
  While the crew, who were few, Looked very queer, too,
And seemed not to know what exactly to do,
And they who'd the charge of them wrote in the logs,
" Wind N. E.—blows a hurricane—rains cats and dogs."
In short it soon grew to a tempest as rude as
That Shakspeare describes near the " still vext Bermudas,"*
  When the winds, in their sport, Drove aside from its port
The King's ship, with the whole Neapolitan Court,
And swamped it to give " the King's Son, Ferdinand," a
Soft moment or two with the Lady Miranda,
While her Pa met the rest, and severely rebuked 'em
For unhandsomely doing him out of his Dukedom.
You don't want me, however, to paint you a Storm,
As so many have done, and in colors so warm:
Lord Byron, for instance, in manner facetious,
Mr. Ainsworth more gravely,—see also Lucretius,
—A writer who gave me no trifling vexation
When a youngster at school on Dean Colet's foundation.—
  Suffice it to say That the whole of that day,
And the next, and the next, they were scudding away
  Quite out of their course, Propelled by the force
Of those flatulent folks known in Classical story as
Aquilo, Libs, Notus, Auster, and Boreas,
  Driven quite at their mercy 'Twixt Guernsey and Jersey,
Till at length they came bump on the rocks and the shallows,
In West longitude One, fifty-seven, near St. Maloes;
  There you will not be surprised That the vessel capsized,

     * See Appendix, p. 254.

Or that Blogg, who had made, from intestine commotions,
His specifical gravity less than the Ocean's,
    Should go floating away,   'Midst the surges and spray,
Like a cork in a gutter, which, swoln by a shower,
Runs down Holborn-hill about nine knots an hour.

You've seen, I've no doubt, at Bartholomew fair,
Gentle Reader,—that is, if you've ever been there,—
With their hands tied behind them, some two or three pair
Of boys round a bucket set up on a chair,
    Skipping, and dipping   Eyes, nose, chin, and lip in,
Their faces and hair with the water all dripping,
In an anxious attempt to catch hold of a pippin,
That bobs up and down in the water whenever
They touch it, as mocking the fruitless endeavor;
Exactly as Poets say,—how, though, they can't tell us,—
Old Nick's Nonpareils play at bob with poor Tantalus.
    —Stay!—I'm not clear   But I'm rather out here;
'Twas the water itself that slipped from him, I fear;
Faith, I can't recollect—and I haven't Lempriere.—
No matter,—poor Blogg went on ducking and bobbing,
Sneezing out the salt water, and gulping and sobbing,
Just as Clarence, in Shakspeare, describes all the qualms he
Experienced while dreaming they'd drowned him in Malmsey.

"O Lord," he thought, " what pain it was to drown!"
  And saw great fishes with great goggling eyes,
Glaring as he was bobbing up and down,
    And looking as they thought him quite a prize;
When, as he sank, and all was growing dark,
    A something seized him with its jaws!—a shark?—

No such thing, Reader :—most opportunely for Blogg,
'Twas a very large, web-footed; curly-tailed Dog!

———

I'm not much of a trav'ller, and really can't boast
That I know a great deal of the Brittany coast;
    But I've often heard say   That e'en to this day,

The people of Granville, St. Maloes, and thereabout
Are a class that society doesn't much care about ;
Men who gain a subsistence by contraband dealing,
And a mode of abstraction strict people call " stealing ;"
Notwithstanding all which, they are civil of speech,
Above all to a stranger who comes within reach ;
 And they were so to Blogg When the curly-tailed Dog
At last dragged him out, high and dry, on the beach.
 But we all have been told, By the proverb of old,
By no means to think " all that glitters is gold ;"
 And, in fact, some advance That most people in France
Join the manners and air of a *Maître de Danse*
To the morals (as Johnson of Chesterfield said)
Of an elderly Lady, in Babylon bred,
Much addicted to flirting, and dressing in red.—
 Be this as it might, It embarrassed Blogg quite
To find those about him so very polite.

A suspicious observer perhaps might have traced
The *petites soins*, tendered with so much good taste,
To the sight of an old-fashioned pocket-book, placed
In a black leather belt well secured round his waist,
And a ring set with diamonds his finger that graced,
So brilliant no one could have guessed they were paste.
 The group on the shore Consisted of four ;
You will wonder, perhaps, there were not a few more ;
But the fact is they've not, in that part of the nation,
What Malthus would term a " too dense population ;"
Indeed the sole sign there of man's habitation
 Was merely a single Rude hut in a dingle
That led away inland direct from the shingle,
Its sides clothed with underwood, gloomy and dark,
Some two hundred yards above high-water mark ;
 And thither the party, So cordial and hearty,
Viz., an old man, his wife, and two lads, made a start, he,
 The Bagman, proceeding, With equal good breeding,
To express, in indifferent French, all he feels,
The great curly-tailed Dog keeping close to his heels.—

They soon reached the hut, which seemed partly in ruin,
All the way bowing, chattering, shrugging, *Mon Dieuing*,
Grimacing, and what sailors call *parley-vooing*.

———

Is it Paris, or Kitchener, Reader, exhorts
You, whenever your stomach's at all out of sorts,
To try, if you find richer viands won't stop in it,
A basin of good mutton broth with a chop in it?
(Such a basin and chop as I once heard a witty one
Call, at the Garrick, a " c—d Committee one,"
An expression, I own, I do not think a pretty one.)
     However, it's clear   That, with sound table beer,
Such a mess as I speak of is very good cheer;
     Especially too   When a person's wet through,
And is hungry, and tired, and don't know what to do.
Now just such a mess of delicious hot pottage
Was smoking away when they entered the cottage,
And casting a truly delicious perfume
Through the whole of an ugly, old, ill-furnished room;
     " Hot, smoking hot,"   On the fire was a pot
Well replenished, but really I can't say with what;
For, famed as the French always are for ragouts,
No creature can tell what they put in their stews,
Whether bull-frogs, old gloves, or old wigs, or old shoes;
Notwithstanding, when offered I rarely refuse,
Any more than poor Blogg did, when, seeing the recky
Repast placed before him, scarce able to speak, he
In ecstasy muttered, " By Jove, Cocky-lecky !"
     In an instant, as soon   As they gave him a spoon,
Every feeling and faculty bent on the gruel, he
No more blamed Fortune for treating him cruelly,
But fell tooth and nail on the soup and the *bouilli*.

———

     Meanwhile that old man standing by
     Subducted his long coat-tails on high,
     With his back to the fire, as if to dry

A part of his dress which the watery sky
Had visited rather inclemently.—
Blandly he smiled, but still he looked sly,
And a something sinister lurked in his eye.
Indeed, had you seen him his maritime dress in,
You'd have owned his appearance was not prepossessing;
He'd a "dreadnought" coat, and heavy *sabots*
With thick wooden soles turned up at the toes,
His nether man cased in a striped *quelque chose,*
And a hump on his back, and a great hooked nose,
So that nine out of ten would be led to suppose
That the person before them was Punch in plain clothes.

Yet still, as I told you, he smiled on all present,
And did all that lay in his power to look pleasant.
　　The old woman, too,　Made a mighty ado,
Helping her guest to a deal of the stew;
She fished up the meat, and she helped him to that,
She helped him to lean, and she helped him to fat,
And it looked like Hare—but it might have been Cat.
The little *garçons* too strove to express
Their sympathy towards the "Child of distress"
With a great deal of juvenile French *politesse:*
　　But the Bagman bluff　Continued to "stuff"
Of the fat and the lean, and the tender and tough,
Till they thought he would never cry, "Hold, enough!"
And the old woman's tones became far less agreeable,
Sounding like *peste!* and *sacre!* and *diable!*

I've seen an old saw, which is well worth repeating,
　　That says,
　　　　　　"𝕲𝖔𝖔𝖉 𝕰𝖆𝖙𝖞𝖓𝖌𝖊
　　𝕯𝖊𝖘𝖊𝖗𝖇𝖊𝖙𝖍 𝕲𝖔𝖔𝖉 𝕯𝖗𝖞𝖓𝖐𝖞𝖓𝖌𝖊."
You'll find it so printed by 𝕮𝖆𝖗𝖙𝖔𝖓 or 𝖂𝖑𝖞𝖓𝖐𝖞𝖓,
And a very good proverb it is, to my thinking.
　　Blogg thought so too;—　As he finished his stew,
His ear caught the sound of the word "*Morbleu!*"
Pronounced by the old woman under her breath.
Now, not knowing what she could mean by "Blue Death!"

He conceived she referred to a delicate brewing
Which is almost synonymous,—namely, " Blue Ruin."
So he pursed up his lip to a smile, and with glee,
In his cockneyfied accent, responded, " Oh, *Vee !*"

    Which made her understand he Was asking for brandy ;
So she turned to the cupboard, and, having some handy,
Produced, rightly deeming he would not object to it,
An orbicular bulb with a very long neck to it ;
In fact you perceive her mistake was the same as his,
Each of them " reasoning right from wrong premises ;"

    —And here, by the way, Allow me to say—
Kind Reader, you sometimes permit me to stray—
'Tis strange the French prove, when they take to aspersing,
So inferior to us in the science of cursing ;

    Kick a Frenchman down stairs, How absurdly he swears,
And how odd 'tis to hear him, when beat to a jelly,
Roar out, in a passion, " Blue Death !" and " Blue Belly !"

" To return to our sheep" from this little digression :—
Blogg's features assumed a complacent expression
As he emptied his glass, and she gave him a fresh one ;
    Too little he heeded How fast they succeeded.
Perhaps you or I might have done, though, as he did ;
For when once Madam Fortune deals out her hard raps,
    It's amazing to think How one " cottons" to Drink !
At such times, of all things in nature, perhaps,
There's not one that is half so seducing as *Schnapps.*

Mr. Blogg, besides being uncommonly dry,
Was, like most other Bagmen, remarkably shy,
    —" Did not like to deny"— " Felt obliged to comply"
Every time that she asked him to " wet t'other eye :"
For 'twas worthy remark that she spared not the stoup,
Though before she had seemed so to grudge him the soup.
    At length the fumes rose To his brain ; and his nose
Gave hints of a strong disposition to doze,
And a yearning to seek " horizontal repose."—

His queer-looking host,   Who, firm at his post,
During all the long meal had continued to toast
        That garment 'twere rude to   Do more than allude to,
Perceived, from his breathing and nodding, the views
Of his guest were directed to "taking a snooze:"
So he caught up a lamp in his huge dirty paw,
With (as Blogg used to tell it) "*Mounseer, swivvy maw!*"
        And "marshalled" him so   "The way he should go,"
Up stairs to an attic, large, gloomy, and low,
        Without table or chair,   Or a movable there,
Save an old-fashioned bedstead, much out of repair,
That stood at the end most removed from the stair.—
        With a grin and a shrug   The host points to the rug,
Just as much as to say, "There!—I think you'll be snug!"
        Puts the light on the floor,   Walks to the door,
Makes a formal *Salaam*, and is then seen no more:
When just as the ear lost the sound of his tread,
To the Bagman's surprise, and at first to his dread,
The great curly-tailed Dog crept from under the bed!—

—It's a very nice thing when a man's in a fright,
And thinks matters all wrong, to find matters all right;
As, for instance, when going home late-ish at night
Through a Churchyard, and seeing a thing all in white,
Which, of course, one is led to consider a Sprite,
        To find that the Ghost   Is merely a post,
Or a miller, or chalky-faced donkey at most;
Or, when taking a walk as the evenings begin
To close, or, as some people call it, "draw in,"
And some undefined form, "looming large" through the
            haze,
Presents itself, right in your path, to your gaze,
        Inducing a dread   Of a knock on the head,
Or a severed carotid, to find that, instead
Of one of those ruffians who murder and fleece men,
It's your uncle, or one of the "Rural Policemen;"—
        Then the blood flows again   Through artery and vein;
You're delighted with what just before gave you pain;

You laugh at your fears—and your friend in the fog
Meets a welcome as cordial as Anthony Blogg
Now bestowed on *his* friend—the great curly-tailed Dog.

For the Dog leaped up, and his paws found a place
On each side his neck in a canine embrace,
And he licked Blogg's hands, and he licked his face,
And he waggled his tail as much as to say,
" Mr. Blogg, we've foregathered before to-day !"
And the Bagman saw, as he now sprang up,
     What, beyond all doubt,   He might have found out
Before, had he not been so eager to sup,
'Twas Sancho!—the Dog he had reared from a pup!—
The Dog who when sinking had seized his hair,—
The Dog who had saved, and conducted him there,—
The Dog he had lost out of Billiter Square ! !

     It's passing sweet,   An absolute treat,
When friends, long severed by distance, meet,—
With what warmth and affection each other they greet !
Especially too, as we very well know,
If there seems any chance of a little *cadeau*,
A " Present from Brighton," or " Token" to show,
In the shape of a work-box, ring, bracelet, or so,
That our friends don't forget us, although they may go
To Ramsgate, or Rome, or Fernando Po.
If some little advantage seems likely to start,
From a fifty-pound note to a two-penny tart,
It's surprising to see how it softens the heart,
And you'll find those whose hopes from the other are
          strongest,
Use, in common, endearments the thickest and longest.
     But, it was not so here ;   For although it is clear,
When abroad, and we have not a single friend near,
E'en a cur that will love us becomes very dear,
And the balance of interest 'twixt him and the Dog
Of course was inclining to Anthony Blogg,
     Yet he, first of all, ceased   To encourage the beast,
Perhaps thinking " Enough is as good as a feast ;"

And besides, as we've said, being sleepy and mellow,
He grew tired of patting, and crying "Poor fellow!"
So his smile by degrees hardened into a frown,
And his "That's a good dog!" into "Down, Sancho! down!"
But nothing could stop his mute fav'rite's caressing,
Who, in fact, seemed resolved to prevent his undressing,
      Using paws, tail, and head,   As if he had said,
"Most beloved of masters, pray, don't go to bed;
You had much better sit up and pat me instead!"
Nay, at last, when, determined to take some repose,
Blogg threw himself down on the outside the clothes,
      Spite of all he could do,   The dog jumped up too,
And kept him awake with his very cold nose;
      Scratching and whining,   And moaning and pining,
Till Blogg really believed he must have some design in
Thus breaking his rest; above all, when at length
The dog scratched him off from the bed by sheer strength.

Extremely annoyed by the "tarnation whop," as it
's called in Kentuck, on his head and its opposite,
      Blogg showed fight;   When he saw, by the light
Of the flickering candle, that had not yet quite
Burnt down in the socket, though not over bright,
Certain dark-colored stains, as of blood newly spilt,
Revealed by the dog's having scratched off the quilt,—
Which hinted a story of horror and guilt!—
      'Twas "no mistake,"—   He was "wide awake"
In an instant; for, when only decently drunk,
Nothing sobers a man so completely as "funk."

      And hark!—what's that?—   They have got into chat
In the kitchen below—what the deuce are they at?—
There's the ugly old fisherman scolding his wife—
And she—by the Pope! she's whetting a knife!—
      At each twist   Of her wrist,
      And her great mutton fist,
The edge of the weapon sounds shriller and louder!—
      The fierce kitchen fire   Had not made Blogg perspire
Half so much, or a dose of the best James's powder.—

It ceases—all's silent!—and now, I declare,
There's somebody crawls up that rickety stair.

The horrid old ruffian comes, cat-like, creeping;—
He opens the door just sufficient to peep in,
And sees, as he fancies, the Bagman sleeping!
For Blogg, when he'd once ascertained that there was some
"Precious mischief" on foot, had resolved to play "'possum;"—
　　　Down he went, legs and head,　Flat on the bed,
Apparently sleeping as sound as the dead;
While, though none who looked at him would think such a
　　　thing,
Every nerve in his frame was braced up for a spring.
　　　Then, just as the villain　Crept, stealthily still, in,
And you'd not have insured his guest's life for a shilling,
As the knife gleamed on high, bright and sharp as a razor,
Blogg, starting upright, "tipped" the fellow "a facer;"—
—Down went man and weapon.—Of all sorts of blows,
From what Mr. Jackson reports, I suppose
There are few that surpass a flush hit on the nose.

Now had I the pen of old Ossian or Homer
(Though each of these names some pronounce a misnomer,
　　　And say the first person　Was called James M'Pherson,
While as to the second, they stoutly declare
He was no one knows who, and born no one knows where),
Or had I the quill of Pierce Egan, a writer
Acknowledged the best theoretical fighter
　　　For the last twenty years,　By the lively young Peers,
Who, doffing their coronets, collars, and ermine, treat
Boxers to "Max," at the One Tun in Jermyn Street;—
I say, could I borrow these gentlemen's Muses,
More skilled than my meek one in "fibbings" and bruises,
　　　I'd describe now to you　As "prime a set-to,"
And regular "turn-up," as ever you knew;
Not inferior in "bottom" to aught you have read of
Since Cribb, years ago, half knocked Molyneux's head off.

But my dainty Urania says, " Such things are shocking!"
    Lace mittens she loves,   Detesting " the Gloves ;"
And turning, with air most disdainfully mocking,
From Melpomene's buskin, adopts the silk stocking.
    So, as far as I can see,   I must leave you to " fancy"
The thumps and the bumps, and the ups and the downs,
And the taps, and the slaps, and the raps on the crowns,
That passed 'twixt the Husband, Wife, Bagman, and Dog,
As Blogg rolled over them, and they rolled over Blogg,
    While what's called " the Claret"   Flew over the garret,—
    Merely stating the fact,   As each other they whacked,
The Dog his old Master most gallantly backed ;
Making both the *garçons*, who came running in, sheer off,
With " Hippolyte's " thumb and " Alphouse's " left ear off;
    Next, making a stoop on   The buffeting group on
The floor, rent in tatters the old woman's *jupon ;*
Then the old man turned up, and a fresh bite of Sancho's
Tore out the whole seat of his striped Calimancoes.—
    Really, which way   This desperate fray
Might have ended at last, I'm not able to say,
The dog keeping thus the assassins at bay :
But a few fresh arrivals decided the day ;
    For bounce went the door,   In came half a score
Of the passengers, sailors, and one or two more
Who had aided the party in gaining the shore !

It's a great many years ago—mine then were few—
Since I spent a short time in old *Courageux ;*—
    I think that they say   She had been, in her day,
A First-rate, but was then what they termed a *Rasée,*—
And they took me on board in the Downs, where she lay
(Captain Wilkinson held the command, by the way).
In her I picked up, on that single occasion,
The little I know that concerns Navigation,
And obtained, *inter alia,* some vague information
Of a practice which often, in cases of robbing,
Is adopted on shipboard—I think it's called " cobbing."
How it's managed exactly I really can't say,

But I think that a bootjack is brought into play—
That is, if I'm right:—it exceeds my ability
    To tell how 'tis done; But the system is one
Of which Sancho's exploit would increase the facility,
And, from all I can learn, I'd much rather be robbed
Of the little I have in my purse than be "cobbed;"
    That's mere matter of taste:
    But the Frenchman was placed—
I mean the old scoundrel whose actions we've traced—
In such a position that, on this unmasking,
His consent was the last thing the men thought of asking.
    The old woman, too, Was obliged to go through,
With her boys, the rough discipline used by the crew,
Who, before they let one of the set see the back of them,
"Cobbed" the whole party,—ay, "every man Jack of them."

MORAL.

And now, Gentle Reader, before that I say
Farewell for the present, and wish you good day,
Attend to the moral I draw from my lay :—

If ever you travel, like Anthony Blogg,
Be wary of strangers!—don't take too much grog!
And don't fall asleep, if you should, like a hog!—
Above all, carry with you a curly-tailed Dog!

Lastly, don't act like Blogg, who, I say it with blushing,
Sold Sancho next month for two guineas, at Flushing;
But still on these words of the Bard keep a fixed eye,
INGRATUM SI DIXERIS, OMNIA DIXTI!

L'Envoye.

I felt so disgusted with Blogg, from sheer shame of him
I never once thought to inquire what became of him;
If *you* want to know, Reader, the way, I opine,
    To achieve your design,— Mind, it's no wish of mine,—
Is (a penny will do 't) by addressing a line
To Turner, Dry, Weipersyde, Rogers, and Pine.

APPENDIX.*

Since penning this stanza, a learned Antiquary
Has put my poor Muse in no trifling quandary
By writing an essay to prove that he knows a
    Spot which, in truth, is   The *real* "Bermoothes,"
In the Mediterranean,—now called Lampedosa;
—For proofs, having made, as he further alleges, stir,
An entry was found in the old Parish Register,
The which at his instance the excellent Vicar ex-
Tracted: viz., "Caliban, base son of Sycorax."
    —He had rather, by half,   Have found Prospero's "Staff;"
But 'twas useless to dig, for the want of pick or axe.—
Colonel Pasley, however, 'tis everywhere said,
Now he's blown up the old Royal George at Spithead,
And the great cliff at Dover, of which we've all read,
Takes his whole apparatus, and goes out to look
And see if he can't try and blow up "the Book."
—Gentle Reader, farewell!—If I add one more line,
"He'll be, in all likelihood, blowing up *mine!*"

* See page 242.